praise for

pomegranate soup

"The recipes Mehran weaves effortlessly into the text add to the novel's delight and depth, as does her pitch-perfect ear for Irish intonations." —*Newsday*

"A stylish entry into the food-lit lineup." —*Good Housekeeping*

"Vibrantly alive and populated with rich characters, this is a delicious first novel flavored generously with Persian spices and Irish temperaments. Marsha Mehran writes with a deft hand and a sparkling imagination."

—*AMULYA MALLADI*, author of *Serving Crazy with Curry*

"The writing in this lyrical debut is matched only by the delicious Persian recipes woven throughout." —*More* magazine

"Marsha Mehran describes the food in mouthwatering detail—with a dash of magical realism." —*Chicago Tribune*

"Heart- and stomach-warming . . . Mehran's lighthearted voice will win readers over." —*Kirkus Reviews*

"These characters come to life; they're as uniquely simple or as deeply complex as the dishes that eldest sister Marjan concocts. . . . Personal demons and questioned loyalties play out like a movie on the page (think Joanne Harris's *Chocolat*), making the reader feel like an eye-witness to all the events. A satisfying summer read or book club pick; highly recommended." —*Library Journal*

"To give the reader a better appreciation for the pivotal role of food in the novel, Mehran includes recipes for some Iranian specialties. . . . Stark contrasts between the sisters' lives in Iran and Ireland and between the Irish and Persian cultures energize Mehran's tale." —*Booklist*

"*Pomegranate Soup*, a delightful debut novel, goes from Iran to Ireland and catches the flavors of both cultures through unforgettable scenes and characters. The three Aminpour sisters enchant us with their optimism and aroma of pomegranate soup, lingering beyond the pages." —*NAHID RACHLIN*, author of *Foreigner* and *Veils*

"A wonderful treat, a flavorful, rich little dish . . . Mehran has an unerring eye for detail, and she applies it well to her description of the three sisters. . . . Even non-cooks . . . will be beguiled by *Pomegranate Soup*'s zest for life." —*BookPage*

pomegranate soup

random house trade paperbacks · new york

pomegranate soup

a novel

marsha mehran

2006 Random House Trade Paperback Edition

Published in the United States by Random House Trade Paperbacks,
an imprint of The Random House Publishing Group,
a division of Random House, Inc., New York.

RANDOM HOUSE TRADE PAPERBACKS and colophon
are trademarks of Random House, Inc.
READER'S CIRCLE and colophon
are trademarks of Random House, Inc.

Originally published in hardcover in the United States by Random House,
an imprint of The Random House Publishing Group,
a division of Random House, Inc., in 2006.

Grateful acknowledgment is made to Lynne Rienner Publishers, Inc., for permission to reprint
an excerpt from "Conquest of the Garden" from A Lonely Woman: Forugh Farrokhzad and
Her Poetry, edited by Michael C. Hillman, copyright © 1987 by Michael C. Hillman.
Reprinted by permission of Lynne Rienner Publishers, Inc.

LIBRARY OF CONGRESS CATALOGING-IN-PUBLICATION DATA
Mehran, Marsha
Pomegranate soup: a novel / Marsha Mehran.
p. cm.
ISBN 0-8129-7248-1
1. Iranians—Ireland—Fiction. 2. Women immigrants—Fiction.
3. Restaurateurs—Fiction. 4. Restaurants—Fiction. 5. Women cooks—
Fiction. 6. Cookery—Fiction. 7. Sisters—Fiction. 8. Ireland—
Fiction. 9. Iran—Fiction. 10. Cookery, Iranian. I. Title.
PR6113.E37P66 2005
823'.92—dc22
[B]   2004051357

Printed in the United States of America

www.thereaderscircle.com

9 8 7 6 5

Book design by Barbara M. Bachman

for Christopher, always

Everyone knows,
everyone knows
we have found our way
Into the cold, quiet dream of phoenixes:
we found truth in the garden
In the embarrassed look of a nameless flower,
and we found permanence
In an endless moment
when two suns stared at each other.

I am not talking about timorous whispering
In the dark.
I am talking about daytime and open windows
and fresh air and a stove in which useless things burn
and land which is fertile
with a different planting
and birth and evolution and pride.
I am talking about our loving hands
which have built across nights a bridge
of the message of perfume
and light and breeze.

—FORUGH FARROKHZAD
"CONQUEST OF THE GARDEN"

pomegranate soup

prologue

DAWN ROSE OVER CLEW BAY and the small Irish village of Ballinacroagh. Had Thomas McGuire stopped to admire the fanfare of saffron rays, he might have missed the beginning of the end of his rule over the sleepy seaside town. But as was often the case with men of his temperament, Thomas had little time for daydreams. The obstinate businessman had charged out of his hard bed at five-thirty that morning, determined as ever to tend to his growing empire of three pubs, two spirit shops, and one inn on Main Mall.

The Mall's slowly winding medieval street began with the greasy Blue Thunder chip and burger shop, and ended with a dusty fourteenth-century church and monolithic memorial to Saint Patrick in the town's square. In between lay the usual combination of pubs, Clarks shoe store, religious relics shop, and Aran sweater and souvenir shop that one has come to expect of Hibernian towns situated in the shadows of Mother Nature's handiwork. Unable to rival the glory of millennial sedimentation and ancient Celtic causeways, such places are happy just to exist on the peripheries with a bland shrug to improvement, for why even try? In Ballinacroagh the natural phenomena are dominated by Croagh Patrick, or the Reek, upon whose perch Saint Patrick had nestled for forty days and forty nights. The solitary mountain sits solemn and monkish, shadowing the village clustered at its base, its weary soul no longer fascinated by the sprawling valley of patchwork fields, stone-bordered lanes, and human folly taking place on Main Mall below.

The first day of spring 1986 found Thomas McGuire standing on Ballinacroagh's main street, shuddering in his boots from the bleak morning drizzle. The burly bar owner had just opened the cellar doors to Paddy McGuire's, the moth-ridden public house he had inherited over twenty years ago from his father. Paddy's untimely death in a tractor accident had made a then nineteen-year-old Thomas the youngest pub owner Ballinacroagh, if not the whole of County Mayo, had ever known. Such early dominion over the town's favorite watering hole had, unfortunately, brought out the worst in the young man's already volatile temperament. Thomas's ill nature was the product of an undetermined mixture of *sard* (cold) and *garm* (hot), which nothing—not even Marjan's famously equalizing recipe for tart pomegranate soup—could remedy. Not only was this lethal combination of humors the catalyst for countless irrationalities but it also left him poorly equipped to deal with the sensuous wafts of cardamom, cinnamon, and rosewater that, this very morning, were blowing his way.

The smell first hit Thomas McGuire as he was directing the underpaid Guinness man down into the pub's freezing cellar. Its spicy, sinful intonations reeked of an unknown evil, a godforsaken foreignness that set off alarm bells in Thomas's large potato head and froze him to his spot. It was not until the Guinness man, Conor Jennings, also paused to catch a sniff of the air that Thomas realized the strange scent was very real indeed.

"Jaysus, Mary, and Joseph. If that doesn't smell like heaven I don't know what does, then." Conor leaned against the keg trolley and snorted through his pug nose. A forty-year-old bachelor who still lived with his thrifty mother, Conor had just come from a disappointing breakfast of watered-down tea (bag used repeatedly) and a rasher sandwich on buttered, day-old bread. As he stood there sniffing, his ample stomach gave a long, mutinous growl.

Thomas scowled. "You'll be seeing heaven sooner than you think if you don't get yer fat arse back in there and finish the stock! Go on with you then, and stop wasting my time. Or would you rather I give Seamus O'Grady a call? I'm sure he'd like to hear how one of his routemen is doing."

It was a particularly harsh slap, even for Thomas McGuire, and Conor's face flushed a deep pink as he hauled another keg from his van. Grumbling under his breath, he disappeared down the cellar steps, leaving the pub owner alone to investigate the source of the scent. Thomas's awakened nose led him next door, to the run-down store that used to be the old Delmonico pastry shop, Papa's Pastries. The Delmonicos had moved into town from Naples shortly after the Second World War and had operated the same doughy shop on Main Mall for over three decades. But ever since Luigi Delmonico's death five years ago, the shop had been an empty shell, deserted and collecting dust. Or rather it *used* to be empty. Because, bleary-eyed as he was, Thomas could not deny the curious glint of light that was shining through the shop's newspapered windows.

The light grew brighter as he crept closer to the old pastry place, the dense, exotic aroma causing his stocky knees to quiver like a shy schoolboy's. Thomas squinted through a small tear in the newspaper, half-expecting to confront the devil himself, but saw instead the glitter of something golden, a bright obscenity that occupied his entire field of vision.

The surly drinks baron growled and spat on the cracked sidewalk below the shop's red door. It was pure witchcraft, that was what. No doubt about it. And he was going to find out exactly who was behind it all.

dolmeh

30–40 canned grape leaves

2 onions, chopped

1/2 pound ground meat, lamb or beef

Olive oil

1/3 cup fresh summer savory

1/2 cup fresh dill

1/3 cup fresh tarragon

1/4 cup fresh mint

2 cups cooked basmati rice

1/2 cup fresh lime juice

1 teaspoon salt

1/2 teaspoon ground black pepper

Rinse grape leaves and lay aside. Fry onions and meat in olive oil over medium flame until meat is brown. Add chopped herbs to pan and fry for 3 minutes. Remove from heat. In a large bowl, combine the meat, onion, and herb mixture with rice, lime juice, salt, and pepper. Lay one grape leaf, vein side up, on a clean surface. Place one tablespoon of rice and meat mixture in middle of leaf, then roll from the base up, tucking the sides to form a tight pocket. Repeat until all leaves are stuffed. Line a greased deep baking dish with stuffed leaves, pour in 1/4 cup of water, cover with foil, and bake in oven at 220°F for 45 minutes.

chapter one

FOR MARJAN AMINPOUR, the fragrances of cardamom and rosewater, alongside basmati, tarragon, and summer savory, were everyday kinds of smells, as common, she imagined, as the aromas of instant coffees and dripping roasts were to conventional Western kitchen corners.

Despite having been born in a land of ancient deserts, where dry soil mingled with the crumbled remains of Persepolian pillars, Marjan had a great talent for growing plants. She had learned from an early age how to tempt the most stubborn seedlings to take root, even before she could spell their plant names in Farsi. Guided by the gentle hands of Baba Pirooz, the old bearded gardener who tended the grounds of her childhood home, young Marjan cultivated furry stalks of marjoram and golden angelica in dark mounds of earth. The dirt drew its moisture from melted mountain snow, which trickled down from the nearby Alborz into Tehran's wealthier suburbs, before flowing into the Aminpours' large octagonal fountain. Bubbling at the center of the walled garden, the pool was lined with turquoise and green Esfahani tiles.

While Marjan trained her eye to spot the first yellow buds of tarragon, or to catch a weed's surreptitious climb up the stalk of a dill plant, Baba Pirooz would recount the long line of celebrated gardeners who had been born on Persian soil. "Avicenna," Baba Pirooz began, clearing his throat, "Avicenna was the most famous plant lover of them all. Did you know, Marjan Khanoum, that this wise physician was the first man ever to make rosewater? He squeezed the soft petals for their oils then bottled the precious liquid for the world to enjoy. What a Persian, what a man!" the old gardener would exclaim, pausing only long enough in his lectures to ignite the strawberry tobacco he smoked in a knobby little pipe.

As an adult, Marjan carried the warm memories of Baba Pirooz and her childhood garden with her wherever she went. Not a day passed by that she was not on the lookout for some mound of soil to plunge her fingers into. Using her bare knuckles, engraved with terracotta dust and mulch, she would massage her chosen herb or flower into the soil's folds, whispering loving encouragements along the way. And no matter how barren that slice of earth had been before, once Marjan gave it her special attention, there was no limit to all that could blossom within its charged chambers.

In the many places she had lived—and there had been quite a few in her twenty-seven years—Marjan had always planted a small herb garden, consisting of at least one stem each of basil, parsley, tarragon, and summer savory. Even in the gloomy English flats she and her sisters had occupied for the last seven years since leaving Iran, Marjan had successfully grown a rainbow of cooking herbs in the blue ceramic flowerpots lining her kitchen windowsill. Always the consummate professional, she could not be tempted to give up planting by any amount of rain.

Marjan tried to keep her past perseverance in mind now as she stood in the old pastry shop's kitchen mixing a second batch of *dolmeh* stuffing. She wished she'd had more time to cultivate a healthy ensemble of fresh tarragon, mint, and summer savory to add to the *dolmeh* that she and her younger sisters, Bahar and Layla, were making. Perhaps if she had planted something here in Ballinacroagh, she could have avoided the anxieties that were now creeping up her spine. But then, Marjan reminded herself, it was best not have such regrets, especially when she couldn't do anything about them. There was still one more batch of the stuffed grape leaves to go—not to mention a half dozen other mouth-watering delicacies—and Time, that cantankerous old fool, was not on her side.

The Babylon Café was set to open in less than five hours. Five hours! In this new town whose name she could hardly pronounce, let alone spell. Ballinacroagh. Ba-li-na-crow. A whole town full of people who would come to taste her fares with questioning eyes and curious tongues. And unlike her other stints in the kitchen, this time she would be responsible for everything.

Marjan's heart quickened as she browned the ground meat and onions together over the low, dancing flame. The satisfied pan hissed as she introduced dried versions of her precious herbs, the only sort she had been able to buy at such late notice. Even in Iran, there had been times when Marjan had had to resort to cooking *dolmeh* with dried herbs. By soaking them overnight, she had discovered, they worked almost as well as their fresher relatives. Using her entire torso, Marjan mixed the herbs with the cooked rice, fresh lime juice, salt and pepper. She stirred with all her might despite the unrelenting ache in her shoulders, for such strong rotations were necessary to the *dolmeh*'s harmony.

Pausing to rub her tired arms, Marjan glanced across the kitchen at her sister Bahar, who was rolling up the first batch of *dolmeh*. With her wide and piercing eyes, Bahar always looked intense when she worked with food—as if her life depended on whichever vegetable or herb was being sacrificed on the chopping block before her.

Surprisingly, of the three Aminpour sisters, it was petite Bahar who possessed the greatest upper arm strength. Fragile in most every other way, Bahar had shoulders and arms that were as powerful as those of a man twice her size, which came in handy whenever jars needed to be opened or there was mixing to be done.

Marjan picked up the wooden spoon and returned to the *dolmeh*. Her sister looked too busy now to help her beat the remaining stuffing, for not only was Bahar concentrating on rolling her own grape leaves but she was also keeping Layla's work in check. No matter how many times Marjan was reminded of the differences in her younger sisters' personalities, there was nothing like the simple act of rolling *dolmeh* to show her how poles apart Bahar and Layla really were.

Bahar, guided by a stern inner compass, smartly slapped each grape leaf (vein side up) on the chopping block. It was a consistent, methodical march that started with a no-nonsense scoop of stuffing with her left hand, followed by a skilled right-handed tuck of the grape leaf. Then, bringing the *dolmeh* to a clean surrender, she briskly rolled the grape leaf from the bottom up. Despite her rather gruff manner, Bahar's method for rolling *dolmeh* was always successful; she ensured that her little bundles of good fortune were secure on the road up, lest all that she had gathered should fall asunder.

Rolling was always where Layla faltered, for her method was more carefree and altogether too trusting. Although Marjan and Bahar demonstrated the right way endless times, Layla would still leave her *dolmeh* vulnerable to the elements. One could always tell which bundles were hers, for if neither of her older sisters was quick enough to catch the spill of stuffing, rerolling the grape leaf while shaking her head, the moment of truth came forty-five minutes later with the opening of the oven door. Among the neat, aromatic green fingers expertly tucked by Marjan and Bahar would be the younger girl's unmistakable burst parcels of golden filling. And for some strange reason, they always smelled of Layla's signature scent—rosewater and cinnamon.

It was a familiar enough smell, this faint perfume that accompanied Layla's every move, but odd for a recipe that did not contain either ingredient. The cinnamon-rose *dolmeh* never really surprised her sisters, though. Layla had a way of raising expectations beyond the ordinary.

WHEN THOMAS MCGUIRE'S spits and curses hit the pavement outside the old pastry shop, Bahar was in the middle of removing a ready tray of *dolmeh* from the oven. After forty-five minutes they were as perfectly symmetrical as the greatest Persian carpets, the tray a clean loom upon which the stuffed grape leaf fingers were lined in even clusters and patterns. Although the kitchen was at the back of the shop, the sound of Thomas's vulgar excretions carried clearly to Bahar's sensitive ears. Gasping with surprise, she reached for the hot tray of *dolmeh* with bare hands and paid dearly for her distraction with the start of smoking blisters.

"Quick! Get under the cold water! Layla—*aloe vera*! Bahar, stop squeezing your thumb like that!" Marjan yelled, pushing her sister toward the sink. As the eldest of the three, Marjan was accustomed to directing her sisters in emergencies.

Bahar shuddered as the cold water ran over her scorched thumb. In the upstairs flat, a small one-bedroom residence that the Delmonicos had used as an office and storage area, Layla scrambled through open cardboard boxes looking for the green bottle of soothing gel.

"I can't find the aloe! Are you sure you packed it?" she yelled down to the kitchen.

"Yes!" Marjan hollered. "Look in the small box that says 'Miscellaneous'!"

"Don't worry. It's stopped already. See? I'll just put an ice cube on it," said Bahar, sticking out her hurt thumb so Marjan could see the rising welts.

Bahar tried to put on a brave face, but inside she felt a lot like that thumb of hers. Born, as her name indicated, on the first day of the Persian spring, she had the superstitious nature of people whose birthdays fall on the cusps of changing seasons. She was forever looking over her shoulder for fear that she had stepped on cracks or wandered under a ladder. Bahar's inherent nervousness had escalated to a deeper malaise in recent years, the result of unspeakable events that had left indelible scars. Although her neurotic tendencies often irritated the more hardy teenager Layla, Marjan's heart just softened a bit more every time she saw her sister jump so.

"Are you sure you're all right? Listen, I'll finish the *dolmeh*. Just mix the rice for me, okay?" Marjan gave Bahar an ice cube wrapped in a torn piece of newspaper and placed the piping tray of *dolmeh* on a low wooden island in the middle of the kitchen.

Made especially for a man of Napoleonic measurements, this rectangular table had been the centerpiece of Luigi Delmonico's kingdom, where he rolled, powdered, slapped, and whipped the exquisite paninis and chocolate-filled brioches he would later showcase in his beloved Papa's Pastries. It was also where Estelle, his bride of forty-five years, had found him dead—three hours after the bowl of meringue he was preparing had stiffened into a pink, cotton-candied tutu.

Of course, Estelle had failed to mention this last point when she had shown the three sisters around the place five days ago, though in reality, it probably would have made little difference. The girls' battered boxes were already shipped over and waiting to be picked up in Castlebar. Besides, the shop, complete with all the appliances and utensils of a working kitchen (albeit outdated and a bit rusty), was perfect for what Marjan had in mind. And it came at a bargain price.

"My niece told me that you are the best chef she has ever seen. Gloria, she's a very good girl, no?"

Mrs. Delmonico had stood in the kitchen after the grand tour, the dying afternoon rays entering lazily through a narrow, stained-glass partition in the back door. The sun rays illuminated the dust particles floating above her peppery hair. All surfaces, from countertops to the stacks of pots and dishes, were cloaked in a good inch of the snowy stuff.

"Oh, Gloria was very good to us when we arrived in Lewisham. A great friend," Marjan said. Behind her, Bahar and Layla both nodded in agreement. "But I think she was exaggerating a bit about my abilities. I was only a sous chef. She was the real talent at the restaurant."

"Yes, Gloria knows how to cook parmigiana and manicotti, but who doesn't? Maybe to those English that is gourmet, but you should have seen my grandmother cook! Pfff! If she was still alive today she would be rich from her cooking, I tell you!"

Estelle Delmonico laughed and placed her chubby hands on her hips. The good-natured widow cocked her head and offered a smile to each of the three young women. Fate had it that, although blessed with the welcoming girth of childbearing hips, she had never been able to give Luigi a baby of their own. It was one of her few regrets in an otherwise fortunate and colorful life. But her barrenness had never turned to resentment, a blessing Estelle often accredited to her niece, on whom she was able to practice all the loving criticisms her own mother had lavished upon her. Gloria was a great source of release for Estelle Delmonico, and now she had sent her three darlings to look after as well.

"Okay, then? You will take the store, eh?"

Marjan turned to Bahar and Layla, both of whom appeared to be asleep standing up. Their drawn, exhausted faces had the look of *torshi*, pickled onions that have been pulled from their bed of vinegar and salt. Who could blame them, really? It had been a long four days since they left London, shipping off their hastily packed boxes and throwing a few personal belongings into two worn plaid suitcases, the same suitcases that had seen them through the Iranian desert a long time ago. The plane ride from London to Knock had been painfully tedious, immigration and customs even worse. Answering the same questions about their religion and ethnic background over and over again. Then two days holed up in a backpackers' hostel in the nearby town of Castlebar, waiting for their boxes to arrive while they survived on white bread and some hard cheese that Marjan had bought from a corner grocery. Layla, of course, had complained all the way (such was the prerogative of her age), but Bahar had remained sullen, her big doe eyes wet with frightened tears.

But, thought Marjan, the worst certainly seemed behind them. Especially now that they were standing in this dusty little kitchen, with this generous Italian woman. It was time for a new start, time for them to take all the money they had in the world and finally make something of those years of hardship.

"You stay, yes?" Estelle Delmonico pulled a heavy, corroded key from a hidden pocket in her black dress. Toothy and archaic, it was the kind of key that would have released Pandora's own demons.

"Yes." Marjan nodded, accepting the key. "We'll stay. How would you like the rent paid? Monthly or weekly?"

"Agh, don't worry about that now. You give it to me whenever you have it, yes? I think what is more important is to get you a big bowl of my minestrone soup. That would put some energy in this pretty face, eh?" Mrs. Delmonico walked over to Layla and lightly patted her left cheek.

Marjan, determined to keep up the momentum that had carried them from London over the Irish Sea and into this land of crazed sheep and dizzying roads, shook her head, more to her sisters than to the jolly widow.

"Thank you, but I'm afraid we can't. There is so much to do. Bahar and Layla have to unpack, and I have to get to Dublin as soon as possible for ingredients. It would be much quicker than trying to find some of the food we need here, I suspect," she said.

"Hah! You are right! My Luigi would sometimes get so red in the face about these village markets. Mini-markets, they call them! I could find more in my mama's back garden in Napoli than in most of these *mini-markets.*"

"Yes, Naples—Napoli, sounds beautiful. I hear the *erberias* there are filled with the most wonderful vegetables. I hope I'll be able to find everything we need for our menu in Dublin. We want to open the café by next Monday. First day of spring," said Marjan.

"Monday? Five days only? No, no. You will give yourselves more time, I think. Why the rushing? Wait a few more days," said Mrs. Delmonico, shaking her head in matronly disapproval.

"Monday is Bahar's birthday," Layla piped up, suddenly awake.

"And it's No Rooz, the Iranian New Year. That's when Persians start their calendar year, the first day of spring," Marjan explained. Originally a Zoroastrian holiday marked by thirteen days of feasting and merriment, No Rooz, or "New Day," is now celebrated by all Iranians. "It'll be a good omen for our first day. And I think we'll make it, if we get started soon," she said pointedly.

"Oh, you young girls. So much ambition! I will leave you alone to do what you have to do. Maybe I come by on your new year's, yes? I will tell you a little about the crazy people that live here. To prepare you. Okay?" Estelle Delmonico planted a departing kiss on each of their cheeks, holding their faces in that warm Italian way of hers that took them all by surprise.

Five busy days had passed since the little widow turned over the key to the old pastry shop, and the girls had worked a great deal of magic in that time. While Marjan took the tortoise CIÉ train across the endless, grassy-knolled countryside to Dublin, Bahar and Layla set about the arduous task of transforming Papa's Pastries into an Eastern-flavored oasis. With its ashy white walls, peeling posters of gondoliers, a burnt-out neon Lavazza coffee sign, faded flags and maps of the boot-shaped country, the old shop had needed a lot of work.

Two large wooden display counters occupied most of the terra-cotta tiled floor. When Papa's Pastries had opened in 1946, a younger Estelle had covered the countertops and the shop's four metal tables with tartan tablecloths. The green-and-red plaid had turned a sickly yellow and orange in the intervening decades, and much of the binding weave crumbled into Bahar's hands as she lifted the musty cloths from the tables. Estelle had fashioned the seating area as a place where customers would mingle, soaking the crusty edges of Luigi's lovingly baked chocolate and anise biscotti in their cappuccinos as they listened to Billie Holiday croon on an old Victrola. But in the thirty-four years the Delmonicos' pastry shop was open, Estelle's checkered tables were hardly used at all, except as a place for tired housewives to dump their grocery bags and rumpled children. These exhausted, sallow-faced women would pay nervously for their crusty country loaves—and an occasional macadamia biscuit to shut drooling infantile mouths—before rushing out again into the rainy streets. After the cappuccino machine broke down in the winter of 1956, its pipes frozen by a freak ice storm raging outside, Luigi did not bother fixing it. Instead, he used the gargantuan installation as extra shelving for the model Ferrari cars he built in his spare time.

The cars were long gone now, but the cappuccino machine had

stayed. Bahar and Layla spent nearly three hours disassembling it before unscrewing the whole contraption from its base. Lifting the machine off the wall, the girls discovered the original color of the centuries-old shop—an ugly greenish brown that looked like cold turf. But that miserable color was gone now, as was the whitewash of the other walls. Bahar and Layla had bathed the entire shop with the house paint Estelle Delmonico had given them the day she showed them the space.

"Take it, take it. There are paintbrushes and rollers too. I bought it all just before my Luigi died, from that good for nothing John Healy. He owns the hardware store near the church. Pfff! I said to him, 'Mr. Healy, I need some good white paint. No cream or yellow. Luigi liked white.' 'Very clean,' he said, 'makes everything big.' So that Healy man, he give me paint on sale. I bring here and open it and look!"

Mrs. Delmonico pried the lids off of two paint cans in the corner of the upstairs flat. The paint, even in the dark room, pulsed out a vermilion that the three girls had seen in only one other place—within the incorruptible flesh of the fruits from the pomegranate tree in the garden of their childhood home.

"I take it back and said to him, 'Mr. Healy. There is a big mistake. This is not white. A beautiful color, but not white.' And do you know what he said to me, eh? 'Mrs. Delmonico, I can't give your money back. You opened the cans already.' Can you believe this? I tell you, that man, he never had a wife. Has a big house with beautiful furniture, but all alone! Why? Because he is miserable! Agh, look, I am getting crazy all over again, and it was five years ago! Maybe the paint is not so good anymore, eh?"

But the paint was just fine. After a bit of a stir the color regulated itself to an even brighter version than the spectacular vermilion

Estelle had awakened. When the girls stripped the walls and gave them a taste of color, the paint changed again, clotting into the dark crimson of Shiraz wine grapes.

On Saturday afternoon, after three days of coughing on sawdust and breathing paint fumes, Bahar and Layla both fell onto the solitary mattress in the upstairs flat. They slept through the whole night without stirring and did not wake until Marjan's return from her shopping excursion early on Sunday morning. Groggy-eyed and with bitter breath, the two girls stumbled down the staircase and followed their eldest sister out the kitchen door. They crossed the small back garden—a fenced-in patch of soggy, overgrown grass—and stepped onto a narrow cobblestone alleyway that was shared by all the businesses on the right side of Main Mall. There, in the predawn moonlight, stood a beat-up, lime green van with peace signs painted on its side panels.

"I found the van in *The Irish Times*. Paid some young kid five hundred Irish for it. Not the prettiest thing, I know, but it braved the rocky roads all right. And the brakes are good, too. I almost ran into a sheep—or at least I think it was a sheep—but stopped just in time. Come on, I bought as much as I could." Marjan motioned to the van's back doors. As soon as she opened them, the memories came spilling out.

A treasure trove of spices that would have made the thieving Ali Baba jealous sat huddled in one corner of the van. The motherly embrace of *advieh*—a mixed all-spice of crushed rose petals, cardamom, cinnamon, and cumin; the warm womb of turmeric; and that spice worth more than its weight in gold—*za'feran,* saffron.

Like their home in Iran, their flat in Lewisham was always filled with these and other sumptuous grindings of barks and plant seeds. Bundles of dried flowers hung from doorway arches, and marble mortars held the remnants of nose-tingling powders. Though they had left Lewisham only a week ago, it seemed much longer. And no matter how intoxicating the smells were, this reawakening of the senses came with the price of memories none of them wanted to think about. At least not yet.

Bahar and Layla helped Marjan unload the boxes of spices, jars of grape leaves, and bags of pistachios, almonds, and dates she had found in an Algerian grocery store on the outskirts of the capital city. Marjan had also purchased five kilos of feta, but she informed her sisters that this would be the last store-bought cheese for a while, as they would start making their own to save time and money. Layla groaned at the thought of squeezing dripping cheesecloth, but Bahar didn't mind; she would make feta every day if it meant Marjan would not be leaving them for another cross-country shopping trip.

The last of the van's inventory came in the form of two long fold-out tables and twelve wooden chairs, which Marjan had found at a secondhand store in the town of Mullingar. The long, communal-style tables would complete the cozy look she had in mind.

Marjan made one more trip in the green hippie van early that Sunday morning, driving to the storage facility outside Castlebar where the shipping company had deposited their eight boxes and four Persian rugs. Unrolled now in the shop's front room, the two larger Qashqa rugs told stories of primary-colored villagers who poured endless cups of golden tea and danced in honor of their sun god. These two covered up most of the shop's cold tile floors, while two smaller rugs—woven slowly by blind old men—hung opposite each other so that their delicate, filigreed patterns could be fully appreciated. The vermilion walls complemented the new artwork wonderfully, bringing out the roses that bordered the corners of one rug while contrasting with the mint green leaves of the other.

From the weary cardboard boxes came the shining tools of their new trade—what would truly set them apart from the rest of the businesses on Main Mall. Bahar unwrapped the items that she had collected over the years from Salvation Army stores and the odd suburban garage sale around London. There were ceramic teapots in aubergine, mustard, and midnight blue (good for one, sweeter still when shared between two drinkers); and forty small, thin glasses with curved handles, set in gold- and silver-plated holders etched with arabesque swirls. Bahar gingerly lined the tea glasses up on the counter where the cappuccino machine had been stationed. She tucked the teapots into the counter's glass-paneled belly, where they sat prettily next to twenty glass containers of loose-leaf teas, ranging from bergamot and hibiscus to oolong.

The larger counter, which sat closer to the shop's front door, had yet to be filled with Marjan's sweet creations. On the wall behind the counter ran a dark wooden shelf. Layla, the tallest of the three, was given the unsavory task of scrubbing it, driving spatula and sponge through the stony clumps of baguettes and currant bread that had petrified after Luigi's death. The shelf was now spotless and exhibiting better-preserved artifacts: etched copper and brass trays, a framed woven calligraphy that read "Tea" in Farsi, five old-style samovars (one that had belonged to the girls' grandmother, which Bahar had bundled up in her coat that day they left Iran for good), and a large print of a painting showing a traditional Iranian teahouse (men only), complete with indoor fountain and hookah pipes.

The brass samovars on display belonged to an older generation, precursors to the large electric machine sitting on the counter next to the tea glasses. The diuretic samovar was plugged in and ready to be filled with water that it would boil for waiting teapots. It was this very samovar, with its enticing golden gleam, that Thomas McGuire had just glimpsed through the cracks in the newspapered window.

The second tray of *dolmeh* was ready for the hot oven. Marjan pushed them into the heat and sighed.

"Well, that should last us the next few days. What do you think?" She fanned herself with an oven mitten. The baklava they had baked earlier that morning was sitting on the kitchen island next to the first tray of *dolmeh,* but there was still so much left to do. And they had only four hours left before opening! She'd have to get started on the red lentil soup next.

Layla clunked down the stairs, pausing on the low landing as she leaned over the banister, swinging her legs. At fifteen, she was already fully aware of the effects these long, exquisite limbs had on men of all ages.

"I couldn't find the aloe anywhere. It wasn't in that box like you said."

"It's all right. It stopped hurting." Bahar held her thumb slanted, like a reluctant hitchhiker. "So much for a good omen."

"Bahar, please. No negativity right now. We need all the luck we can get our hands on. Look how far we've come already," Marjan said, waving her wooden spoon around the warm, inviting kitchen.

Bahar and Layla set aside their private thoughts to survey the fantastic bounty of tastes and colors around them. The ambrosial food and neat, cozy rooms were a real testament to their efforts, a great accomplishment for only a handful of days.

Yes, they had come very far. Very far indeed.

red lentil soup

2 cups dry red lentils

7 large onions, chopped

7 garlic cloves, crushed

1 teaspoon ground turmeric

4 teaspoons ground cumin

Olive oil

7 cups chicken broth

3 cups water

Salt

2 teaspoons nigella seeds*

*Ground black pepper
may be substituted

Place lentils in a saucepan, cover with water, and bring to a boil. Cook, uncovered, for 9 minutes. Drain and place aside. In a large stockpot, fry 6 of the chopped onions, garlic, turmeric, and cumin in olive oil until golden. Transfer lentils, broth, and water to the pot. Add salt, nigella seed or pepper to taste. Bring soup to a boil. Lower heat, cover, and simmer for 40 minutes. Fry the remaining onion in olive oil until crisp but not blackened. Add as a garnish over individual bowls of soup.

chapter two

FROM HER BEDROOM WINDOW, in a flat above the Reek Relics shop, Dervla Quigley could see the universe. Or its equivalent, which for her was the comings and goings of all who ventured up and down Main Mall.

A proud Ballinacroagh native through and through, Dervla had lived with her spinster sister, Marie Brennan, ever since her husband of forty-one years passed away. Although most in town knew the circumstance of Jim Quigley's ignominious death (a horse breeder from County Kildare, he met his grand demise being squashed under the flanks of a spotted filly), no one dared speak about it. As Ballinacroagh's primary gossip, Dervla kept mouths shut with a combination of canine hearing and a vicious tongue that knew no boundaries.

At most times of the day—except during six o'clock Mass—Dervla could be found spying out of her bedroom window. Bolstering her hunched torso with large pillows, she stared with beady, rhubarb gray eyes out into the damp street below, determined not to miss a minute of provincial drama. It was an admirable feat of endurance, this constant watch over all Ballinacroagh, especially considering the old gossip's unfortunate medical condition. At the height of her autumn years, and without warning, Dervla Quigley had been stricken with incontinence, an embarrassing bladder problem that left her housebound and dependent on her long-suffering sister. Unable to control her own body, Dervla soon became obsessed with manipulating everyone else's. Gossip was not only her friend and solace but a source of great power.

The week that the Aminpour sisters moved into the old pastry shop would prove especially fruitful for Dervla Quigley. By Sunday, she had almost met her weekly quota of scandals: on Wednesday, at 1:17 A.M.: Benny Corcoran stumbled half-blind and drunk out of Paddy's, his hand on the arse of someone other than his saintly wife (Dervla blamed the broken streetlamp over the pub for obscuring the floozy's face); on Friday, at 2:47 P.M.: a caravan of ten decrepit trailer homes—tinkers with no shame to them, no shame at all—climbed up Main Mall toward the lower levels of the craggy mountain heap.

Tinkers. Just the word made Dervla shudder. The old gossip's fury, of course, was a direct product of her ignorance. Despite her boundless curiosity, Dervla had never stopped to learn the tumultuous history of Ireland's traveling people. Tinker, or "Tinceard" in Gaelic, referred to the tin pots and cooking pans that, until only a few years ago, were mended and peddled by the freckly, pale-eyed Celtic nomads. Before plying their tin trade, these travelers had been storytellers, descendants of medieval Irish bards who earned their daily bread by belting out high-pitched ditties:

> She went to live with a gentleman; one day came a
>   tinker to solder her pan.
> He slyly got her behind the door, and gave her kisses over and o'er.
> Fa la la lero liddle lie day, fal la la lero li gee whoa!

This clan of caravan dwellers, having survived centuries of famine and the follies of wigged Englishmen, no longer traveled in horse-drawn trains. Instead, they opted for mobile homes topped with shiny roofs of chrome, peach, and Tipperary gold.

No matter how colorful they may have seemed to the outsider, Dervla told herself, *she* had little patience for the train of itinerants who took hold of road and field alike. Maybe she couldn't change Ireland's ridiculous bylaws, which allowed travelers to squat in any open field, but it didn't stop the old gossip from trying. Dirty, disgusting things, those tinkers, Dervla muttered. Dirty, disgusting things. She picked up the telephone and dialed the town council office. Someone had to tell Padraig Carey about those filthy beasts. If she wasn't around to look after things, just imagine what sort of scum could come cruising down her beloved Main Mall!

What came in the form of a bright green van, Sunday morning, 4:00 A.M. sharp. Dervla awoke to acrid exhaust fumes billowing into her open bedroom window. Annoyance turned to gratitude when she spotted the peculiar vehicle, for Dervla knew a juicy bit of news when she saw one. The van ambled around the corner into the back alley, its bright orange peace sign reflecting in the moonlight. She might be sixty-two, Dervla thought to herself, but she was well aware of what went on in the backs of those hippie vans: lewd animal acts and drug use, that was what. No two ways about it.

Dervla sat frozen with anticipation, waiting for the shadowy driver (some sort of heathen hippie no doubt) to park and saunter into view, but nobody came. She waited an hour, then two, hobbling out of her bedroom only for an urgent toilet run. No one was on the street at that time of morning; it was too late for pub crawls and too early for the delivery vans, so any suspicious footsteps could be heard easily. Dervla waited and waited, but nobody came.

The foggy light of morning brought Dervla little relief. There was the usual pedestrian bustle of Sunday bests parading toward the church, the same penitent drunks peeling themselves out of roadside ditches with warbled promises to do better next time. No mysterious hippie, though; no details of back alley dealings, no chugging exhaust fumes. Hours of sitting and watching, and all she had to report back to the hungry beaks of Ballinacroagh's ten o'clock parishioners was a sinful Benny Corcoran and a bunch of dirty tinkers. It was simply not good enough for a week's work.

Monday would prove to be much more rewarding. Not only did Dervla spot a light beaming through the cracks in the newspapered windows of the old Delmonico pastry shop but her sharpened ears detected murmuring voices coming from behind its red door. She couldn't understand what was being said, but it didn't sound like English, that was for sure. Italian, more than likely. No doubt a version of Latin the Pope himself wouldn't have approved of. Had Estelle Delmonico lost her marbles altogether and decided to start up that sad excuse for a shop again? Hadn't she learned her lesson the first time around?

Dervla sniffed the air outside her bedroom window.

Yes, a nasty reek of foreignness was definitely in the air. It was a different smell than what she remembered coming from Papa's Pastries all those years ago. She recognized the same unyielding yeasty scent of rising bread and perky almond intonations, but there was also a vast and unexpected array of under- and overtones she could not name. The wicked, tingling sensation taunted Dervla's sense of decency, laughing at her as if it knew her deep, dark secrets, as though it had heard all about her dead husband's wanton ways.

When the crusty gossip witnessed Thomas McGuire's own fierce reaction to the new scent, she knew that she was on to something all right. She watched with glee as Thomas stormed up Main Mall (to the town council, no doubt) in his Land Rover, rubbing her wrinkly hands over her thickly veined thighs in a moment of unrestrained happiness. She was sitting over a gold mine of news, enough to last for weeks to come!

Dervla Quigley would not have to wait long for further entertainment. Soon after, Thomas charged off toward the town council building, the shop's red door opened, and out walked Layla.

It seemed that Marjan, in all her meticulous attention to the extraordinary details on her grocery list, had failed to buy sufficient bags of white onions, those humble servants of so many magical dishes. Her initial stock was already used up in the *dolmeh* and the pot of red lentil soup simmering away on the stove top, and she would need more to complete her opening day menu. Panicked, Marjan pushed Layla out the shop door with instructions to buy as many bags of onions as she could carry in her long, slender arms.

Red lentil soup, although quite seductive in scent, is as simple to make as its name suggests. Marjan preferred to boil her lentils before frying the chopped onions, garlic, and spices with some good, strong olive oil. Covering the ready broth, lentils, and onions, she would then allow the luscious soup to simmer for half an hour or so, as the spices embedded themselves into the compliant onion skins.

In the recipe book filed away in her head, Marjan always made sure to place a particular emphasis on the soup's spices. Cumin added the aroma of afternoon lovemaking to the mixture, but it was another spice that had the greatest tantric effect on the innocent soup drinker: *siah daneh*—love in the midst—or nigella seed. This modest little pod, when crushed open by mortar and pestle, or when steamed in dishes such as this lentil soup, excites a spicy energy that hibernates in the human spleen. Unleashed, it burns forever with the unbound desire of an unrequited lover. So powerful is nigella in its heat that the spice should not be taken in by pregnant women, for fear of early labor.

Indigenous to the Middle and Near Easts of the girls' past lives, nigella is rarely used in Western recipes, its ability to soothe heartburn and abolish fatigue quite overlooked. Modernity, it seems, prefers over-the-counter pills to the advice of ancient seers. Marjan, aware that the spice would not be readily available in Ireland, had packed several envelopes of seedlings in the boxes they had shipped over from London. Layla would never fully realize how fortuitous a move this shipping of seeds had been, for she was already following the destiny its perfume had assigned her, undulating as it was from Marjan's simmering pot all the way out to the sleepy street.

Benny Corcoran, owner of Corcoran's Bake Shop, was the first townsperson Layla encountered as she made her way down to Fadden's Mini-Mart. Rather than buy a van for delivery runs, Benny transported the loaves and rolls he packed for Fadden's in a large red wheelbarrow. He had just finished his second delivery trip to the grocery store, sweat running down the creases in his freckled face and onto his wheelbarrow of bread, when he saw Layla. Almost at once, Benny was stung by the cloud of nigella that had blended with the young girl's own rosewater and cinnamon bouquet. The poor man didn't know what hit him. One minute he was wandering around in his own lonely vacuum, the next he was in an Eden of tempting fruits, standing before an Eve whose long, dark hair and fragrance soothed his very heart.

It would be easy to attribute Layla's effect on the opposite sex (and the occasional Sapphically inclined female) to her youth or sweet, natural perfume, but the real reason behind her attraction was far more complex. Of course, there was no denying her beauty, the consistency of her angled, porcelain features, that tilt in her almond eyes, which shined like half-moons across her celestial face. Unlike her two older sisters, who sported wayward brown ringlets, Layla had hair that was long and jet black. Tied up or let down, moussed or gelled, nothing could excite her stubbornly straight locks. They were a definite throw-back to some latent Oriental chromosomes roaming deep inside of her.

Had he still been alive, their father would have wasted no time in making a point of this Eastern descent. Javid Aminpour often boasted a lineage to Genghis Khan, beating his chest while yodeling Mongolian war songs, in imitation of an ancestry he was determined to stake a claim to. He died two months before Layla's first birthday, so she could barely recall her father's theatrics, but Bahar's many bedtime stories over the years had given Layla ownership over her own set of memories.

Layla never knew her mother either, for she died shortly after pushing her out into the harsh world. After a nine-year drought, it seemed that this last child had released in Shirin Aminpour an inner tourniquet that kept on flowing until there was nothing more to give. The weary doctors in Tehran General Hospital had no explanation for the merciless bleeding and just shrugged with defeat when they told her father the news. They failed to mention that, as the last drops of blood seeped into the hospital's sea green bedsheets, a tiny bud had popped out of his wife's womb. When the flower seed fell into the pool of blood, it blossomed into the face of a full-grown rose. The fearful doctors had kept this to themselves, partly to avoid a malprac-tice suit, and partly because the rosewater and cinnamon scent that accompanied the flower's miraculous unfolding reminded them of a time when military guards did not hover behind every surgery room door. So it is that people who are denied hope become greedy hoard-ers when granted even the smallest of drops.

But the doctors' selfish motives had made little difference in Layla's fate. Even from those first minutes in the outside world, she was charming all who crossed her path. In Layla's hopeful aura, men like Benny Corcoran were free to relive the ambitions of their idle youths, dreams that were once entertained behind closed doors as they rubbed away under sweaty teenage quilts. Those were the moments of pure self-indulgence, before the repercussions of manhood were thrust upon them in the form of soul-breaking jobs and nagging wives.

Sensing Benny's adoring eyes on her, Layla quickened her pace down Main Mall. A gaggle of primary school children milling about outside the news agency were too busy sucking gobstoppers between crooked teeth to notice her. On the opposite side of the street, a beauty salon, Athey's Shear Delight, was just opening up its flamingo pink window blinds. Still too early for customers, the three hair-dressers were enjoying their morning tea inside as they flipped through old magazines. When Layla walked by, the beauticians dropped their *Irish Women's Weekly* and *Celtic Hair* and stared with open mouths out the window.

"Now who do you suppose that is, then? Would you look at the length of skirt on her!" Joan Donnelly, hair colorist and sister to the proprietor, slammed her teacup down and marched over to the window, widening the gap between two blinds with her fingers. Joan was a small, nervous woman. Although blessed with a talent for both hi- and low-lites, she had found no cure for the barrage of dandruff that fell daily from her own bowl-cut fringe; the flakes sat like a conscience on her pointy little shoulders. "She looks right foreign to me. Spanish or Italian, wouldn't you say?"

"Haven't ya heard, so? Sure, I was meaning to tell ya!" Nineteen-year-old Evie Watson's sparrow voice piped up. "That Delmonico woman, she's got the old pastry place up and running again. With some sort of foreign hippies, no less. To listen to Dervla Quigley tell it she's ready to put Corcoran's out of business."

In spite of her bulimic frame, or perhaps because of it, Evie was always hungry for approval and did her best to gather tidbits of

Ballinacroagh information that might prove useful. Evie's eagerness, though, was quite different from Dervla Quigley's lust for gossip. Her chatter was grounded on good intentions and hopes that it would boost her position from salon apprentice to full-time stylist, like she had always dreamed.

"If you ask me, Estelle Delmonico has better things to do than break her back in that dustheap again," said Fiona Athey, chief stylist and owner of the salon that bore her name.

Fifty pounds and another lifetime ago, Fiona had been on her way to great glories, reenacting the entire opus of Irish fairy tales before delighted audiences in the theatrical capital of Ireland, Galway City. But an illicit romance with Gerhard, a German puppeteer, had rendered her bed bound with a pregnancy that would produce the bane of her existence, her seventeen-year-old daughter, Emer. After having her child, Fiona suffered a double blow of indignity when she discovered Gerhard under the theater rafters, in a compromising position with her very own understudy. The upstart bottled blonde—a primary reason why Fiona stuck to cutting hair and left coloring to her sister Joan—had taken advantage of Fiona's incapacitation to move in on her man and her starring role. Heartbroken, and vowing never to tread the boards again, Fiona had returned to her hometown with baby Emer in tow, taking over her sickly father's barbershop and eventually turning it into a nifty little business. Athey's Shear Delight was popular with the town's children and womenfolk, but most men steered clear of its peroxide-filled rooms—mainly to spare themselves the embarrassment of donning one of Fiona's flowery smocks. Pass Athey's Shear Delight on any given afternoon, and you will find it a hotbed of estrogen, where gossip mingles with the acetate fumes of nail polish and hair spray.

Fiona, who had endured tittering giggles and reproachful shakes of heads when she first arrived back in town, usually refrained from voicing her opinions. She detested the constant gnawing condemnations that went on inside her small, pink salon but understood the necessity of such gossip for the health of her business. Because of her neutrality, when the odd moment arose that Fiona Athey actually did make her thoughts known, anyone within earshot would pause and pay her particular deference.

"I'd say Estelle's done the smart thing and rented the place out," Fiona reasoned. "That might be our new neighbor, so. Let's hope it's not another salon, that's all."

"Sure, I was walkin' past the other day and saw the lights on through the small bit of window there. Something was cooking. I can't put my finger on it, but it wasn't anything like the Eye-talian food in that spaghetti place in Westport. It was something different altogether," Evie keenly offered.

"Humph! Well, I don't care who they are or what they do, so long as that there hussy doesn't go distracting my boys from their Leaving Cert studies. They'll be going to seminary school whether they like it or not," Joan retorted, pursing her lips and releasing the vertical blinds with a snap.

Fiona and Evie both nodded, well-acquainted as they were with the drama of Joan Donnelly's identical twin boys, Peter and Michael. Convinced that her precious boys were intended for a higher power, Joan had been pushing nightly catechisms into their mushy brains since an early age. Her ecclesiastical ambitions, however, had done little to curb the twins' appetite for weekend carjackings, brothels, and drunken cow-tipping parties. The boys were a constant source of worry for poor, neurotic Joan, and the real reason behind her falling scalp tissue. Lucky for Joan, she was not watching when her devilish sons nearly knocked Layla off her feet in front of Fadden's Mini-Mart.

"How's it going?" Peter winked at Layla as his brother let out a low whistle.

Layla, having just sidestepped Benny Corcoran's admiration, was not prepared for the wily twins' attentions. With an enchanting combination of teenage timidity and self-assurance, she nodded briefly in their direction before ducking into the mini-mart.

"Jaysus. Did you see her?"

"See her? Michael, I think we've just witnessed a miracle."

The Donnelly twins, with their salacious grins and gawking eyes, were not affected by Layla's bloom in the same way as nostalgic older men. They were, after all, only eighteen, with the prospects of a whole world of debauchery and mischief before them (hang what their mother had in mind). The sight of Layla's long legs, tanned even under her thin stockings, produced the basic, primitive lust expected of boys their age. On any other day, the twins would have followed Layla into the shop. But this was Monday. The boys never stepped into Danny Fadden's mini-mart more than once on Mondays.

As a matter of tradition, and to spite their mother for making them sit through two Sunday Masses, Peter and Michael Donnelly habitually paid a visit to Fadden's Mini-Mart on Monday mornings before school. In a ruse that had started their first year of secondary school, Michael would keep Mr. Fadden busy at the counter with some obscure mythology question, to which only the grocer, a devoted fan of Irish lore, would know the answer. Meanwhile, Peter would swipe two bottles of Beamish from the beer shelf, stuffing them into the pockets of his large duffel coat. The twins gleefully chugged their beers before school, passing them among the thick-necked boys who congregated in the woods beyond the football field. This ritualistic passing of backwashed ale was merely a frothy afterthought for the twins, though, for it wasn't the beer or the thrill of stealing it but the rather cruel game they played on poor Danny Fadden that tickled them the most.

Every time Peter swiped two bottles of beer (always from the back of the shelf), he left a piece of green felt in their place, along with an IOU note signed Finnegan. It didn't take long for Danny (a man who starred in his own daydreams as a love-struck Diarmuid eloping with a witchy Grainne) to put two and two together to get five. The green felt, the missing stout, the name Finnegan. It all pointed to one thing: the mini-mart had its very own leprechaun. Danny Fadden counted himself supremely lucky to be blessed by the touch of the little people, and he awaited the leprechaun's Monday morning visits with barely contained excitement. Of course, everyone in Ballinacroagh joked of "Fadden's Fairy" and would often ask the shopkeeper, when stopping in for some milk or potatoes, how his little friend was getting along. Danny's wife, Deirdre, by contrast, did not find her husband's leprechaun fixation at all funny, and after nearly five years of his lunacy, she left Danny on the eve of their thirtieth wedding anniversary.

The shy grocer was softly tiptoeing up to the beer aisle when Layla walked into the store. Knowing full well the precarious temperament of leprechauns, with their complete dislike for anything human, Danny was always careful not to disturb his little friend's hiding place. He steered clear of the beer shelves from noontime Sunday to eight o'clock Monday morning, lest he stumble upon his unsuspecting visitor and frighten him away altogether. This meant, of course, that he never made the connection between the notes and the Donnelly twins' Monday morning visit. While Layla scoured the produce stands for onions, Danny was hunched over in the beer aisle, deciphering the meaning behind the little person's latest note: "I like barley, I like rye, I like stout in my pie. IOU. Finnegan." Neither of them saw Malachy McGuire standing patiently at the register counter.

The younger of Thomas McGuire's two sons, eighteen-year-old Malachy had somehow managed to sidestep the male McGuire DNA of turnip torsos and butchered complexions. Nor had he taken much from his mother's side, who along with Malachy's three plump sisters would have given a modern-day Rubens much to concentrate on.

Peaking at six foot one, and slender with the hands of a pianist, Malachy sported a mop of unruly black hair and sapphire eyes that sparkled like midnight suns. His luminous youth was something to marvel at indeed. He was nothing like his older brother, Tom, who at twenty-one was an almost carbon copy of their father, though without the latter's ambition and talent for subversion. Tom Junior spent most of his time scurrying between amateur hurling matches and playing henchman for his father, while Malachy much preferred the complementary hobbies of football and astronomy, balancing the terrestrial with the heavenly, and excelling in both equally. Unknown to Malachy, the cosmos that he pored over so many nights from his bedroom window was in perfect alignment that Monday morning.

Like Peter and Michael Donnelly, Malachy was on his way to school when he decided to stop into Fadden's for his morning Lucozade. But unlike those of the devious twins, Malachy McGuire's soul was as old as the constellations themselves. To him, Layla's promising aroma was not a reminder of a long-lost boyhood or the instigator of teenage lust. No, for Malachy, the sight of Layla's exotic profile filling up a bag of white onions was a sign, a resounding *yes* to the age-old questions of the divine.

Yes, there was a God. Yes, there was life beyond the sleepy valleys of Ballinacroagh. Yes, there *were* undiscovered universes waiting just for him. And one of them was standing right before him, in all her astounding milky ways.

Malachy felt suddenly weak and dizzy. As his vision fuzzed over and his legs gave way, he grabbed the nearest stationary object—a grocery shelf. Unfortunately for the star-gazing romantic, the shelf happened to hold a pyramid display of feminine hygiene products, and before Malachy knew it he was in a heap on the floor, covered—to his mortification—in specially priced, two-for-one boxes of super-size tampons.

The clatter awoke Layla to her surroundings, and as she turned to the front of the shop, a burning sensation instantly took hold of her body. There, down the aisle before her, was the most beautiful boy she had ever seen. Layla tried to breathe but found instead the start of debilitating hiccups—catches of love-bitten air that would not end until she had taken a good swill of Marjan's famous *dugh* drink.

"Are you all right there, lad? Didn't hurt yerself now, did you?" Danny Fadden asked, rounding the corner of the beer aisle, his fishbowl eyes blinking behind thick glasses.

Poor Malachy. For the first time in his life his natural grace had forsaken him. Surrounded by such private tokens of femininity, all he could do was bow his red, tender face and make a run for it. He didn't dare look back at Layla as he pounded through the grocery's door; didn't acknowledge the twins' mocking calls of "I think ye forgot yer tail, McGuire," or even notice that he was running in the opposite direction from school, so lost was he in Layla's lovely perfume.

While her youngest sister was hiccuping romance in the minimart, Marjan was busy in the kitchen chopping her last onion, impatient for Layla to return with reinforcements. Frying the chopped onion with some olive oil, she flipped the pieces about until they were crunchy but not blackened, then set the fried charms aside for later, to be sprinkled on bowls of soup ordered by expectant customers. Marjan considered this sizzled garnish to be the best part of her red lentil soup, for after all, the humblest of moments can often be the most rewarding.

Layla would not appreciate the significance of this simple lesson until she had paid for her bag of white onions, smiled at Danny Fadden's dazed look, averted the loitering Donnelly twins' low whistles, and quickly returned to the warmth of her sisters' kitchen, hiccuping all the way. Only then did she realize that she was still holding an onion in her palm, the last one she had picked up before seeing Malachy McGuire's wondrous face. When she unclenched her tight fist, she found that, just like her heart, the little white vegetable was sautéed to a crisp.

baklava

4 cups brown sugar

1 cup water

1/2 cup rosewater

1 pound shelled pistachios, chopped

1 pound blanched almonds, chopped

2 tablespoons ground cardamom

1 teaspoon ground cinnamon

15 frozen phyllo pastry sheets

1/2 cup unsalted butter, melted

Bring 2 cups of sugar, water, and rosewater to a boil in a medium saucepan. Set aside to cool. Grind pistachios, almonds, cardamom, cinnamon, and remaining 2 cups of sugar in a food processor for 1 minute. Set aside. Lay 5 sheets of buttered phyllo pastry into a greased 13-by-9-inch pan. Spread a thin, even layer of nut mixture, then cover with 5 more buttered sheets of pastry. Repeat until all mixture is used. Cover with 5 more buttery sheets. With a sharp knife, cut across and diagonally to form diamond shapes. Bake in oven at 350°F for 1 hour. Pour cooled sugar and rosewater syrup over top. Let cool before serving.

chapter three

THE PEACH OFFICES of Ballinacroagh's police station sit at one end of the town square, across from Saint Barnabas Roman Catholic Church and immediately adjacent to the decaying Palladian building that houses the town council.

The Garda station, with its pasty, popcorn stucco façade, is nothing to boast about; nor does the crumbling plaster crest above the door, engraved with the words "An Garda Síochána," intimidate anyone who crosses its creaking, musty threshold. "An Garda Síochána," or "Guardians of the Peace" for those unschooled in the Gaelic tongue, is the official title of the blue-vested, potbellied police officers comfortably stationed all over the Irish countryside. To the uninitiated, *Garda* may seem like a badge of glory, a name that alludes to winged, mythical protectors, the kind that hover above their human counterparts with ready crossbows in case trouble strikes. But such grand titles can often be misleading, as evidenced by the police station's two most regular (and reluctant) inhabitants.

Sergeant Sean Grogan sat in the processing room, feet up on his desk with eyes half-closed as he listened to the day's weather pattern on a handheld radio. Flaccid in both body and soul, Grogan could usually be found listening to Mid-West FM; news of union disputes, foot-and-mouth epidemics, and war-torn African countries always made him thankful for the monotony of his chosen occupation.

"Is that tea on its way, Kevin?" Sean Grogan asked, briefly popping open one eye to his second in command, Guard Kevin Slattery.

Every morning Kevin Slattery would ignite the hundred-year-old stove—a turf-powered range kept in a side room—before filling the dented tin kettle with cold water and arranging Grogan's favorite shortbread biscuits on a tea plate. On this particular Monday morning, though, Kevin had arrived late for work, having been detained by his pregnant wife's premature contractions.

"I was meaning to get to that now, Sean," he replied, lighting the range. He didn't know who was more demanding of attention—his water-retentive wife or his lazy superior officer. Calling it a draw, Kevin returned five minutes later with a gray circle of turf ash on the tip of his round nose. "The range's goin'. It won't be long now, so."

Grogan grunted testily. He needed his morning tea and shortbread boost in order to concentrate fully on the International News.

To bide the time until the water boiled, Kevin crouched before a two-shelf bookcase set against one corner of the processing room and removed eight dusty ledger books from its shelves. Although most Garda stations in County Mayo were furnished with at least one humming new typewriter, Ballinacroagh still used the crumbling ten-pound ledger books of yesteryear to record the town's illegal activities. Kevin Slattery had the wearisome job of handwriting the police reports, meticulously printing in the ledger columns each crime, with its corresponding date, time, and alleged perpetrator.

Opening the most current ledger, Kevin read the last entry on the fourteenth of February, the day the Cat, Ballinacroagh's resident drunk and all-around malcontent, had delivered a two-fingered salute to the Saint of Sweethearts. The wizened alcoholic (no one in town *really* knew how old the Cat was) had decided to bring his Valentine's Day party to the rectory's roof, climbing up there with the uncanny ease of the scraggy animal for which he was named. The Cat spent a good three hours on the rectory's roof, lamenting lost loves and wailing into an unmarked bottle of misery, until Grogan and Slattery finally managed to bring him down with a cattle prod.

The young officer shook his head at the memory and closed the ledger, sending up a poof of dust that made his eyes water. The kettle whistled sharply in the side room just then, overriding the news crackling on the radio. Annoyed, Grogan leaned forward to turn the receiver's volume up and happened to catch sight of Thomas McGuire's Land Rover gunning into the town council's parking lot next door.

Both guards scrambled to the window and watched as Thomas thundered up to the council office. The hefty bar owner pounded on the closed door for a full two minutes, driving his fist senselessly into the wood panels and giving himself a right old nasty splinter, which worsened his mood altogether. It was only eight in the morning, too early for the lazy sods on the board to show up for their stab at municipal work. Still, the wee hour didn't stop Thomas from kicking the blue council doors in unadulterated rage before retreating to his Land Rover to await Councilman Padraig Carey's arrival.

"Doesn't look like he'll be filing any complaints at the town hall just yet," observed the mild-mannered Kevin. He would not have admitted it for the world, but the sight and sound of Thomas's violence frightened him something awful.

Grogan sighed. "Better get to the tea now, Kevin. It's going to be a long day yet. I'd put my money on it," he said out of habit, for Grogan was a man who regularly lost his week's wages to the horses.

He nodded knowingly and turned the weather report up on the crackling radio.

. . . Well now, folks, this just in from the lovely Kathleen at our weather desk—be prepared 'cause it looks like the rain's coming and it's here to stay. Winds will be gale force eight, with a chance of strong gusts to storm force ten. Don't forget yer umbrellas, and do yer shopping before lunchtime! This is Irish Western Radio. Mayo, Ireland, and the world are listenin'!

Thomas turned the radio on in his Land Rover with his splintery hand, hoping to drown out the beats pounding in his head. That gobshite Padraig had better open the council office soon, he thought angrily to himself, or there was no telling what he'd do. If he didn't get some answers for what he had seen in the old pastry shop, God help him, he'd tear the place apart with his own two hands. He was fecked if he was going to let that Eye-talian witch rob him of his dream a second time around, that was for sure.

For Thomas McGuire, the dream had started on December 31, 1961, the fateful birth night of Irish television. The country's foray into technology that night brought him face-to-face with the debonair moves of the Working Boys Band, swinging live from Dublin's Gresham Hotel. As his entire family sat gobsmacked before the fuzzy receiver, fifteen-year-old Thomas stood behind the line of straight-backed chairs set in the front parlor and felt his toes move with a life of their own. Before he knew what was happening, his pointy, two-toned shoes were swinging in uncontrollable dips and turns, following the televised rhythms of the Motown-inspired Irish sextet into a whole new world. Those feet of his mash-potatoed out of the parlor, did the twist up the stairs, and set a syncopated beat knocking about in Thomas's usually vacuous brain, a beat that did not stop thumping, not even when he was asleep.

Aware of the stigma that his growing obsession with popular dance steps would incur on the Gaelic football field at his all-boys' secondary school, Thomas hid his passion from everyone and indulged only under the invigorating stream of a scalding showerhead, shimmying as the shampoo bubbled down the drain. Sometimes, while his snotty brothers slept in the bed next to him, he would fish out a flashlight to pore over the latest *Teen Beat* magazine he had "borrowed" from under his sister Margaret's pillow. Pictures of apple-cheeked American teenagers on Dick Clark's *American Bandstand* and bowl-headed Brits bopping away to Top 40 hits from the Yardbirds and Herman's Hermits filled his gut with yearning. If only he was older, young Thomas would whisper to himself. He'd be off like a shot to London or New York. To make a name for himself. Thomas McGuire could be the next Elvis Presley or Paul McCartney, he knew he could.

Alas, it was not to be. With his father's untimely demise came the responsibility of an empire, or the start of one, which for young Thomas turned out to be Paddy McGuire's Pub. He put his dreams of dancing fame aside for the more staid occupation of drink lord and town bully. Between 1966 and 1976, with the help of a much-touted marriage to Cecilia Devereux, the county mayor's two-hundred-and-twelve-pound nymphomaniacal daughter, Thomas McGuire would secure for himself a tidy monopoly on the town's precious leisure money. He relegated his six wayward siblings to the daily maintenance of his growing businesses, while he oversaw the whole machine with the eyes of a hungry beast. And it had served him well, this diligence of waking hours, his insistence on upgrading the Wilton Inn's upholstery (from an early-century leather to a paisley velour) and pub menus (adding a bottle of sticky port wine to his growing list of stouts and ales). In a time when the average yearly wage hardly topped eight thousand pounds, Thomas McGuire had managed to become a very rich man. With his six thriving establishments and nearly a third of the town's residents working under his fungied thumb, Thomas might even have taken a respite from it all. He might finally have set aside some time to tend to his ever-expanding wife and his growing litter of children. Yes, had Thomas not decided (in a rare moment of generosity) to treat his three hardworking brothers to a trip to the Spanish island of Majorca in the summer of 1980, he probably would have stopped for a stale breath or two. But destiny, it seemed, had other plans. For it was on that trip that Thomas finally became free to relive his adolescent dream.

The idea hit him as he was standing on the patio of Discoteca de Amor, listening to the opening strains of Thelma Houston's "Don't Leave Me This Way" pump out into the sultry Spanish sky above him. Prompted by the liberating ecstasy of synthesizers, the comforting approval of slippery polyester, and a pretty brown girl in enormous platform shoes jutting into his groin to the rhythm of a funky beat, Thomas's feet suddenly began dancing again. Swaying with abandon to the loud disco music, the bar owner felt like a newer, better version of himself. And it didn't take long for him to decide that what he needed more than anything, what he desired above all else, was his very own discotheque.

Back in Ballinacroagh, a rejuvenated Thomas set about pursuing his goal with the greatest fervor. He sported bushy sideburns, grew his curly hair out to his shoulders, and squeezed his sausage legs into a pair of denim bell-bottoms. At Kenny's Record Shop, he combed through thousands of disco records, produced in exotic American locales such as Bushwick, Brooklyn, downtown Detroit, and Jamaica, Queens, and in December 1980 he took in a total of twenty-two screenings of *Saturday Night Fever* in Castlebar's one-screen cinema. By the new year Thomas McGuire was ready to implement the second step of his nightclub plan: finding the perfect dancing space.

It was no contest, really. There was only one spot Thomas would consider for his disco—Papa's Pastries next door. Chance had it that the wall separating the Delmonicos' pastry shop from Paddy McGuire's Pub was nothing but a shaky layer of plaster and rotting wood, an anomaly among the brick and stone of other shops. A three-man crew would need a day, two at most, to clear the way for the rip-roaring nightclub Thomas had already christened Polyester Paddy's. It was the perfect venue. All that mattered now was figuring out how he could get his hands on it.

Thomas McGuire wouldn't have to wonder for long; his disco prayers were soon answered with Luigi Delmonico's meringue-coated death in the spring of 1981. The sudden coronary waltzed Luigi out of this world and into the next. It also left the door open for Thomas McGuire to move in.

At least, that was the plan.

Knowing it would not sit well with the town's more religious factions if he rushed into demolition the day after the chubby pastry chef's wake, Thomas waited a whole month before knocking on Estelle Delmonico's door. Tradition must be adhered to, he reasoned, if only for appearances' sake. The green-shuttered, four-room Delmonico cottage was situated on a remote and perilously steep mountain road that proved far too narrow for Thomas's mammoth Land Rover. Forced to park his prized vehicle at the bottom of the hill, the big man puffed his way along the rocky mile and a half to the cottage on foot, coughing on vapors of cow dung and pig fat that hung in the air. The hike felt to Thomas like penances paid in advance; his hairless inner thighs burned with every step, his self-preoccupations blinding him to the beauty of the surrounding verdant valleys.

The lanes winding uphill toward the cottage are those quaint, postcard snapshots one has come to expect of the Irish countryside. Lined with rusted fences and stone borders, the leafy farm roads are liberally embraced by thousands of drooping, wet tree branches and stinging blades of nettle. But it is the clearing that suddenly springs upon the walker as he turns to the cottage that showcases the ultimate fairy tale, the Druids' dream. For there is the ocean. The Atlantic feeds into the southern end of Clew Bay like a doting parent. On a clear day the view through the cottage's windows, bordered with sills of African violets, is simply magnificent. One can even see, wedged into the side of neighboring Croagh Patrick, the graying blocks of a stone altar, where most climbing pilgrimages end and the redemption of souls begins.

Thomas reached the whitewashed cottage and paused to wipe his sweaty meat brow. Yes, he had done what decency required. He had waited long enough, and now the pastry space would be his. All he needed to do was offer the old widow a tidy sum—probably more than she had ever seen come through that greasy wog excuse for a bread shop—and Polyester Paddy's would become a reality.

Thomas tried to restrain his excitement as he knocked on the low cottage door. A minute later a short, plump woman in her mid-sixties opened up, her ample, apron-covered bosom jutting out toward him in a way that brought back childhood memories of secretive peeking. For indeed, as a young boy, Thomas had been drawn to the decadent colors twinkling through the pastry shop's windows. Schoolboy Thomas had loved to watch Estelle Delmonico administer sweet toppings to lemony yellow meringue pies and frozen scoops of orange gelato, smiling as she went along. He remembered quite vividly how her then younger breasts heaved passionately as she placed a single, pearl-glazed maraschino cherry on top of each dessert, from Danish to chocolate éclairs. But that was a long time ago, Thomas reminded himself. He didn't know any better back then.

"Yes?" Estelle's puzzled greeting shook Thomas back to reality. She cocked her head quizzically—for she had difficulty remembering faces—but Thomas interpreted the gesture as a shrewd bargaining tactic from the Old Country. Well, two could play at that game.

"Don't think we've met. I'm Thomas McGuire," he said, puffing out his broad chest. The bully did not extend his hand or even acknowledge the old lady with a nod, a basic Ballinacroagh extension of courtesy. He just stood there, looming over the Italian widow in unmistakable hubris, waiting for her to recognize his assumed superiority.

"Of course. How silly of me, eh? You know, I would not even know my own mama's face, may she rest in peace, if she was right in front of me. It's my eyes. They don't remember faces like they do recipes." A surprisingly girlish giggle escaped from Estelle's mouth. Pools of sweat glistened on her downy upper lip and began to trickle down the cracks above her lipstick line. She rescued them with her darting tongue, slurping the water in sweet delight.

Thomas stared down into the widow's playful face and felt an unexpected shiver of fright. Was she not right in the head, then? Her husband was not yet cold in the ground and here she was licking her lips and laughing like it was Christmas morning. He had always heard she was a bit strange, but crazy?

What Thomas McGuire did not know, as he stood cultivating his jumped conclusions, was that Estelle Delmonico had sweated nothing but a highly potent mixture of pure sugar and water ever since she was a day old. Unlike the musk of normal feminine perspiration, her glands exuded no smell—but the taste! Her late husband, Luigi, himself anything but ordinary, had caught on immediately to the magic of those sugary drops. Sweet Estelle was the greatest muse an ambitious pastry chef from Naples could ever wish for, and theirs was a match made in plum-sugared heaven.

"Would you like to come in? I'm making baklava. Can you smell the happiness? The recipe is a special Persian dessert sent to me by my niece in London." Estelle wiped her floury hands on her apron and stepped aside to welcome him in.

Thomas squinted into the dark house, expecting to see strange shadows and lacy doilies. He wasn't prepared for the strange smell that punched him in the gut. Stunned by the erotic mixture of cardamom and toasted almonds, he reeled two steps back down onto the gravel. Unknown to Thomas McGuire, this very aroma had once induced a lusty Achaemenian king to declare sixty-nine nights of lovemaking in his kingdom of honeysuckle fortresses. Concubines were ordered to comb their dark locks with powdered cardamom, as harem slaves drizzled their white belly buttons with a mixture of warm honey and almonds. But rather than have a similar amorous effect on Thomas, the scent tied his bowels into a disturbed knot.

"No, no. I'm here on a business matter," he said, raising his hands in revulsion. There was something very wrong about a smell so strong. "Sorry to hear about yer husband's death. See the shop's been closed since. Would ya be leaving for yer niece's soon, then?"

"Gloria? No. She's young, free, in London. No, I don't go anywhere. Anyway, what would my Luigi do without me, eh?"

"Luigi? Yer husband?" Thomas was already crafting his speech before the town council. This old bird was ready for the loony bin, for sure. She certainly was not fit to keep her hold over such prime Ballinacroagh real estate.

"*Si, si,* my husband. Luigi," said the widow.

She stepped beyond the door's threshold and pointed past Thomas, toward the gravel path. There, at the beginning of the walkway, a large rosebush sat clinging to the ocean wind. Unlike the prim, Anglicized bushes spattered outside various Ballinacroagh houses, this plant burst with deep, primal magenta blossoms. Thick thorns curved around the flowers' petals like good chaperones guarding virginal yet very hormonal schoolgirls. Estelle Delmonico didn't seem to notice the thorns as she patted the flowers.

"Luigi. My Luigi. You see the ribbon?" She pointed to a thin white sash tied tightly around the bush's trunk.

Shivers ran up Thomas's spine as he realized that the sash he was looking at was no ordinary string. It was an apron string. A pastry chef's apron, to be exact. Now there was no denying it: the woman was mad.

"My Luigi is sleeping here. No, Luigi, I never leave you," Estelle whispered. Leaning down toward the gritty soil, she kissed her hand and gently patted the base of the rosebush, where she had secretly sprinkled her late husband's ashes.

"Good. Right. Nice to meet you there, Luigi. And the shop? Is Luigi going back there as well?"

"No. That shop killed my Luigi. No more work for him. Now he rests." She sighed, patting the mound again.

"Well so, that's that then! Just let me know what yer asking for the shop and I'll take it off yer hands right away. Just name yer price," he said.

"No, I'm sorry, Mr. McGuire. The shop is not for sale. No sale, but I rent it to you at a good price."

"Well now, Mrs. Delmonico. Renting is no good for me. It's a sale I'm after. Wouldn't you rather be free of the whole lot? Just spend yer days looking after, er, Luigi there?" He nodded uncomfortably toward the rosebush.

"No, no. Luigi says to me not to sell. I have to listen to him. He's so good with business. Me, no. I love the cooking, the baking, the bread." Estelle turned toward the cottage. "I'm sorry, Mr. McGuire. No sale. But I give you some baklava before you go, yes? It's a new recipe. You can be the first to taste." Estelle disappeared into the dark cottage. Situated as she was on the lonely crag heap, the little widow had few visitors and no one to taste her baklava besides a couple of confused hillock sheep, so she took the pub owner's visit to be positively providential.

"Look what I have for you, Mr. McGuire. It's a lucky day for your sweet tooth."

Estelle had returned to the doorway with a colorful plate piled high with baklava. She was humming an improvised aria under her sugared breath; a snippet from the second act of *Don Giovanni,* when the arrogant, sinful nobleman plunges into the open arms of hell. Little did Estelle know that the passionate chorus, "such is the fate of a wrongdoer," combined with the overpowering seduction of the rosewater-soaked baklava pastry, would send Ballinacroagh's own misanthrope hurtling down her gravelly pathway and into the thorny hands of Luigi's rosebush.

"Oh, Mr. McGuire! Do not move! You will get bad cuts from my Luigi's thorns if you do!" Estelle exclaimed, hurrying to where Thomas lay prostrate, atop a hundred and one sharp rose thorns. She was about to help Thomas off the rosebush, the hopeful plate of baklava still in hand, when the big man held up his beefy paw and roared.

"No! Stay away! Don't you come near me with those feckin' things!" Thomas lunged forward on the thorny stakes and managed to land on his feet. Backing down the rest of the path, he held up his two fists in front of his red face, an amateur pugilist shamefully defeated in the first round. "And if ya know what's good fer ya, you'll sell that bloody shop to me! You'll be sorry if you don't!" he threatened weakly, before turning and running down the cottage lane.

Stunned, Estelle Delmonico watched the hulking man scurry away, his broad back pierced by curling rose spikes that resembled Beelzebub's own cowardly tail. And all the while, the operatic chorus chimed in her ear, "such is the fate of a wrongdoer," "such is the fate of a wrongdoer."

THAT WAS FIVE YEARS AGO. Thomas cursed under his breath and punched his good fist into the Land Rover's steering wheel. Five feckin' years.

He should have kept on Estelle Delmonico like he planned instead of letting things go the way he did. But even he hadn't been able to forecast the series of travesties that had sent him lurching through the first part of the new decade.

The trouble had started with Kieran, that gobshite brother of his who had abandoned his managerial duties at the Ale House to run away with some dope-smoking actress. The last Thomas heard, the two lovers had formed a performance troupe called The McGuire Family Circus and were traveling the countryside in caravans, reenacting the "Feast of All Saints." Put the whole family to shame, that Kieran. And then, of course, fortune had dealt another blow with the flood of 1982. Torrential rains washed through half the businesses on Main Mall as if it was laundry day. Nearly took the Wilton Inn off the map, the flood did. The gushing water burst into the carvery room and floated silver trays of roasted meats onto the hilly street. For weeks people were picking soaked pieces of parsnip and rotten ham out from the soles of their shoes. Getting the old inn back to working order had left Thomas with little time to devote to his disco cause.

Bleedin' nature and all her feckin' rain. Thomas shook the morning drizzle from his thick hair. Ah, who was he kidding? The truth was he had become lazy, let things go. Taken it for granted that the pastry space would always be there for him when he was ready. It had never crossed his mind that the place could have a new life without his say-so.

Jaysus! Thomas growled and punched the steering wheel again. He should have known the old bat was holding out on selling the shop for a better reason than her husband's dying wishes. She was planning to get back into business for herself all along. Well, that Estelle Delmonico was in for a surprise, Thomas told himself. A big surprise.

The synthesized vibrations of disco beats were suddenly pounding again inside Thomas McGuire's potato head. He was going to heed them this time around. No doubt about it.

=

dugh yogurt drink

2 cups plain yogurt

3 cups mineral or spring water

3 tablespoons freash mint, chopped

1 teaspoon salt

½ teaspoon ground black pepper

Mint leaves for garnish

Mix ingredients in a large pitcher or jug. Add ice slowly as you stir. Garnish with mint leaves.

chapter four

PADRAIG CAREY NEVER had much luck with timing. If he had known that Thomas McGuire was waiting in the town council parking lot to unleash his wrath upon him, he would have stayed for another nine holes at Westport Pitch and Putt. Instead, he'd left in the middle of a great round, driven by guilt for having spent another workday morning putting the greens. Padraig drove his car into the town council parking lot and turned the ignition off. Another day of mindless slogging before he could tee off again, he wistfully thought.

A thin and unusually hirsute man, Padraig was in the unenviable position of being intimidated by the McGuire name in both domestic and public sectors. Having married Thomas McGuire's Amazonian sister Margaret (who, as the smartest of the McGuire clan, had the difficult job of balancing all of Thomas's books), Padraig was completely cornered in his home life. He acquiesced to his wife's every decision, whether it was who controlled their finances (she did), when to have a rough-and-tumble in the bedroom (once a month), or what to have for dinner (salty bacon and boiled cabbage). In his public life Padraig seemed to be set up comfortably as head of Ballinacroagh's two-manned council post. His lofty position as council speaker required little of him: occasionally managing road-to-farmland ratio and cutting ribbons at foreign-owned factory openings. But in reality Padraig had little peace in his job. His bully of a brother-in-law was always meddling in every aspect of Ballinacroagh's daily administration. Hardly a week went by without the councilman getting a complaint from Thomas, be it as trivial as the height of the hedges around the town council building or as dangerous as that time he had wanted to throw Estelle Delmonico into Saint Mary's Mental Institution. Still, Padraig thought, as long as he could get himself onto the putting green most mornings, he could stand just about anything his job entailed. Even if it meant pandering to Thomas McGuire's every whim.

Oblivious to the bar owner's hulking approach, Padraig reached out across the backseat and absently traced the brass buckle on the strap of his golf bag.

"Padraig Carey."

Thomas's booming voice made the short councilman jump in his seat.

"Hello there, Tom. Yer up and about early as usual, I see." Padraig gulped. He hurried out of his car, angling his thin body to block the golf bag in the backseat from Thomas's view.

"Can't say the same for you, now can I? I want some answers, Padraig Carey! Just because you got my sister up the pole years ago doesn't mean I won't have you out on your feckin' arse before you can blink twice!"

"Sorry now, Tom." Padraig could almost feel himself shrink before the steaming bully.

"Sorry now, Tom? Sorry now, Tom! You've got some nerve, Padraig Carey! Why wasn't I told about the old witch's place? Why do you think I keep you in this shite post, if you're no good to me then?"

Thomas's eggplant face contorted grotesquely. Standing on his toes, he towered above poor, inconsequential Padraig like a mighty skyscraper over a feeble pigeon.

"Now, now, Tom. Calm yerself. What do you mean? The old Delmonico place, is it?"

"Yes, the Delmonico place, you *eejit*! I've been waiting five years fer the bit of expansion any man in my position has the right to. Now she's gone to openin' that pisshole of a shop again without any prior warning from yer bleedin' end! I have a good mind to tear the place down myself!"

"Estelle Delmonico? Another shop? She couldn't be thinking about that now—not at her age."

"How the feck would you know? You with your golf clubs up the arse while I slave away looking after this town! Where would this place be without me and my business, eh?" Thomas punched the air, grazing Padraig's shoulder. He climbed into his car like an angry gorilla and rolled down his window. "I want you to find out what that old bag is up to. And meanwhile, tell Margaret and all she knows that if they want to stay on Thomas McGuire's better side they'd better stick to Corcoran's fer their daily bread."

"Are you sure it's a pastry shop she's got running again, then?"

"Whatever it is, I want it empty and closed within the week."

Thomas revved the Land Rover and tore out of the parking lot, leaving Padraig numbed and unanchored. The feeble councilman placed one hand on the hood of his car for support as his blood pumped furiously through his small, hairy body.

ESTELLE DELMONICO carefully maneuvered her croaky Honda into the cobblestone alleyway behind the café. The little widow had gotten up earlier than usual that morning, the gale-ridden moans of neighboring Croagh Patrick echoing her own as she pushed her brittle legs out of her feathery bed.

Despite Estelle's hearty laugh and steady eyes, she suffered from a degeneration of cartilage that caused her great misery. It had started with a seasonal prickling of wrists and fingertips that first year she and Luigi arrived in County Mayo, and had slowly but surely expanded like a piece of pulled dough until it wrapped her in a cannoli of excruciating pain. Years of helping Luigi knead and punch endless loaves of currant bread had exacerbated her affliction, and by the year preceding her husband's death, Estelle's arthritis had reduced her to sitting on a stool behind the store counter while Luigi ran around tending to customers and ovens alike.

Of course, Estelle had tried the prescribed doses of steroid but found that it did nothing but give her unusually unmanageable underarm hair. She had even traveled to a Chinese acupuncturist, who in the height of the free-loving seventies, had set up shop in Dublin's Henry Street. Although she was impressed by the Chinaman's fortitude—Li Fung Tao practiced his morning tai chi in undisturbed serenity while fruit and veg hawkers spat their shrill wares all around him—his needles did nothing but make her feel like a piece of anchovy strung in an *Alici* marinade of oregano and chili flakes.

Estelle had even tried her own concoction of rosemary and lavender, which she plucked from the little herb garden around the back of her cottage. Boiling the leaves down until only their dark oils remained, she would then mix in a good amount of Umbrian olive oil sent by her niece, Gloria, from London. The oil left her Mediterranean skin taut like snappy brindle berries, a fact that spurred envy among the old townswomen and prompted Dervla Quigley to spread rumors that Estelle Delmonico had made a deal with the fairies, for sure. Estelle didn't mind the suspicious stares, even enjoyed them to be honest, wishing there was some truth to it all. Because no matter how aromatic and moisturizing, the rosemary and lavender massage was not magical enough to put an end to the arthritis.

The Italian widow's aches were acting up as usual on this day of spring reckoning, but she was not going to let them stop her from whipping up her famous osso buco for her sweet new tenants. She even made a side of her own mother's gremolata, toasting the woody pine nuts until they turned dark brown. This veal masterpiece used to be Luigi's favorite dish, and Estelle saved it for special occasions when the frangipani of her sunny homeland was especially missed.

"Hello?" Estelle knocked on the old shop's back door with her right fist and peered into its blue, yellow, and green stained-glass window. From inside the kitchen, her round face looked like that of a medieval Venetian harlequin come to life.

Bahar, sitting closest to the back door, jumped at the unexpected knock. Her large brown eyes popped with anxiety, and she tightened her grip on the sharp knife she was using. It had been a long time since a knock had not set off a flutter of fear in Bahar's small birdcage chest or made her duck for cover. Ten seconds, counted out in thudding heartbeats, passed before she realized the knock was benign, but by then her complexion had grown ashen, the color of unwanted oatmeal.

Darkest among her sisters, Bahar considered her brown skin tone as yet another sign that she was the least desirable Aminpour sister. As the middle child, Bahar was inevitably stuck between Marjan's intuitive compassion and Layla's willowy optimism. And, as for many children who find themselves bookended by extraordinary siblings, the gnawing desire to stand out, to take center stage, became for Bahar an all-consuming, if subconscious disease. Drama is vital to this sickness's survival, and many middle children are thrown from one emotion to another, within minutes going from extreme anger to acute sadness to euphoric gaiety.

Marjan measured Bahar's unpredictable temperament according to the ancient and treasured Zoroastrian practice of gastronomic balancing, which pitted light against dark, good against evil, hot against cold. Certain hot, or *garm*, personalities tend to be quick to temper, exude more energy, and prompt all others around them to action. This energy often runs itself ragged, so to counter exhaustion, one must consume cold, or *sard* foods, such as freshwater fish, yogurt, coriander, watermelon, and lentils. Most spices and meats should be avoided, for they only stoke the fires inside. (Tea, although hot in temperature, is quite a neutralizing element.) By contrast, for the person who suffers from too cold a temperament, marked by extreme bouts of melancholia and a general disinterest in the future, hot or *garm* dishes are recommended. Foods such as veal, mung beans, cloves, and figs do well to raise spirits and excite ambitions.

To diagnose Bahar as a *garmi* (on account of her extreme anxiety and hot temper) would have been simple enough, had she not also suffered from a lowness of spirit that often led to migraine headaches. Whether in a *garm* or a *sard* mood, Bahar could always depend on her older sister to guide her back to a relative calm. Marjan had for a long time kept a close eye on Bahar and knew exactly when to feed her sautéed fish with garlic and Seville oranges to settle her hot flashes, or when a good apple *khoresh*, a stew made from tart apples, chicken, and split peas, would be a better choice to pull Bahar out of her doldrums.

"Marjan? Who's that?" Bahar got up from the round table where she had been chopping mint sprigs, still clenching the knife.

"It's all right. It's only Mrs. Delmonico," Marjan reassured her sister. "Did you eat anything this morning?" Without Marjan forcing her to take a bite, Bahar would not look after herself, often skipping meals altogether.

"No. Too much to do," Bahar said tiredly, relaxing her tensed jaw.

She placed the knife on the table and opened the back door. At once she was greeted by a friendly smile and the zesty smells of lemon thyme and fresh tomato sauce.

"Hello, Mrs. Delmonico. Come in, please. Let me help you." Bahar leaned over and took the red enamel casserole dish Estelle was balancing on her left arm like a precocious baby.

Marjan left the pot of soup she was stirring at the stove and, taking Estelle's aching arm, gently led her to a kitchen chair. "Mrs. Delmonico, you look so tired," she said. "You are welcome here, of course."

"I bring you my best cooking. Osso buco with pine nut gremolata. It's good luck, you know. In Napoli we eat it on special times. So I bring it for your new year's and birthday." Estelle sat down at the round table, relieved.

"You shouldn't have," said Marjan.

"Please, Mrs. Delmonico. Would you like some tea?" Bahar was already running into the front room to pour a cup of hot water from the boiling golden samovar. Having worked for a year as a nurse in a Lewisham rest home, she immediately recognized the signs of osteoarthritis.

Estelle coughed and unwound her twisted spine. "Thank you, darling," she said, wincing. "And call me Estelle. Mrs. Delmonico was my mama-in-law, and you know, she was a very hard woman to like. Believe me."

Bahar returned and placed a steaming cup of bergamot tea in front of the old woman.

"Thank you. Agh—this Irish weather is going to kill me!" Estelle threw her hands up with all the Italian dramatic flair she could muster. Leaning into the vapor of the steaming tea before her, she inhaled the bitter orange oils of the bergamot flower. "Mmmmm, just like Napoli!"

"Yes, drink. And you have to have some of my red lentil soup. It will warm you up." Marjan smiled at the sweet woman as she ladled out the fragrant soup and placed a bowl next to her teacup.

The combination of cumin, turmeric, and nigella seed produced a healthy blush in Estelle Delmonico's face. Transporting her back nearly fifty years, the smell conjured up her first night of wedded bliss in Morocco. There, under a magical crescent moon, and with the smells of the spices rising from the bazaar below their open hotel window, the tumbling, bronzed bodies of the twenty-year-old honeymooners Luigi and Estelle made love with all the vigor of their Latin blood.

"Mmmmm, wonderful, wonderful. So much food here, my goodness!" Estelle said, emerging from her romantic daydream.

At only nine in the morning the kitchen was already pregnant to its capacity, every crevice and countertop overtaken by Marjan's gourmet creations. Marinating vegetables (*torshi*s of mango, eggplant, and the regular seven-spice variety), packed to the briny brims of five-gallon see-through canisters, sat on the kitchen island. Large blue bowls were filled with salads (angelica lentil, tomato, cucumber and mint, and Persian fried chicken), *dolmeh,* and dips (cheese and walnut, yogurt and cucumber, baba ghanoush, and spicy hummus), which, along with feta, Stilton, and cheddar cheeses, were covered and stacked in the enormous glass-door refrigerator. Opposite the refrigerator stood the colossal brick bread oven. Baking away in its domed belly was the last of the *sangak* bread loaves, three feet long and counting, rising in golden crests and graced with scatterings of poppy and nigella seed. The rest of the bread (paper-thin *lavash,* crusty *barbari,* slabs of *sangak* as well as the usual white sliced loaf) was already covered with comforting cheesecloth to keep the freshness in. And simmering on the stove, under Marjan's loving orders, was a small pot of white onion soup (not to be mistaken for the French variety, for this version boasts dried fenugreek leaves and pomegranate paste), the last pot of red lentil soup, and a larger pot of *abgusht*. An extravaganza of lamb, split peas, and potatoes, *abgusht* always reminded Marjan of early spring nights in Iran, when the cherry blossoms still shivered with late frosts and the piping samovars helped wash down the saffron and dried lime aftertaste with strong, black Darjeeling tea.

"If you think this is something, you should see the front. We've been working since midnight," said Marjan, smiling with the realization that the hardest part of the day was nearly over. Everything was finally coming around, taking shape, in this place with such a funny name.

Bahar continued chopping mint on the round table, every now and again stealing a glance at Estelle as she slurped the last of her soup and leaned back, satisfied and refreshed.

"Oh, so delicious. I am a new woman. So, it is your birthday today, no? How old?"

"Twenty-four." Bahar's shy smile was returned by a large set of teeth sparkling with various fillings of gold.

"Ah, so young!" Hands over head again. "And what are you making there with the mint?"

"It's for Layla. I'm chopping this for her *dugh*." Bahar's knife expertly sliced across the mint leaves, striking emerald mines. Helping Marjan in the kitchen had given her years of experience in peeling and slicing. If Bahar hadn't taken up nursing in London, she would have made an excellent sous chef, even gone to work alongside her sister in one of those trendy English restaurants. But then, that would have required her to spend hours over a hot stove, the burning pots staring up at her with gaping mouths, crucibles of a past that threatened to become present. No, Bahar was certain she could never do that. Even now she went to the stove only in emergencies. Only when Marjan had too little time and not enough hands for stirring all that she had cooked up.

"Doo-oo-gghhh?" Estelle emphasized the word's guttural ending, letting it tickle her throat. "What is that?"

"*Dugh* is a yogurt and mint drink. We usually have it with *chelow kabob*—that's rice and barbecued meats. But Layla's been suffering from hiccups for an hour now, and it doesn't look like they'll stop. This *dugh* will put an end to them," said Marjan, as she grabbed a container of yogurt from the refrigerator.

Estelle watched as Marjan combined the yogurt, mint, salt, pepper, and water in a large pitcher, stirring vigorously until the color became a uniform creamy mint. She added some crushed ice to the pitcher and threw in a garnish of mint to remind Layla of the calming quality found in its green leaves.

Layla was indeed still in the throes of a hiccup fit, but she was nowhere near suffering. The young girl was lying upstairs on the mattress the three sisters shared, splayed out like a star fruit with soliloquies of love-struck Shakespearean heroines running across her muddled brain. The image of Malachy's sapphire eyes sent tremors through her body; the hot node below her belly tingled and sent waves of pleasure down to her toes.

So this was how love was supposed to feel, Layla thought, like the ecstatic cries of a pomegranate as it realizes the knife's thrust, the cesarean labor of juicy seeds cut from her inner womb. Like the gleeful laugh of oil as it corrupts the watery flour, the hot grease bending the batter to its will and creating a greater sweetness from the process—*zulbia,* the sugary fried fritters she loved so. Falling in love was amazing. Why hadn't anyone ever told her so?

Layla hiccuped again. Those sapphire eyes. Maybe she would see them again tomorrow, at her new school. For once Layla would not mind standing before a classroom full of staring faces.

"Layla! Your *dugh* is ready. Come down! Mrs. Delmonico is here for a visit!"

"I'm coming!" Layla answered. Marjan's voice sounded tired, and Layla felt a twinge of guilt for not helping her sisters more with the cooking.

Downstairs, Estelle Delmonico was drinking her second cup of bergamot tea.

"So, my Gloria tells me that you girls escaped the revolution. Yes?"

Marjan stopped stirring and cast a quick glance toward Bahar. Except for a dark shadow over her sister's soulful eyes, there was no sign that the word *revolution* had caused Bahar any agitation.

"Actually, we left Iran a little bit earlier. Just before," Marjan said tentatively, still watching Bahar.

The foggy control towers of Heathrow Airport flashed momentarily into Marjan's mind. February 1, 1979, a date they would later learn had also welcomed a previously exiled Ayatollah, one with a penchant for mystic poetry, into power in Tehran. Ushered into the clear-paned interrogation cubicles of the airport's immigration offices, the girls were completely unprepared for the barrage of accusatory questions and embarrassing searches of pockets and undergarments. Marjan recalled how little Layla had been forced to step out of her ratty panties, to reveal a wad of prerevolutionary exchanged sterling hidden where her underwear's elastic should have been, financial stability in untouchable hearths.

Marjan knew the kind widow was waiting expectantly for their story of escape but found that she could not tell that tale. Not yet. At least not in front of her sensitive sister.

"We were lucky to get visas to the U.K., lucky to get good jobs with the economy so bad. . . . Layla was only seven, so she doesn't remember much."

Despite her madcap moments, Estelle had an acute sense of boundaries and decided to leave the subject alone.

"Yes, very young, seven. And where is that pretty girl, eh? She is not sick?"

"No, just a teenager. Layla, come on!" Marjan yelled toward the staircase again, unaware that Layla had been standing the whole time at the top of the landing. No one could see her from there, but she had heard. And it wasn't true. She remembered it all.

She remembered the sirens. The blaring horns, mounted atop military jeeps that appeared without notice to signal the nightly curfew; circling in and out of the soft-hued residential streets lined with marigolds, households stocked with both *dugh* and Coca-Cola. Soon after came the flapping. Funny how she remembered hearing it before actually *seeing* it, the funeral tint of that female tent that was lately becoming so commonly worn, even in the more affluent northern suburbs. *Chador, chador.* Three square yards of scratchy wool strategically wrapped and clenched in chattering teeth, revealing nothing above blinking pupils, nothing below dripping nostrils. *Chador, chador.*

Posters of these multiplying fabric ravens were popping up on university walls and shop windows daily, headlined with thinly cloaked threats. Bahar, who was sixteen at the time of the upheaval and very much under its influence, had used those same threats to induce Marjan and Layla to wear full-length veils. She would return home flushed with excitement after attending one of the many student revolts in Tehran's central and southern streets, filled with stories of bullet-ridden banners and a stern-browed Ayatollah that made so many chadors swoon with delirium.

The chants, the demands for death, were heard everywhere. *"Death to the traitor Shah! Death to all things from the opiate West!"* An end to the America that had brought Layla the Tom and Jerry cartoons and peanut M&M's she loved so much. That had been enough to make her cry (secretly, of course), late at night in bed.

Bahar was sixteen then, just a little older than she was now. Layla shook her head to dispel those dark thoughts. Maybe Marjan was right to change the subject, to try to put it all behind them. Layla hiccuped again, the sound releasing her from her hiding place. She walked down the stairs and smiled.

"Finally! Your *dugh*'s on the counter there. Drink it before it settles. And say hello to Mrs. Delmonico," Marjan barked, her nerves getting the better of her.

"Estelle. Call me Estelle."

abgusht

4 pounds boned leg of lamb, save bone

5 large onions, chopped

1 teaspoon turmeric

10 cups water

1 cup yellow split peas

1 teaspoon paprika

4 teaspoons salt

1 teaspoon ground black pepper

5 large potatoes, peeled and quartered

7 tomatoes, sliced

2 tablespoons tomato paste

1 dried lime

2 strands saffron dissolved in 7 tablespoons hot water

2 teaspoons advieh*

*Optional: equal amounts crushed rose petals, cardamom, cinnamon, and cumin, mixed

Brown meat, 1 onion, and turmeric in a large stockpot. Add water, split peas, paprika, and bone. Lower heat and simmer, covered, for 2 hours. Add remaining ingredients. Simmer, covered, for 40 minutes. Remove bone. Remove all vegetables and meat, and mash them together in a large bowl. Serve mash in a separate bowl alongside remaining broth.

chapter five

MAYBE IT WAS ALL Thomas McGuire's doing. Not trusting Padraig Carey to the effective dissemination of his message of hate, Ballinacroagh's chief publican had promptly set up camp inside McGuire's Ale House after leaving the town council parking lot. From his favored stool at the high end of the oak bar, Thomas deftly expounded, like a seasoned politico of the Roman Forum, on the dangers of foreign smells.

Perhaps Dervla Quigley had a finger in it as well, hissing the news up and down Main Mall until all of Ballinacroagh knew exactly what to avoid. "Forget the infested ways of the tinkers," Dervla would have whispered darkly to anyone standing beneath her window. "It's these foreign hippies we've got to hold fast against."

Or it could have simply come down to the uncontrollable caprices of Lady Luck, Bahar's blistery thumb and the persistent Atlantic rains, signs of imminent trouble ahead.

Whatever the culprit, the opening of the Babylon Café that first day of spring was not half as grand as Marjan had hoped. To her utmost disappointment, not a single customer had stepped inside the inviting café the whole of Monday.

"Maybe we need to put up a big Open sign. What do you think?" Marjan said on Tuesday morning. She stood perplexed before the café windows, with folded arms and knitted eyebrows.

"A sign? Open your eyes, Marjan. We had the curtains opened and all the lights on yesterday and no one even stopped to look through the windows. A sign!" Bahar sniffed, shaking her head.

"I just don't understand it. Not even one customer! Maybe it's the rain." Marjan pressed her forehead against the cold glass windowpane.

The rainstorm had started Monday around noon, blasting down in stinging sheets, rattling hinges and windowpanes, and wiping Main Mall of any pedestrians. Most shops had soon shut down for the day, their tired proprietors heaving sighs against the wind as they struggled to lock their storefronts. Battling gusts with overturned umbrellas, they quickly scattered home on foot or, the luckier ones, in freezing, water-clogged cars. Even Dervla Quigley, who hardly counted the daily village drizzle as a reason to leave her window, had retreated behind the pleats of her chintz curtains at the height of the storm.

"Well, it doesn't look like the rain'll stop anytime soon. Look at it! I didn't think any place could be wetter than London," Bahar commented, gazing outside. The street gushed with an unappetizing soup of broken glass, stray turf blocks, cigarette stumps, and the salty tears of a darkened sky that had yet to end its purge.

"I bet we'll get at least fifty people in today. Right, Marjan?" Layla looked up from her breakfast of *lavash* and feta. She was already running late for her first day of school and was scarfing down her food as fast as she could.

"Of course, *joon-e man*. We'll have the whole town in here soon," she replied, trying to sound upbeat.

"It's a good thing you made Mrs. Delmonico take some food home with her yesterday. We'd never get through all the pots of soup and *abgusht* you made," Bahar said disapprovingly.

"Okay, wish me luck!" Layla rose abruptly from her half-eaten breakfast. She was decked out in her newly starched uniform of light blue sweater, crisp white blouse, and brown tweed skirt. Grabbing an umbrella, she slung her schoolbag on her shoulders, smiled radiantly at her two sisters, and swung open the café door.

The dense mist that usually sat upon Croagh Patrick's shoulders had descended on the village, insidiously inhabiting all crevices and street corners. Layla eagerly joined the train of high school kids braving the cold rain and fog, pushing through a shrouded Main Mall up toward Saint Joseph's Secondary. She paused for a moment to wave excitedly at her two sisters before disappearing in the heavy veil of mist. Bahar, worried for Layla's well-being, waved back anxiously, but Marjan looked on with delight, happy to see Layla so energized. In a decade of regularly televised hijackings and terrorist bombings carried out by masked Middle Easterners, new schools for Layla tended to be breeding grounds for endless taunting sessions; accusations of "terrorist" and "hijacker" were thrown around the school yards like recess diversions. Their youngest sister would usually be too terrified to sleep the night before she started at a new school. But Layla had surprised her sisters this morning, getting up early with bright eyes to pack her own lunch of basil, tomato, and yogurt-cucumber dip wrapped in *lavash* and to iron out her school uniform. There was no nervousness in her gestures, no fear on her beautiful face as she nearly skipped up a drenched Main Mall.

Layla's unexpected cheerfulness was a good sign, Marjan decided. Any optimism was welcome, especially in light of yesterday's failed opening.

A SAVIOR, AND THE BABYLON CAFÉ'S first customer, came that very Tuesday afternoon, in the merry shape of Father Fergal Mahoney.

Father Mahoney was on his way down to Marie Brennan and her sister Dervla's dimly lit parlor for the first meeting of the 1986 Patrician Day Dance committee. For the past thirty-nine years, the good-natured priest had served as coordinator of the dance that celebrated the annual pilgrimage to the peak of Croagh Patrick. Every summer a stream of pilgrims climbed the mountain's stony shoulders—some with bare feet—as penitence for choosing sinful paths during the rest of the year. To commemorate this turn for atonement, Ballinacroagh celebrated the first Sunday climb in July, Patrician Day, by hitching up coarse canvas tents, stringing up Japanese lanterns, and brandishing life-size, cutout posters of a rather soused Saint Patrick. Foldout tables were loaded with Thomas McGuire's latest ale and enough bacon and cabbage from his carvery at the Wilton Inn to give everyone in town heartburn, with a three-pound charge, of course.

As coordinator of the Dance, Father Mahoney had a lot on his plate: not only was he in charge of choosing a band (always a success but for that unfortunate year a group of three Dublin nuns shocked the crowd with their a cappella renditions of "99 Red Balloons" and "Relax"), but he was also designated Master of Ceremonies. It was a delicious role for the extroverted priest, who often peppered his Masses and homilies with humor. As MC, Father Mahoney happily indulged in a good half hour of jokes that, for one time each year, were unfettered by his religious duties.

Preoccupied with new punch lines, the funny priest did not notice the Babylon Café's welcoming glow until he was standing right in front of its sparkling windows. Having prepared himself for the committee's usual fare of afternoon tea, crumbly digestive biscuits, and gossip, the priest was stopped dead in his tracks by the savory aroma of lamb *abgusht*. Dumbfounded, he peered in at the warm blush of the café's walls with his mouth open, not even minding the cold raindrops that pierced his round face and priestly overcoat.

Marjan was just making her way out to the café's front room with a tray of washed teacups when she spotted Father Mahoney's hungry face outside the window.

"Hello! Please come in! We're open for lunch," she enthused, thrusting the shop door open. Were priests allowed to eat outside their homes? Marjan wasn't so sure. But now was not the time to hesitate.

"Lunch? Ah, so this is what Estelle Delmonico's been up to. I heard a thing or two about it from the ladies after Mass. Are you a relative of Mrs. Delmonico's, then?" Feeling a bit woozy from the saffron perfume that hit him when Marjan opened the door, Father Mahoney had forgotten the introduction he customarily dished out with a joke or two on the collared profession.

"No. We just met last week, actually. I'm Marjan Aminpour. My sisters and I are renting this place from Mrs.—ah—from Estelle." She pointed to the sign hanging over her head and smiled. It was a simple wooden square that Bahar had made with the leftover wall paint, writing out the café's name in red cursive flourishes, one side in English, the other in Farsi.

"Ah, yes. The Babylon Café. Very clever. The Hanging Gardens of Babylon. Birthplace of Nebuchadnezzar the Second and all that he created."

"Not far from where we come from."

"Is that so? And where, may I ask, is that?"

"Iran. We left over seven years ago, though. For London."

"London. Fabulous town. Lots of fantastic theater on the West End there. I'm not keen on the English sense of humor, though. Monty Python and all that Holy Grail stuff. I much prefer the Americans for a bit of a laugh. Richard Pryor and Bill Cosby. Fantastic, they are."

"Yes, I suppose so," Marjan replied, laughing, surprised by the incongruity of a priest with a sense of humor. He reminded her of a ripe quince fruit, pale-skinned and tart-flavored. Unexpected.

"I'm Father Mahoney. It's my parish you'll be coming under. Right up the Mall there."

"Oh, but we're not Catholic."

"Right so. I won't tell if you won't." He laughed, his little blue eyes twinkling beneath folds of fat and skin. "Ah, sure, I'm a bit of a tease. You'll learn that about me sooner than later, I'm afraid. Mmmmm . . . but that smells fantastic. What is it?" He sniffed, his round nostrils moving with a life of their own.

"It's called *abgusht*. Lamb and potato stew. Are you sure you can't come in—for a cup of tea at least? You'll be our first customer."

Father Mahoney glanced at his watch; fifteen minutes to spare before Dervla Quigley rang the parish looking for him. Besides, it would only be a cup of tea. How long could that take?

"Your first customer, you say? Well, I can guarantee I won't be your last! You'll be the first café we've ever had in Ballinacroagh, as far as I can remember. Sure, the Wilton Inn's carvery doesn't even come close. No lovely smells like this lamb and potato stew," he said, stepping inside. "Hmmm, Iran, did you say? Have you heard the one about the Priest, the Rabbi and the Mullah?"

"JUST WHO DOES she think she is? I hear they're Indian or Pakistani or something of the like," Dervla Quigley said churlishly. The crabby gossip had taken up her usual roost at her bedroom window and had just witnessed Father Mahoney's encounter with Marjan across the street.

"I think it was Iranian. Danny Corcoran was telling me so himself just now." Marie Brennan leaned over her sister's curved back, gawking. "That one there was at the market looking for tarragon of all things. Tarragon! Now what do you suppose that is?"

The two old women watched as Father Mahoney took off his coat and settled into one of the front tables with the look of a man possessed.

"Whatever they are, it can't be civilized. And what do you suppose that Father Mahoney is thinking now, sitting there like some Romanian beggar and just before teatime? He knows very well we're expecting him. If he's even one minute late—I'm counting, it's seven minutes to three on my watch—I'll be telling him a thing or two."

"It's a café! Babylon Café! Says so right there on the sign!"

"I can see it with my own eyes, Marie," Dervla snapped at her younger sister. "Babylon! Sinful, that is."

"It's in the Bible, as I recall," Marie muttered, hurt by Dervla's mean tone.

"So's Sodom and Gomorrah. Humph! Will you look at him sitting there! That Father Mahoney better have a good excuse. Is that a meal now he's having? Marie?!"

"Looks like it, Dervla," Marie answered weakly, as she edged out of the room. Dervla sure knew how to suck her dry. Years of tending to her bitter sister's every need, whether it was helping her onto her toilet seat or into the black pleated skirt Dervla favored for Sunday Mass, had left Marie Brennan a ghost of a person. Sometimes, God help her, Marie wished she'd come home to find Dervla at her window, staring at nothing but the pearly gates of Saint Peter himself. Every time she imagined this, though, she made a beeline to Saint Barnabas to see Father Mahoney. The kind priest always made time for the lonely spinster's frequent, guilt-ridden confessions.

"Marie!"

"Yes, Dervla?"

MARJAN LEFT A FASCINATED Father Mahoney to take in all the fineries of the café's front room and returned to the warming pot of *abgusht* to taste its progress. She lifted the lid and breathed in the slowly simmering lamb stew, which she had cooked with a large, round *limuomani*—or dried lime. Just one of these limes is enough to add an intense flavor to any savory dish, its tart essence rising to the occasion.

As Father Mahoney gaped at the radiant vermilion walls and the curious belly of something that looked like it belonged in a fairy tale—the samovar bubbling with contentment—Marjan placed a bowl of broth on an oval, silver serving plate that was etched with a village scene of children dancing around a donkey. Next to the bowl she arranged a plate heaped with *gusht kubideh* (mashed meat and veg), warmed *lavash* bread, mixed-spice *torshi*, sliced onions and radishes. Marjan would have loved to have included some fresh tarragon, but it was one of the few key ingredients she had forgotten to bring back from Dublin, so she settled for fresh sprigs of mint and basil, and made a mental note to get some seedlings on her next trip to the city. She was going to turn that craggy patch of a backyard into a blooming herb garden yet.

Marjan steadied the heavy platter and pushed through the swinging doors. Father Mahoney stood next to the northern wall, running his fingers over the hanging tapestry.

"Extraordinary, absolutely extraordinary. Handmade, I take it?"

"Yes, from Iran," Marjan replied. "You know, each region in Iran has its own specific rug pattern. Tribal families would weave their histories into their rugs, passing down their secrets to the next generation. So, you could say that in a way, they were magic carpets."

"Enchanting!" exclaimed the priest.

Marjan smiled, placing the platter on Father Mahoney's table. She noticed that his cup of jasmine tea was already drained dry. "Here's the *abgusht* I promised. I hope you enjoy it."

"I'm sure I will. You are too kind. My goodness! What smells, what smells indeed. This ab-abba-goosht is not a Portuguese dish by any chance, is it? I used to be quite the connoisseur of Portuguese dishes in my day, that's why I ask." Father Mahoney sat back down, looked into the platter, and instantly forgot about the committee meeting he was about to be late for.

"No, it's Persian, through and through. It's hearty, but contains some very delicate ingredients. Would you like another cup of tea? Or a pot, perhaps?"

"Oh, well, I can't say no now, can I?" He peered at the various *abgusht* components, at a complete loss for where to start. Father Mahoney picked up his spoon but paused over the broth as if afraid he was going to hurt it.

"The broth is clear enough. You can take it throughout the meal, but the real treat is the meat paste there. The thin bread is called *lavash*. Use it to scoop some of the meat, then add onions and herbs and whatever else you like there as you go along. It is a very nourishing dish, especially during the winter months," Marjan explained, pointing to the food as she went along.

She took the priest's empty cup to the samovar for a refill. Instructing him on the finer points of eating *abgusht* had somehow stirred Marjan's memories of home. She pushed the lever down on the samovar and watched the tawny liquid fill the glass and gold-plated teacup. If she was in Iran now, this tea would be accompanied by angelica-powdered pomegranate seeds, toasted nuts, or sticky saffron and carrot halvah. On the night of the winter solstice, everyone in her family would gather on the living room rug to share such treats and tell stories. If it was particularly cold, they would snuggle around the *korsi,* a low table covered in a quilt and wrapped a second time in a pretty embroidered cloth. Underneath the table would be a small electrical heater that warmed their hearts and laps as they sat, recounting memories and their hopes for the year ahead.

One year her cousin Mitra had kicked the heater, nearly burning off her big toe in a fit of passionate storytelling. Another time, her great-aunt Homa had made everyone scour the snowy garden and front yard until dawn, convinced that her prized ruby bracelet had been lost, only to realize in the morning light that the piece of jewelry had surreptitiously crept into the folds of the blanket she had been sitting on. Why were these memories coming back to her now of all times? Marjan wondered. Now that she was the furthest she had ever been from her place of birth? Why this homesickness today?

The tea overflowed the cup and gushed over the edges of the saucer Marjan was holding. With a noisy clatter, she released the samovar's lever and grabbed a towel, soaking up the hot puddle beneath her feet. The commotion, however, did not wake Father Mahoney from his own reverie. He was softly brewing over his *abgusht,* his round cheeks rosy and full of life. Marjan finished cleaning the spilt tea and leaned against the counter, not wanting to disturb the priest. She understood exactly what was happening to Father Mahoney.

If Layla inspired lust in younger men and youthful dreams in their older counterparts, then Marjan worked her magic over both men and women in a more practical, yet equally intriguing manner. Through her recipes, Marjan was able to encourage people toward accomplishments that they had previously thought impossible; one taste of her food and most would not only start *dreaming* but actually contemplate *doing.* It was no different for Father Mahoney. As the priest chewed his last bit of meat-filled *lavash,* he felt a little lump in his stomach. It was a seed that would not bloom for at least another month, for ever changing the course of his life, but for now it rustled against the *abgusht* and gave him an unsettled feeling. Father Mahoney did not know what had happened to him exactly, but he knew that he was a very different man from a half hour ago.

The priest stood up. He reached for his coat hanging next to the door, his arm shaking slightly.

"Oh, are you leaving already?" Marjan smiled at the euphoria in the priest's hazy eyes.

"Yes, I'm afraid I've got to run. I'm sure I had an appointment somewhere, but for the life of me I just can't remember what it was. How silly of me." Father Mahoney's confusion was sweet, steeped as it was in a greater force. He needed to lie down somewhere, anywhere. There was a lot to think about. He was not sure what it all was, but he knew that he needed to think about it.

"I hope you enjoyed your *abgusht* and tea," said Marjan.

"Enjoyed it? I have never, in all my years traveling, tasted anything as divine—excuse me, Father." The pudgy priest looked up to the ceiling and quickly crossed himself. "Never. You, my dear, have a true talent, a calling. I have no doubt that this enchanting little place will be filled with customers in no time. Enchanting!" He shook his head and placed a few notes on the table.

"Oh, no, it's on the house, Father. You are our first customer, after all." Marjan shook her head.

"Nonsense. That's precisely why I insist on paying. I wouldn't have that fine distinction if it was a freebie, now would I? And I'll be back, you can count on it. Well, good-bye. And thank you, young lady!" With that he left the Babylon Café, heading in the direction of the parish without a second thought to the Patrician Day Dance committee.

Marjan stuck her head outside the café door, chuckling softly to herself as she watched Father Mahoney toddle up the rainy street, too dazed even to bother opening his umbrella. Hearing a rustling behind her in the shop, she turned around. Bahar, rumpled and woozy from the remnants of a headache-induced nap, was crossing the room toward her.

"How's your headache?"

"I've had worse. It's fine. Who was that?" Bahar asked, blinking to readjust her blurry eyes.

"Our first customer," Marjan replied.

"Well, let's hope he's not our last."

"He won't be." Marjan turned back to the wet street. The funny priest receded into the horizon, but she knew he would be back soon for more of her *abgusht*. Lunchtime had been a success as far as Marjan was concerned. Even if Father Mahoney was to be their only customer for the day.

elephant ears

1 egg

1/2 cup milk

1/4 cup sugar

1/4 cup rosewater

1/2 teaspoon ground cardamom

3 3/4 cups all-purpose flour

6 cups vegetable oil

GARNISH:

1 cup confectioners' sugar

2 teaspoons ground cinnamon

Beat egg in a bowl. Add milk, sugar, rosewater, and cardamom. Slowly
mix in flour, kneading into a dough. Roll out on a clean surface with a
floured pin until it is paper-thin. Using the rim of a wide-mouthed glass
or cup, trace and cut out a circle. Pinch the center of the circle with your
thumb and forefinger to form a bow. Set aside. Repeat until all circles
(approximately 15) are done. Heat oil in a deep pan. Fry each ear for
1 minute. Lay pastries on paper towels to cool. Sprinkle with sugar and
cinnamon mixture.

chapter six

"COLM CAHILL AND THOSE Donnelly twins, now. They're after one thing only. Best give them the cold shoulder, Layla. They think they're God's gift, those three."

Emer Athey's blond curls bobbed as she pointed out a group of fifth-year boys, the same hooligans that congregated around Peter and Michael Donnelly's fermented offerings before school. It was only midmorning recess, and Layla's second day of school, but already every boy in that group was set on winning the exotic new girl's attentions.

"And steer clear of the rest of the lot there." Emer frowned at the beefy boys before returning to her snack of marmalade and chocolate Jaffa Cake biscuits.

Fiona Athey's fiery daughter had taken Layla under her wing immediately, giving her a thorough tour of Saint Joseph's expansive grounds. Before its latest incarnation as a coeducational secondary school, the medieval buildings had, through the ages, served as a monastery, an experimental love shack for a Gallic viscount, and a shelter for unwed mothers. Emer had also introduced Layla to Regina Jackson, a pert redhead who wore argyle kneesocks pulled tight over her skinny legs. Although by no means unpopular, Emer and Regina were rarely involved in the Saint Joseph social scene, which consisted mainly of Friday night piss-ups and Saturday morning football matches. Saturday afternoons spent bowling in Castlebar and the occasional traditional music *seisiún* in Westport were more to their liking.

Layla was surprised by how simple it had been for her to make such quick friends in Ballinacroagh. Emer and Regina listened attentively to Layla's concentrated version of her life story (Tehran, Lewisham, and now Ballinacroagh), and Layla in turn, appreciated their advice on boys.

"What about Malachy? Is he like them as well?" Layla asked, praying hard under her thumping heart that he wasn't. Malachy with the sapphire eyes had not been in any of her new classes, so she had learned his name only that day from Regina.

"Malachy McGuire? Na—though there's a bit of a surprise he came out looking and sounding the way he does, going by who his dad is," Emer replied.

Emer, Regina, and Layla watched the boy in question from under a large oak tree. Malachy was crossing the rugby field in gallant strides, deep in his own amorous thoughts, when he caught the girls looking at him. Blushing profusely, he walked toward them and waved shyly.

"What do you mean? Who's his dad?" Layla asked, her eyes still glued to Malachy.

"Don't you know? Well, you will. Thomas McGuire, the original egomaniac. Thinks he owns the town, he does. The pub next to your café is his. And the rest of the drinking holes on the Mall. That's why I go to Westport for my beer. He won't be getting my money anytime soon. My mum hates his guts and isn't afraid to say so," Emer pronounced.

Regina snorted.

"Well, she's isn't, Regina! Not when she needs to. Don't you remember the summer we both turned five, or do I have to remind you?" Emer retorted hotly. While she and her mother often had screaming matches that rang out from the salon all the way up Main Mall, Emer loved Fiona very much and was always the first to defend her against gossips.

"What happened?" Layla asked.

"He tried to buy out the salon," said Regina, munching on a bag of prawn-flavored crisps.

"Let him try, that feckin' gobshite!" Emer's round face turned a bright shade of magenta. Besides a streak of Athey stubbornness, Emer had inherited little else from Fiona. It was from her philandering puppeteer father that she took her Germanic features and hearty Braunschweigan appetite—endless reminders to Fiona of tangled marionette strings and an ache that seventeen years had not dulled.

"Well, he did own half of the place," Regina muttered. She too had a deep hatred for the uncrowned king of Ballinacroagh. Her alcoholic father had lost seventy-five percent of his farm to Thomas McGuire, after running tabs the size of the river Shannon in all three of his pubs. Regina's good Catholic upbringing prevented her from fully expressing her resentment, though. For this she looked to Emer. Regina would often push the louder girl's buttons as a way to release her own bottled-up anger.

"Own, my feckin' foot! More like wormed his way in when no one was looking. Anyway, that was all my granddad's fault. My mum owes Thomas McGuire nothing." Emer pouted.

By August 1974, after nearly five years of snipping thinned hairlines and nodding through endless rounds of mind-bending gossip, Fiona had finally saved enough money to buy out Thomas McGuire's shareholdings—only to discover that the man had his own plans for the beauty parlor. In a moment of unmistakable egotism, Thomas had invested half of his money (even giving the bank the deed to the Ale House and news agency) into the 10 Minute Tan—a chain of tanning salons that, as the name implied, promised ten minutes to bronzed beauty. From Cong in the south to Belmullet in the north, Thomas McGuire—with the help of the Turbo Tanner 200, a new line of sun beds straight out of the corrugated sheds of a Limerick wholesaler—was determined to bring pasty pores and blue-veined thighs out of their woolen shells. Starting with Fiona Athey's beauty parlor as his flagship tanning salon, Thomas was going to make Mayo the Saint-Tropez of Ireland.

Underhanded wrangling and legal maneuvers followed, with the pub owner visiting Fiona daily to issue threats that just made the former stage queen even more determined to see her business through to the last act. She hired a big-time lawyer from Galway (one of her many admirers from her theater days) and embarked on a defense that gave Dervla Quigley enough news to munch on for months. A week before the two parties were to meet in the county courthouse, tragedy struck. As a preview to sunnier days to come, Thomas had set up a tanning bed in the back of one of his quieter pubs, the McGuire Ale House, and invited the whole town to have a test run of it. Filomina Fanning, the town's librarian and most devoted churchgoer, was to be the first (and last) victim of the shoddily built Turbo Tanner 200. At 8:30 A.M. Filomina walked into the Ale House white, round, and heaving from the extra hundred and forty-six pounds she carried on her small frame. At 8:40 A.M. she was wheeled out on a stretcher headed for Mayo General Hospital, blistered and burned by a tanning bed turned torture chamber. The Turbo Tanner 200 was really just a large microwave gone haywire, and Thomas McGuire was the eejit who had bought into it all.

"He sold my mum his share of the salon after that. Even Thomas

McGuire couldn't afford to have two court cases on his head. I'd tell your sisters about him if I were you, Layla. Word's out he's got his eye on—"

"He's had his eye on that Delmonico place for years," Regina interrupted.

"Yes, thank you, Regina. Anyway, he'll come hassling, sooner or later. Layla?"

But Layla was not listening. She was lost in Malachy McGuire's blue eyes, already too entangled in her own enchantment to heed Emer's warning.

IN ITS FIRST WEEK of business, the Babylon Café could count the number of its regulars on one hand. But within a month, its daily clientele had increased to nearly two dozen, with many more hesitant customers pausing before the café windows in wonder. The glint of the samovar and the smell of frying elephant ears were reasons enough for most to step inside. For a look, at least.

Gush-e fil, or elephant ears, like their fellow fritters, are fried until golden and dripping with all things forbidden. In shape each pastry resembles a giant bow, much like farfalle pasta, but in taste it belongs to the doughnut family of treats. *Gush-e fil* is normally made in celebratory moments, when the satisfaction of its simplicity is unmatched by more complicated desserts. On that day in April, Marjan had decided to make elephant ears to celebrate the good fortune that had come their way since they had moved to Ballinacroagh, nearly a month to the day. Not only were lunchtimes filled with steady orders but the cloud that had followed Bahar around the first couple of weeks was dispersing. Who knew, Marjan thought to herself, maybe this time things were really going to work out.

Marjan smiled with contentment as she beat an egg in a large bowl. After adding the flour, she vigorously kneaded the dough, not even minding the tenderness that the constant pushing and pulling created in her lower left shoulder. Hidden there, just at the juncture of her arm and shoulder, was a raised one-inch scar, so silver and slight that no one could have guessed the vulgar weapon that had created it. Through the circular windows of the kitchen's swinging doors, Marjan could see Bahar taking Mrs. Boylan's order as Father Mahoney nodded in approval. The friendly priest had kept his word, returning every day for lunch, and sometimes a second time for afternoon tea with several elderly ladies in tow. The only days he hadn't shown up were Sundays, which Marjan assumed were the busiest in his line of work. Today he had brought his housekeeper and had begged Marjan to give away her elephant ears recipe, so that Mrs. Boylan could replicate the doughy treats whenever he had a midnight craving. More than happy to lend out her expertise, Marjan found a green index card and wrote in neat, round letters:

Roll dough out on a clean surface with a floured pin until it is paper-thin. Using the rim of a wide-mouthed glass or cup, trace and cut out a circle. Pinch the center of each circle with your thumb and forefinger to form a bow. Set aside. Repeat until all circles (approx. 15) are done.

"That priest of yours is really funny. Did you know that they're allowed to drink, these priests? No women, but alcohol is fine!" Bahar walked in waving Father Mahoney's order. Her usually skittish eyes were bright and—dared Marjan hope?—happy.

"They drink beer like water here. Last Saturday I saw an entire family, with young kids, leaving the bar next door. At eleven at night!" Marjan replied with awe. She read Father Mahoney's order:

1. *Pot of Darjeeling × 2*
2. *Bread and cheese platter*
3. *1 chicken salad*
4. *1 abgusht*

"Sure likes the *abgusht,* doesn't he? It's the fifth time he's ordered it this week." Bahar shook her head in amazement. She enjoyed *abgusht* like the best of them, but too much made her feel sluggish.

"Father Mahoney's raved about it to everyone. The shopkeeper at the mini-mart told me this morning that 'his Finnegan'—I think that's his son—had heard all about us. He was wondering if we do takeaway packages! If this keeps up, we'll be out of debt in no time!" Marjan said cheerily.

Besides Father Mahoney and Mrs. Boylan, the regular lunchtime crowd in the Babylon consisted of Evie Watson and Fiona Athey. It wasn't only Father Mahoney's praises that had drawn the two hairdressers inside but three days of intense curiosity heightened by the smells of fried elephant ears and cinnamon-roasted walnuts. The perfume blew into the beauty salon on the ocean breeze, creeping through the door's crevices and floating above the bouffant hairdos and hair spray fumes. Evie and Fiona sat at one of the window-side tables now, each drinking her own bowl of red lentil soup as vague ruminations—prompted by Marjan's magic—swam in their heads: Evie could see neon pink letters spelling out her name over the salon's door, while Fiona imagined hers lighting up a theater marquee once again.

Even the elderly ladies of the Patrician Day Dance committee had heard Father Mahoney's descriptions of the sweet, exotic pastries and teas to be had at the Babylon Café. Forgoing their usual meat and two veg lunches at the Wilton Inn, they now sat at the café's long communal table before platters of minty chicken salad and bowls of sweet onion soup.

Unlike her sister, Marie, Dervla Quigley never took part in these girlie lunches. She considered Father Mahoney's absence from their first committee meeting a personal affront to her already overwrought dignity and officially moved her vigil to the Thomas McGuire camp. Upon Thomas's request, Dervla was to continue her watch over the café and report back to him daily on the exact nature of the Babylon's epicurean operations. Thomas wanted to know the types of food supplies that were being bought and delivered, the start of each day's lunchtime rush, and the average turnover of tables, hoping to pinpoint in such rudimentary details the mysterious alchemy behind so many diners' glowing smiles and rounded, satisfied bellies. Excited by her new patrol, Dervla bought a small spiral notebook and with her claw-like fingers wrote down the name of every soul who walked in and out of the café, even recording the times when Marjan opened the windows or Bahar crossed the street for the butcher's. In addition to ranting from her bedroom window, the old gossip dialed every parishioner in her tattered address book and repeated the same indignant spiel: "There's no tellin' what's in that food. Unhygienic, I'd say. Downright dirty. Babylon Café! Sinful, that's what it is!"

Orders slowed down after lunch, giving Marjan the opportunity to finish up the last batch of elephant ears. The morning tray was already sold out, gobbled up by schoolchildren who had given up their usual sticky taffy runs for the flaky pastries. Soon, afternoon tea junkies and the occasional passerby would once again wipe the silver platters clean of her baklava, fried *zulbia*, wafflelike window cookies, and elephant ears, so she had to be ready.

Marjan plunged two pinched elephant ears into a deep pan of hot oil for one minute, then transferred them with a slotted spoon to a paper towel. Beads of excess oil dripped luxuriously off each pastry and were instantly swallowed by the thirsty paper towels. When the entire batch cooled, she sprinkled the glistening ears with a mixture of sugar and cinnamon that made her nose tickle. Ever since childhood, Marjan had adored these fried pastries. After all, she thought, a little oil every now and again never hurt anyone. Not unless you were standing too close to the pan, that is.

MALACHY MCGUIRE WAITED five weeks before he roused the courage to ask Layla for a date. The young man proposed a walk along the hilly roads leading to Clew Bay Beach, holding out his hand and locking Layla in his jewel-toned gaze. Sitting atop the crest of a high dune, the teenagers masked their timid hand-holding in the long sea grass as they watched the effervescent tide and felt the warm, powdery sand beneath their heated bodies.

Layla stole a shy peek at the boy sitting next to her. Was he going to make the first move, she wondered, or should she take the helm? And what if he did try something? What would she do then? She could feel droplets of sweat dampen her school uniform and trickle between her breasts, settling in her belly button. Her cinnamon-rose perfume was growing denser by the second, emanating from her flushed skin in heady waves. Hoping Malachy hadn't noticed her growing blush, Layla turned her face away from the boy and pointed up toward Croagh Patrick, which was staring down on them with grandfatherly approval.

"That's a beautiful mountain. Such a perfect triangle," she squeaked

"That old heap? It's nothing special. Nothing like the places you've been. What was your old home like?" Malachy inched closer.

"England?"

"No—Iran. Isn't that a very dangerous place?"

Layla's almond eyes were suddenly very far away. She slipped her hand out of Malachy's and planted it deep in the sandy mound next to her, as if to steady herself.

Now it was Malachy's turn to blush hotly. He sure knew how to stick his foot in his big gob, didn't he? What was he thinking of, asking such personal questions? Maybe she didn't want to talk about Iran; maybe she was just humoring him by coming here; maybe he should apologize— Midway through his consternation came the kiss. It was a quick one, on the lips, but it still counted.

"Oh," Malachy whispered, his voice cracking with pleasure. He returned Layla's soft kiss, drawing her against his thumping chest as he inhaled her cinnamon-rose scent.

Malachy's warm arms were a cushion of comfort for Layla's confused emotions. What was wrong with her? she wondered. Was she ashamed of Iran, of being Iranian? Was that why she had cut Malachy off so abruptly? He only wanted to know about her childhood home; there was nothing complicated in that, was there? This boy with the beautiful sapphire eyes wasn't afraid of her foreignness, he wouldn't judge her for the violent country of her birth. But what should she tell him exactly? Where to start?

Prickles shot up her right arm. Her hand had fallen asleep. Lifting it off the sand, Layla noticed the impression her palm had made in the white powder. A perfect handprint. The deep fate lines engraved in her palm, the forked markers of destiny, rose in curving ridges of sand across the hollow. She lightly traced the lines with her finger, feeling a shiver of recognition run down her spine, other sets of handprints suddenly clouding her mind.

THE NIGHT THEY LEFT Tehran forever was a September night like no other. It was still the twilight of summer, but the anorexic trees outside had already shed themselves of all delusions, scattering their leaves on the pavement below. From their kitchen window, on the fourteenth floor of the decaying apartment complex they lived in, a seven-year-old Layla had watched the sun set behind the neighborhood mosque, its brilliant turquoise dome changing into a mystical, deep lapis in the gathering dusk. There had been no wailing of bedtime prayers that night, no ardent devotions blaring from the mosque's high minaret. In fact, there had been no prayers at all since Friday. Even the usual gunfire had died down, with only a sporadic *rat-tat-tat* coming from the former South Street Bazaar. Most of the neighborhood's revolutionaries were holed up in the empty bazaar; they had been there ever since the Imperial Guards gunned down demonstrators in Jaleh Square. Only three days had passed since the students, marching peacefully against the Shah's regime, had been greeted by indiscriminate military bullets. Thousands had met their immediate deaths, falling on the pale stone ground of the open square.

Layla glanced down the street toward the bazaar before turning her attention to the flow of blood, still seeping, still weeping its way along their leafy boulevard. The bloody handprints were spattered all over the dirty sidewalk, bright and fresh, though the hands that had been raised to the cause were long gone. Several handprints were even slapped on house walls, the blood dripping from the bases of palms like new sets of fingers. The red rivulets seeped into the sidewalk cracks, greeting their compatriots on the ground with a shake, a wave of defiance that acknowledged the mutual source of their misery. Jaleh Square, only ten blocks away from their apartment.

Black Friday, they were calling the massacre, but all Layla could see was red. Red everywhere.

"Bahar, can I go to school tomorrow?" Layla asked, even though she already knew the answer. There would be no school tomorrow; there had been no school for many days. That was what *martial law* meant, Marjan had explained to her. That was what the Shah had declared, sending his Imperial Guards, the "Immortals," to scour the streets, looking for radicals and the odd, confused Communist.

"Stop asking me stupid questions and get down from that chair! Do you want someone to shoot you?" Bahar pushed Layla off her perch. As she pulled the flowery curtain across the window, her head scarf slipped, revealing a crusty cut near her right ear. The skin around the wound was blotchy and jaundiced, matching the purple-and-yellow stains on Bahar's forehead and cheeks. Bruises. Layla couldn't help staring at them.

"Stay in the living room until Marjan comes home," Bahar commanded. "I hope to God she got our passports," she said, more to herself than to Layla, as she returned to the hot stove.

"But I'm hungry," Layla complained. She eyed the pot of pomegranate soup that Bahar was stirring.

"You're such a brat. Marjan could be caught by the Guards by now and all you can think about is your own greedy stomach. Move it!" Bahar whacked her wooden spoon against the pot.

Layla stifled her tears and padded out of the kitchen. She hadn't thought about Marjan being out on the bloody streets past curfew. What if Bahar was right and Marjan had been caught by the Imperial Guards? What if she never came back and Layla would have to live alone with Bahar forever?

Salt water blurred Layla's eyes and landed on her tongue as she crept through the hallway toward her favorite hiding place, the pantry where Marjan stored her dry goods and spices. She opened the wicker door and slipped into the comforting darkness, touching the wooden shelves, the grains and powders asleep in their jars. Reaching behind a tall terra-cotta jug, Layla's little fingers clasped the familiar glass container of sumac. The ground-up product of the astringent *Rhus* berry, sumac was a brick red spice that Marjan used sparingly on her kabob dishes. Layla would sneak into the pantry at least once a day, more when she was feeling particularly blue, to scoop some of the lemony spice into her puckered mouth. She was reaching for her second scoop when she heard Bahar scream.

It was a primitive jungle holler. A bloodcurdling howl that was suddenly cut short by a terrifying blow. To Layla's young ears, it sounded like the pounding of *kubideh*—the tender kabob meat Marjan flattened with a mallet, hitting the beef over and over until it sighed, finally defeated. The hammering grew louder and more frequent. The shadowy spices jumped in their jars around her, mimicking Layla's own lurching, acidy stomach. She clenched the lump of sumac tightly in her fists, so tightly that the sour powder began to burn her palms. Suddenly, a high-octave cry broke from within the pantry's suffocating walls, shocking her tender senses. She was the one screaming.

She never heard the pounding stop, her cries were so loud. She didn't hear the soft feminine sobs outside the pantry walls, or even sense Marjan seeking her out in the darkness. When her eldest sister finally rescued her from the overturned jars of dry fava beans and quince-lime syrup, Layla's eyes and ears were welded shut in agony.

"Shhhh . . . Layla *joon. Joon-e man.* Shhh . . . don't cry." Marjan stood in the kitchen holding Layla in her arms, kissing her face and sumac-tainted fists. With her wet lids anointed by her sister's kisses, Layla felt safe enough finally to open her eyes. The mangled body lying on the kitchen floor made her wish she had kept them closed.

Legs clothed in dark men's trousers lay spread apart on the linoleum. Bony, boyish ankles, matured by irregular tufts of black hair, met a pair of green army boots caked in mud. A dark, thick liquid seeped from beneath the thin calves, spreading so quickly that it momentarily lifted the man on its surge before engulfing the body in its crimson flow. Layla's eyes followed the sharp crease ironed into the man's rigid pants, the cheap gabardine kind worn by street vendors.

Her gaze settled on his thin, splayed knees just as Marjan showered her tearstained eyes with kisses once again.

Fourteen flights of crumbling stairs never went by so quickly, Layla remembered thinking with surprise. Any other day and her sisters would have scolded her for jumping two steps at a time, but Marjan and Bahar skipped three and four steps themselves on their way down to the street. The fallen leaves and bloody handprints were underfoot, but Layla kept her gaze on the night sky as she held tightly on to her sisters' clammy palms. Marjan's face was outlined by her black chador, ashen yet determined, her other hand lugging a heavy suitcase. Bahar was to Layla's right, her full-length robe and veil covering everything but her bloodshot eyes, which blinked rapidly with fear. Neither said a word to Layla, not when they reached the end of their neighborhood walls, not when they crossed the vacant railroad lines, not even when they made it to Tehran's Downtown Bus Terminal, which was teeming with other suitcase-carrying, silent, chador-framed faces, and climbed onboard the bus heading for the east.

East, to the lawless town of Zahedan, a den of opiate dealers set on a scrap of transitory land, a trepidation of shifting sands. Iran's Dasht-e Lut desert, the province of tribal lords, with their lifeblood of camels, carpets, and caravans. And the last stop before the Pakistan border.

The bus dropped them off at the edge of Zahedan, where several Baluchi tribal men were busy setting up their night's camp. Each of the camp's twenty tents was lined with handwoven kilims, the brightly colored carpets extending beyond the lips of oilcloth and canvas openings. A few of the men loaned them a tent, hitching it up as their womenfolk spooned *mast-o khiar,* their traditional yogurt and cucumber soup, into earthen bowls. The cooling liquid soothed Layla's dry throat and brought some welcome color back to both Marjan's and Bahar's faces.

Still, good as it was, the yogurt and cucumber soup did not loosen her sisters' tongues. Nothing was said about what had happened back there, in the middle of their apartment's kitchen floor, in the midst of a revolution, deep into a Tehran night.

"JAYSUS." MALACHY WHISTLED under his breath. "Did your sisters ever tell you what happened that night? Who that man was in the kitchen?"

Layla shook her head, unable to speak for the lump in her throat. She did find out, eventually, but that story wasn't ripe for the telling. Maybe she shouldn't have shared so much with Malachy, but she needed to confide in someone after all these years of silence.

"Don't worry, Layla. You're safe here in Ireland. With me," Malachy said tenderly. There were still many questions he wanted to ask, but sensing a peculiar sadness stirring within her, he instead put his arms protectively around Layla and kissed her again.

Though she felt the burning sensation of love more than ever, Layla's mood remained solemn. Her mouth puckered up again, the tissue in her cheeks remembering a sourer time, the taste of sumac suddenly everywhere.

lavash bread

1 tablespoon quick-rising yeast

½ cup warm water

¼ cup olive oil

1 cup milk

2 tablespoons sugar

2 teaspoons salt

4 cups all-purpose flour

½ cup poppy and sesame seeds

Preheat oven to 500°F. Mix yeast and water. Set aside for 15 minutes. Combine yeasty water, oil, milk, sugar, and salt in a large bowl. Slowly mix in flour. Knead into a dough. Divide into 3 even balls. Cover with a clean towel and leave to rise for 30 minutes. Roll out one ball of dough on a clean surface with a floured pin until it is paper-thin. Sprinkle with poppy and sesame seeds. Place on a buttered cookie sheet and bake in oven at 500°F for 5 minutes. Repeat with remaining balls of dough.

chapter seven

THOMAS WASN'T TERRIBLY surprised when he finally heard that his youngest son was cavorting with one of those "foreigners." Dervla Quigley had seen him strutting down Main Mall—in broad daylight, no less—hand in hand with that darkie girl.

Shameless, good-for-nothing gobshite, that Malachy. It was just like him to dip his toe into bog scum, Thomas thought to himself. Probably going back to his own bleedin' kind, for all he knew. Because self-assured as he was, Thomas wasn't blind to the obvious: Malachy, with his unnatural mop of black curls and a tongue that named major constellations before ever sputtering a reluctant *Da-Da* or *Mam*, was not like the rest of his children. If Thomas could have attributed Malachy's tall frame and razor-sharp intelligence to his wife's genes, then maybe he could have looked at the boy without needing to punch something. But squat Cecilia, with her flat features, brittle blond hair, and triple chins, was as different from Malachy as Thomas was. Like it or not, he had to admit that his suspicions about the summer of 1967 were correct.

Just around that time, Thomas had been busy expanding his empire with a second pub on Main Mall. While he was knee-deep in the new Ale House's punctured septic tank, a boatload of swarthy Andalusian fishermen had surreptitiously docked in Clew Bay Beach. The frisky Spaniards had come up from Galway, mistaking Clew Bay for the Aran Islands after a drunken night of potcheen poker. Their two-ton fishing boat hit a sharp limestone shelf, driving a foot-wide hole into the *Hermosa*'s oak belly and leaving the fishermen no choice but to camp out on the beach while they patched their ruptured vessel. Other than a few food and *vino* runs, the Spanish sailors kept to themselves, so Thomas had no major complaints. It wasn't until a week after the seamen left for their sunny homeland that the bar owner began to notice an unusually sated smile on his wife's face. Only then did he detect the strange smell of crayfish that had crept into every corner of his house, and notice for the first time the strings of seaweed that floated curiously into tubs and basins whenever he turned on the water taps. And then a dark-haired Malachy arrived eight months later, premature and completely alien.

Feckin' foreigners, thought Thomas, laying their filthy paws on what was rightfully his. And now it was happening all over again. Not only was his so-called son blatantly disobeying orders by stepping foot in that stinking café but he was shagging one of those Arabs as well. All behind his back. Just like his cheating mother, that Malachy.

Determined to give the young man a fine bollixing, Thomas sent his elder son, Tom Junior, to fetch his wayward brother. It was a charge that the sadistic bully in training carried out with utmost glee, as he had little love in his small heart for Malachy. Marked since infancy by their differing constitutions, the McGuire boys never shared anything minutely resembling a brotherly bond. Malachy did not understand Tom Junior's penchant for pub piss-ups and violent martial arts films, and Tom Junior hated how the younger boy buried himself in his books and telescope, with that faraway smile like he knew something the rest of them didn't, as if the pub life was below him. He couldn't wait to see what their father had planned for the bloody bastard. Tom Junior chuckled cruelly to himself as he pounded down Main Mall. He found Malachy in Fadden's Mini-Mart, engrossed in a conversation with the shop owner on the origins of fairies.

"You see, lad, each country has its own race of fairy folk. No two fairies are alike. Anywhere," said Danny sagely, pushing his thick glasses up the bridge of his bulbous nose.

"Are there fairies in Iran?" Malachy asked, with a twinkle in his eyes.

"Oh, yes. The Peries of Persia. Lovely little things with wings. Mind you, you can't see them with the human eye, but they're there. Like to roam the forests looking for perfumed flowers."

"Fairies! Should've known it'd be the sort of thing yer into," Tom Junior cut in with a harsh laugh from just inside the mini-mart's door.

Malachy glared at his brother in silence, though he was surprised to hear Tom Junior address him. Weeks could go by without either of them saying a word to each other, and when necessity called for one of them to speak, it was usually Tom Junior coming at him with a biting insult.

"Move it, gobshite. Dad wants ya at the Ale House."

"What for?"

"Just get yer arse down there now, ye poofter!" Tom Junior bellowed.

Malachy turned to Danny Fadden, who was cowering behind a stack of Bisto gravy cans on the counter. "Sorry, Mr. Fadden. I'll be back soon to hear more about those Persian fairies."

"Take your time, lad," Danny whispered meekly.

Tom trailed Malachy up to the Ale House, muttering insults with every step. A furious Thomas was sitting in a booth at the back of the bar waiting for them both.

"Here now, boyo." He sneered, rising from his seat. "What's this I hear about you and that Arab whore?"

Tom Junior grinned uncontrollably behind Malachy's back. The McGuire money was as good as his now. No chance of any of the pubs going into Malachy's hands when their dad finally croaked.

"She's Iranian, not Arab. And don't you ever call her a whore or I'll—"

"Or you'll what? You better watch who yer talkin' to, boy! And I'll tell you something else, whore or not she's still the enemy. Her and her darkie sisters. They're stealin' what feeds that gob of yours nightly, and I better not see you anywhere near them." Thomas's face was so close that Malachy could count the burst capillaries on his slack, beet red cheeks. The boy stood his ground and narrowed his eyes, even as his father threatened him with his shaking fists.

"What's with the sudden interest in what I do? Didn't think you even knew I was alive," Malachy pushed.

"Another word out of you and yer going to wish you were dead. Am I making meself clear?"

Thomas had certainly made himself clear, but his threats wouldn't stop Malachy from seeing Layla every day after school. After all, his defiance was just further evidence of the independent streak that had marked him from birth. Malachy knew the future held in store for him greater things than nights of coughing up tar and misery in one of his father's pubs. He was going to catch Orion from under an Arizona desert sky and watch as Cassiopeia danced over Norwegian fjords. And he was going to do it all with Layla by his side.

It was as much of a proposal as an eighteen-year-old could make, and for her part, Layla agreed wholeheartedly to a lifetime of thrilling adventures with Malachy. Neither mentioned their future plans to Bahar and Marjan, though, when two weeks after their first date, Layla introduced him to her sisters. Dressed in a formal button-up shirt and school jacket, Malachy came by the café after closing time. Seated at the round kitchen table, the young man was alternately discouraged by Bahar's unresponsive eyes and heartened by Marjan's warm food.

"Layla tells us you're an astronomy buff. Is that what you want to study after high school?" Marjan flashed Malachy an encouraging smile as she handed him a cup of oolong tea.

Malachy nodded. "I'd like to take a year off and travel first," he said. "See the world."

"Travel?" Bahar said, sharply. She squinted disapprovingly at Malachy, her lips pressed in a hard line.

Marjan shot Bahar a reproachful look.

"Malachy loves your plants in the backyard, Marjan," Layla offered, rescuing the awkward moment.

"It's a grand looking garden," Malachy said. "Astronomy and gardening aren't that different, when you think about it. Mythically speaking."

And with that inspired observation, Malachy charmed his way into Marjan's heart. A few minutes later he found himself standing at the kitchen island with Layla, peeling onions and sifting through piles of basmati rice for Marjan's *chelow*. The young man had never known there to be such joy in cooking, subjected as he was to the gristly pork sausages and limp carrots of his usual home meals. Marjan, the eternal gardener, was only too happy to answer his questions on the fickle nature of Irish topsoil and the medicinal uses of sweet basil leaves. Together they spent the afternoon detailing the similarities between the heavens above and the earth below, marveling at the diverse palette of creation. Bahar remained silent throughout the boy's visit, but it did not go unnoticed by anyone in the room that she got up to refill Malachy's teacup not once but twice.

After Malachy left, with a good amount of *zulbia* packed in his schoolbag, Layla turned to Bahar and Marjan, unable to hide her excitement any longer.

"Well? Isn't he beautiful? Do you like him?"

"He's wonderful, Layla! Your first boyfriend! And those eyes, my goodness! He reminds me of a boy I knew in school. Before the revolution, of course. He had green eyes," Marjan said, wistfully.

She stopped wiping the kitchen island and stared dreamily into space as she thought of Ali, the green-eyed boy of her youth. Such thoughts were usually limited to private moments when Marjan could sneak into the flat's tiny blue bathroom and lock the door behind her. Reaching into the upper shelf of a four-tiered medicine cabinet the Delmonicos had bought on their Moroccan honeymoon, Marjan would gingerly remove a small brass jewelry box etched with beautiful desert roses. Inside she kept a few golden trinkets and the childhood identity bracelets given to them by their father. The box's rose satin lining was worn in spots, and grains of sand had become embedded in the holes, reminders of their flight through the Dasht-e Lut desert.

Settling on the covered toilet seat, Marjan would pull a faded photo out from beneath the jewelry. The picture, now slightly yellowed and crinkled at the edges, was taken on a school field trip to Istanbul. Her senior class had caught a ferry on the Black Sea shore, arriving in Istanbul just as the sun was setting over the city's Grand Covered Bazaar. Ali had led her through the Grand Bazaar's labyrinthine aisles, past insistent *bazaari* hocking their wares, clusters of carpet stalls, and tents filled with copper serving trays and brassy samovars. At the center of the Grand Bazaar sat the jewelers' booths, piled high with gems and stones that would eventually be brought home by eager husbands. It was in one of these bejeweled stalls, alongside a line of half-price, multicolored bangles on a low table, that Marjan first saw the brass jewelry box. Although it was humble in appearance, to her the jewelry case looked like it could hold all the treasures of the Magi. On the ferry heading back home to Iran, Ali surprised Marjan with the small box and made her promise to keep a picture of him always tucked inside its satin pockets.

For ten years Marjan had kept that promise. Whenever she felt like breaking down, she would cling to the fading photograph of Ali, sitting there in his white polyester shirt and frayed bell-bottom jeans, with the Turkish sun in his eyes. He was smiling then, life pulsing through his beautiful body. But of course, Marjan reminded herself, that was before the revolution, before everything changed.

Unaware that her two sisters were witnessing her tender reminiscence, Marjan smiled sadly at the cleaning rag in her hand. Bahar's stern voice brought her out of herself, and she blushed for her indulgence.

"Well, he's smart, I suppose. But that still doesn't mean you're ready for a boyfriend, Layla. You're fifteen, for God's sake! Still a child!" Bahar slammed the kitchen table with opened palms. "Besides, we haven't even been here two months. Certainly not enough time to start trusting people." She pushed her chair away from the table and walked tiredly up the stairs. Her left hand gripped her temples, the right held tightly on to the banister. "I'm going to lie down. It's in your hands now, Marjan."

"Don't worry," Marjan whispered, sensing that Bahar's pessimism had dimmed Layla's excitement. "She'll come around. Did you see how she offered Malachy another helping of baklava when she thought we weren't looking?"

Layla nodded slowly, but Bahar's sadness was infectious; she could taste its metallic flavor in her mouth. Still, no matter how much Bahar's neurotic behavior aggravated her, Layla understood why her sister was so anxious, so untrusting.

"Marjan?"

"Yes, *joon-e man*?"

"What ever happened to that boy with the green eyes?"

"We just lost touch with each other after Baba died, when we moved to the south. These things happen sometimes." There was no point in telling Layla the truth now, Marjan thought. Best to spare her the details.

JAVID AMINPOUR DIED not long after that senior class trip to Istanbul, more of a lonely heart than from the attack doctors diagnosed. He was happy at last, joining their mother where she lay in Zahirodoleh cemetery, but for Marjan it was more tragedy than she could bear. At seventeen, she became sole guardian of fourteen-year-old Bahar and baby Layla, who hadn't even turned five yet. Their great-aunt Homa, cousin Mitra, and the rest of their closest relatives had heeded the sinister winds of an oncoming revolution and escaped to a land of endless sunshine and fertile valleys—California. With no family to take them in, Marjan was forced to sell their childhood home and move into a small apartment on the southern edge of Tehran, where the pristine Alborz mountains were obscured by the New City, a rampant brothel settlement only a few blocks away. Marjan took a job washing dishes at the Hilton Hotel's famed Peacock Restaurant, and it was there that she picked up the tricks of the trade while cleaning up the chefs' messes. Two years would pass before she saw Ali again, this time in the laboratories of Tehran University, where she was studying for her degree, cramming classes in between restaurant shifts.

Marjan had been in the lab for half an hour, legs stretched across the stool in front of her, hands cupping her chin. She was listening to the *splat* of the city rain outside and trying hard to ignore the rapid germination taking place on the slide under her microscope. There was nothing affirming about molecular parasitology, Marjan decided. She abhorred the slaughterous trails of cannibalistic cells, their lack of compassion, the endless specimen slides. Botany had been her first choice, but botany wasn't going to put food on the table, or school uniforms on Bahar's and Layla's backs.

Closing her left eye, Marjan squinted through the microscope once again. When she lifted her head, she found Ali staring at her in disbelief. He was standing in the doorway with transfer papers in hand, his light brown hair shorn tightly at the sides. He had grown a beard, which bristled against Marjan's face as she buried herself in his chest.

Not long after their reunion in the university lab, Ali introduced Marjan to the revolutionary students who constituted his circle of friends. They were beginning to distribute their own underground newspaper, *The Voice*, printed in the basement of Ali's uncle's house with a rotary printing press from the era of Reza Shah, a time of complete stupidity and ignorance, Ali explained to her. And now his idiot son was squeezing the country dry and senseless. Claiming an improbable connection to the great Zoroastrian rulers of the Persian Empire, the short Shah crowned himself King of Kings and robbed the last shreds of dignity from the Persian people. As most of his subjects rotted away in mud huts devoid of electricity and proper sewage, barely existing on pittance wages, the Shah filled his coffers with American-bought weaponry, African diamonds, and Parisian furs, financing it all with the land's vital bloodline, oil. But they weren't going to let him get away with his pillage, Ali told her. Did she want to join him in his journey to freedom?

At first Marjan found Ali's radicalism frightening. She felt especially uncomfortable around the girls in his group, whose gray faces and black chadors were so different from the rest of the women on campus, who preferred liberal coats of lipstick and swinging miniskirts. Marjan couldn't see how covering herself would better society, but she soon came to accept it as one of the many facets of the new Iran they were all dreaming of. Taking up the chador was too drastic a change for her, but she did stop wearing miniskirts and makeup, and covered her hair with a *roosarie,* a head scarf of dark colors. For his part, Ali made no comment on the addition to her wardrobe. He just smiled his beautiful smile. He never pressured her but merely coaxed her with those eyes. Soon enough, Marjan was in the middle of it all, writing and printing revolutionary articles for *The Voice,* organizing weekly meetings, painting banners, and stuffing straw effigies of Uncle Sam in the newspaper's underground offices, all the time not realizing the consequences, the inevitable price of her involvement. For unbeknownst to Marjan, her world was about to break open, bursting and bleeding like the rich yolks of quail eggs cracked over a hot skillet.

Late one spring morning in 1978, as she was arranging type on the aging printing press, an ax broke through the basement door and immediately reduced it to splinters. Marjan later remembered feeling thankful that no bullets were fired, as Ali's desk was close to the door and he would certainly have been hit. How naïve of her really, to give such quick thanks, to have such belief. She made a desperate play for the telephone on her desk, but the handcuffs were quicker. The cold metal sliced into her soft flesh, forcing her hands to her back. There would be no calling home from where she was going.

A rough blindfold was yanked up her face, tightening over her eyes. The final glimpse Marjan had, before the light was extinguished by the dark rag, was the back of Ali's shorn head. It was the last time she ever saw him.

GOHID DETENTION CENTER. A maze of inter-connecting injustices, where the walls were covered in shame. A temporary ground where revolutionaries were taken by the Shah's secret police, slated either for a quick death or for days of torture and mind-bending interrogations. If, God forbid, you ever find yourself inside Gohid's walls, Ali had once warned her, don't say a word. Don't tell them anything, Marjan.

A hand grabbed Marjan's neck and led her, still blindfolded, deep into the center's subterranean levels. These floors, assigned to female revolutionaries, were hollow-sounding and smelled of kerosene and burning skin. A high-pitched wail echoed in the distance, then faded. Countless footsteps and metal hinges clanged, doors opened and slammed shut. Then, suddenly, the black blindfold was ripped away and the iron door of her cell was bolted behind her.

Marjan's pupils slowly adjusted to the harsh light; a naked bulb dangled on a chain in the center of the cell, shining on rough brown walls that curved in a semicircle from the door. A strange, slobbering creature sat slumped in one corner on a straw mat. At first, Marjan thought her eyes were playing tricks on her, because the leering woman was an almost identical twin to her cousin Mitra. Or, rather, she could have been her cousin had Mitra spent the better part of her life hopping beds in flea-infested brothels.

Khanoum Zanganeh was a rather jovial prostitute whose body rose in bumps where fat had accumulated and then sank into bony, hungry areas that were black and blue with bruises. She was dressed in a tattered black shirt and red miniskirt whose sequins she picked at for entertainment.

"Welcome to the Palace!" She chortled. She patted the stony ground next to her. "Sit, sit!" When Marjan did not move, the prostitute narrowed her eyes and pursed her lips. "Who do you work for? No, don't tell me—you're one of Toothless Taraneh's girls, aren't you?"

Marjan swallowed hard and slid down to the floor, closing her eyes. Frenzied thoughts looped through her head as she pictured her sisters waiting for her back at the apartment. Who would make them dinner if she wasn't there? What would happen to Bahar and Layla if she didn't make it out of this terrifying place? How could she have been so stupid, getting involved with Ali and his friends? Curling her knees up to her chin, she laid her head in her arms and began sobbing deeply. Fortunately, Khanoum Zanganeh had stopped her alcoholic banter, leaving Marjan room to mourn her fate alone. She cried for most of the night, never looking up from her arms until the cell door was thrust open once again.

A yellow-skinned, big-boned woman dressed in military fatigues strode into the cell, her heavy boots pounding the damp concrete. She wound a woolen blindfold tightly around Marjan's eyes, her breath stinking of cheap fried meats and stewed okra. Two sets of muscular hands painfully clasped under her armpits and dragged her through the crumbling corridors, her feet skimming over cracked tiles, then tumbling down steep stairs to lower, denser levels. Soon a stool was shoved under her, and grating male voices knocked around her head and body.

What was your role in the newspaper? Who is this Ali you're working for? What were you planning to do with all this propaganda?

The booming voices echoed over and under her like an earthquake.

Your boyfriend Ali is in for a good, long bleeding session if you don't talk. Did you hear me? Your little editor is going to rot in here! Did we tell you about his accident? No? We didn't tell you how he tripped over his own shit and knocked his ugly eye out? All because of your disgusting deeds. We know what you did already!

The laughter of animals in heat; panting and the smell of sweat surrounded her. Someone touched her breasts then, cupping them in his grubby palms before tweaking her nipples so painfully that she was forced to break her silence with a gasp.

Tell me, which would you like more, your pimp's lips or that sausage of his you love to eat so regularly? We know what your real occupation is, Khanoum Journalist!

She remained silent amidst the roaring voices, remembering Ali's advice. Don't say anything, Marjan, she told herself. Don't say a word about Ali, or *The Voice,* and for God's sake, don't tell them about Bahar and Layla, waiting back at the apartment, all alone. It was the same routine, every day, for an hour; a volley of violent groping and unanswered questions, after which the voices threw her back into her cell, unable to be satisfied. Not even starvation—a denial of her daily rations of water, *lavash* bread, and rancid sheep's cheese—would induce Marjan to speak.

"Khanoum Aminpour, take this piece of *lavash* bread from me. Go on, don't be shy! I've the fat to stave the hunger, believe me."

The stale piece of *lavash* bread crumbled in Khanoum Zanganeh's hand. When Marjan finally accepted the rationed food, the weathered prostitute settled back against the cell wall and told her how she had come to be arrested by the Shah's secret police.

"The bastards think I know something about the Committee. Me! What do I know about these political things? I'm just a whore with good teeth!"

Marjan had heard about the infamous Committee, a militant minority that had ballooned seemingly overnight, bringing with it a plethora of undernourished beards and a hunger for vengeance against the capricious Shah and his supporters. Fundamentally inclined, this ragtag group of Islamic vigilantes answered only to the Turbaned One, the exiled Ayatollah with all the answers, as they set about intimidating local neighborhoods in the name of God. Although the Committee was the most powerful organization to emerge in the last year, it still held loose associations to many revolutionary movements, especially those involving university students. Friends of Ali's, supporters of *The Voice*. The Committee.

"Don't worry," Khanoum Zanganeh continued, cocking her henna-colored head toward the cell door. "You'll be out of here in no time. The secret police have no patience for women. It's the men they want."

Somehow, Marjan knew then and there that she'd never see Ali again. She had been mistaken about so much, gotten involved in a business she didn't really understand, didn't really want a part of. And for what? For love? Was that it? How could she have bartered safety for a taste of romance?

By the time she was released from Gohid four days later, thrown out of an unmarked van with a kick of disgust, Marjan had an excuse lined up for her disappearance. She would tell Bahar and Layla that an emergency had kept her from calling them, maybe a fire in the Peacock Restaurant's kitchens. She'd tell them that she had been injured—only a slight burn, nothing major—and had spent the last four days in the hospital, recovering. And then she'd take her sisters and run. They would go to America, to California. Do anything to get there. Sell everything and try for new lives, away from this revolution, this murdering. Just go.

But she was too late. By the time Marjan got home, the revolution had already begun.

"KHANOUM AMINPOUR, *take this piece of* lavash *bread from me.*"

Eight years on, and the memory of the old prostitute's kind offering still set Marjan's stomach rumbling with unexplainable hunger.

And as much as she loved the smell of baking *lavash* bread, she couldn't deny the hint of dread she felt each time she rolled out the dough for a new batch.

Marjan bent over the wooden work island in the café's kitchen, the soft morning light illuminating her floury hands as they kneaded the tough dough before her. There was definitely something wrong with her technique today, she thought to herself. No matter how much she pushed and prodded the white mass of yeasty flour, it kept catching in chalky clumps beneath her fingers.

"Hello there? Anybody home?" The singsong voice behind her gave Marjan a start. The unlocked back door creaked open slowly to reveal Fiona Athey, with an apologetic look on her face. She was holding a stack of flyers under her left arm. "I hope I didn't wake you up, now. I'll come back another time, then. Sorry." She turned to leave.

"No, stay," Marjan replied. "I've been up since five. Making a new batch of bread. Why don't you come in for a cup of tea?"

"I couldn't."

"Don't be silly. Please. I could use the break."

"All right then. Just for one cup so, and then I'll let you go," Fiona said, closing the back door behind her.

Wiping her floury hands with a checkered tea towel, Marjan placed the kneaded dough back in its bowl and covered it with a clean cheesecloth. She was glad to be free of its memories, even for a little while. While Fiona settled into one of the window-side tables, Marjan measured three big tablespoons of Darjeeling leaves into a pretty yellow teapot. The samovar was already bubbling away happily when she pushed its lever down to release boiling water into the pot. Fiona Athey, who had befriended many an Eastern European traveling troupe in her Galway theater days, recognized the shiny electric water boiler instantly.

"That's a Russian-made samovar, isn't it?"

"Yes. How did you know?" Marjan was surprised.

"I haven't always lived in Ballinacroagh. I was an actress once. Met a lot of performers from all over the world in my day," replied Fiona, smiling proudly.

"How exciting! And have you done anything lately?" Marjan asked, filling a platter with elephant ears, *zulbia*, and almond delights.

"I stopped right after my Emer was born. At the time I thought quitting the theater was what I wanted, but now I realize my mistake. I threw away so many years, so much of what I loved for a man." Fiona sighed and told Marjan all about Gerhard and the seduction that had left her out in the cold.

"Yes, it's a wonder what we do for men," Marjan reflected.

"Have you ever been married, Marjan? I hope I'm not being too forward by asking."

"Me? No, never married. I wouldn't have been able to cram it into my busy schedule." Marjan cracked a wry smile and shrugged shyly.

"Ah, sure, men will always be there when you're ready. But look at what you've done! This café, your food—now that's something. This town doesn't know how lucky it is," Fiona said. She reached over and patted Marjan's hand warmly.

"Thank you. That means a lot," Marjan said, feeling a sudden rush of gratitude for the caring hairdresser. She should definitely make a point of coming out of the kitchen more often, she thought to herself. "Now, are you going to tell me what those flyers are for?"

"Oh, these?" Fiona waved her hand nonchalantly over the stack of papers, but her squeaky voice gave away her excitement. "Actually, I'm a bit terrified about it all. Seeing it's been so long since I've tried my hand in the theater."

"Are you putting on a play?"

Fiona nodded. "I thought it'd be just the thing for Patrician Day."

She handed Marjan a light purple flyer from the thick stack. "It's for a bit of a laugh, really." Fiona giggled nervously.

Marjan held the flyer before her and studied the vibrant, fuchsia-colored print:

OVER THE HILL PRODUCTIONS PRESENTS:

FRUITS OF LABOR

a play in two acts

by FATHER FERGAL MAHONEY

ANY INTERESTED PARTIES PLEASE ATTEND AUDITIONS:

Wednesday & Thursday, 3 PM

New Gymnasium, St. Joseph's Secondary School,

BALLINACROAGH

"Father Mahoney has written a play!" Marjan exclaimed.

"I was surprised about it myself. He's no stranger to the stage, so it seems. Used to be a comedian, would you believe! Told me so himself on the phone the other night," Fiona relayed.

Father Fergal Mahoney had indeed been a seasoned stage ham before he entered the seminary. A rising comedic star, to be exact. As a young man he played the circuit of crumbling town council halls, festivals, and fairs around his hometown of Listowel, perfecting his repertoire of impersonations and bawdy jokes. Fergal Mahoney's comedy routine had become so popular that by the age of twenty he was opening for the great Jimmy O'Dea in Dublin's famed Gaiety Theatre. Onstage his rendition of the British Royal Family's bathroom etiquette left the whole house rolling in the aisles, but it was backstage that Fergal really learned the meaning of impropriety. After his performances, he not only mingled with third-tier celebrities and dodgy politicians but also enjoyed intimate moments with a surprisingly flexible Portuguese showgirl named Pepita. All in all, it was a grand life for a farm boy from County Kerry. Little did Fergal know then that, within a year, he'd be knee-deep in sacramental studies and endless readings of the Pentateuch at a Tipperary seminary.

On one misty autumn night in 1945, after a session of piss and puns in the Brazen Head, the mother of all Dublin pubs, Fergal Mahoney was ambling across O'Connell Bridge on his way back to his swanky bachelor's pad when Fate intervened. Fergal was so busy replaying the jokes he had delivered that night onstage, the roaring laughter and thunderous applause that had followed, and Pepita's throaty love moans in his well-lit dressing room after the show, that he did not notice the rotten banana peel beneath his shiny shoes. Before he knew it, he had slipped on the peel and was sliding head-first over the bridge's great Georgian wall toward the infested waters of the river Liffey.

Time stopped for Fergal then. He heard nothing as his soft body tumbled into the Dublin night. For the longest five seconds of his life, Fergal was surrounded by complete silence. Just when he thought he was going to somersault all the way to the peaks of the great Himalayas, Fergal's body abruptly stopped its cartoonish defiance of gravity and plummeted toward the dark river below. In a last-ditch effort to save himself, Fergal shut his eyes and prayed hard and fast for a divine intervention. He pleaded with God to save him; he promised Him that he would do anything, if only he could see his sweet Pepita's sparkly face once again. Fergal didn't expect his prayers to be answered, but he prayed anyway, hoping, like all last-minute converts, for a sign.

The young comedian did not die that night. Nor did he even splash into the dreaded muck of the river Liffey. Fergal's life was spared, his prayers answered when he landed on his whiskey-filled belly in the most reliable of river vessels—a hardy little tugboat. It took a full minute for Fergal to realize that he was alive and that his fall had been cushioned by the tugboat's mountainous cargo load—cartons of bubble-wrapped, silver-crossed, Guatemalan rosary beads.

Fergal Mahoney knew a *sign* when he saw one. He had been given a second chance by the big man Himself, and now he had a promise to fulfill. Bidding farewell to a tearful Pepita, Fergal left for Tipperary's best seminary the very next day.

Not until the moment he first tasted Marjan's *abgusht* had Father Mahoney allowed himself once again to entertain his comedic ambitions. But after a monthlong battle with his conscience, he was finally able to pinpoint the strange exuberance that always coursed through his body after tasting Marjan's delicious lamb dish. Hastily finishing his lunch one afternoon, the priest rushed home to the parish, pulled out his old electric typewriter, and began writing. He didn't stop for Mrs. Boylan's usual Thursday ham and chive colcannon and nearly missed the Henley twins' christening that Sunday, he was so immersed in his new project. When Father Mahoney finally stopped writing a week later, he had before him a two-act play dedicated to the pleasures of the mind and body.

"And I agreed to direct it for him!" Fiona gulped, her eyes fluttering with excitement.

"How wonderful for you both!" Marjan exclaimed. "I'll take two flyers, please. One for the window here and one for the door, so there's no missing them. Are you making your way up the street with the rest?"

"Thought I would. Start early and all, before I open up the salon. Besides, it gives me a bit of headway before all those bleedin' gossip tongues start flaring." Fiona gave Marjan's arm a friendly squeeze and wriggled her fingers as she left through the café's front door.

Gathering the dregs of their impromptu breakfast and tea, Marjan returned to the kitchen with a new spring in her step. She wouldn't have thought so, but it felt good to talk to Fiona. It had made her strong somehow to hold a positive conversation with a new acquaintance. She felt lighter, as if something pressing had been raised from her chest.

Marjan slowly lifted the cheesecloth off the bowl of *lavash* dough. The airy, white mass had risen in the time she had been away and felt almost weightless in her hands. She rolled the dough out once again, marveling at how much more easily it worked under her fingers this time around. Perhaps she too was like the *lavash* bread, thought Marjan; given some time and a warm, comforting environment, anything was possible.

torshi

2 large eggplants, cubed

1 pound small cucumbers, cubed

1 pound carrots, cubed

2 large white potatoes, cubed

8 garlic cloves, peeled

3 cups cauliflower florets

1 pound pearl onions, peeled

½ pound green beans

4 quarts white wine vinegar

4 cups chopped fresh herbs (parsley, basil, tarragon, mint, cilantro)

2 tablespoons salt

2 teaspoons ground black pepper

½ teaspoon cayenne pepper

1 tablespoon nigella seeds

Torshi all-spice mix (½ teaspoon ground turmeric, 1 tablespoon ground cumin, 1 teaspoon ground saffron, 1 tablespoon ground cardamom, 1 teaspoon ground cinnamon)

Wash vegetables and dry well with paper towels. Combine all ingredients in a large bowl. Ladle out the mix into sterilized canning jars. Leave lidded jars in a dry, cool place for a minimum of 1 month.

chapter eight

UNLIKE THE STANDARD pickled cucumbers one finds on supermarket aisles in most Western countries, gentrified and cut into slices or wedges, vegetable *torshi* comes packed in a variety of sizes, shapes, and colors. On Persian tables or upon the venerable spread of a *sofreh*, a hand-sewn cloth which requires limber, cross-legged positions from picnickers, *torshi* is nearly always the first platter served. The most common variety is a combination of fresh vegetables and herbs, pickled in good-quality white wine vinegar, but the list expands to mango chutney, date pickle, eggplant *torshi*, and fruit chutney, all marinated in all-spice and a pinch or two of salt. Integral to most Persian meals, not only does *torshi* complement dishes but its briny, vinegary crunch reminds the palate never to take any taste for granted.

Bahar was given the task of preparing the twenty jars of *torshi* that Marjan had promised the ladies of the Patrician Day Dance committee for their table of charity. Although a great fan of sour cauliflower florets herself, she wasn't keen on the lasting spray of vinegar that would take several showers to scrub off. Drying the clean vegetables thoroughly, she added them to a large bowl of salt, pepper, cayenne, and the *torshi* all-spice. After ladling the *torshi* into six canning jars, she tightened the lids, pumping her powerful forearms with a renewed gush of blood.

Bahar's muscles had always served her well, especially when she had worked as a nurse in Lewisham's Green Acres Home for the Newly Retired. Her sturdy arms had pushed many decaying, insubordinate Englishmen back into their bedpans whenever they insisted on showing her their withered willies. Despite her stern hand, though, Bahar's heart broke every time she witnessed her elderly patients' sad attempts at virility. It was this very withering away of life, she knew, that was behind the second and less appetizing definition of the word *torshi*.

In a tradition where fifteen was the average age of marriage and twenty full-blown motherhood, twenty-five was the hallmark for spinsterhood. As a result, many an unmarried Iranian woman had been branded with the dreaded T-word. Of course, in the latter part of the twentieth century, the marriage age in Iran had risen considerably, but the use of *torshi* to describe a girl who had a certain use-by date, and who was left to dust away on the shelves of love, was still common in gossipy circles. As a teenager, Bahar would never have thought that by the age of twenty-four she would be not only single again but also quite happy to see the vast lonely road before her. The single life was actually quite satisfactory, in her opinion; maybe Layla had her little boyfriend, and Marjan, well Marjan had her planting and cooking and the café and who knew, probably some white-faced Irishman with a good appetite on the horizon, but *she* was content to see her days out alone, in peace, God willing. She did not want a man in her life—never again.

Shaking her head, Bahar twisted shiny purple ribbons around the lips of the *torshi* jars, tying them into proud bows. No, she would not be ashamed of being labeled a *torshi*, she decided. Despite the assault of vinegar, *torshi* vegetables somehow managed to survive their pickling period. And that was what she wanted to be: a survivor, afraid of nothing.

Having packed and decorated the fat jars, Bahar lined them beneath the stairwell, where they would sleep and acquire their distinctive sizzle, the piquant edges of cayenne and nigella softened by the sour vinegar. The *torshi* would have sufficient time to marinate by the Patrician Day Dance in July.

"Mrs. Delmonico's just come in. She wants a bowl of lentil soup, a hummus and grilled eggplant wrap, and a pot of bergamot. Later she wants baklava and two pieces of *zulbia*," said Layla, pushing into the warm kitchen. She slapped Estelle's order on the kitchen island. "Can I go now, Marjan? Ms. Athey's posting the audition results outside the school offices this afternoon."

"Yes, but be back soon. We might get a rush later on like last Saturday," Marjan replied.

"Thanks!" Layla shot out the back door.

"I suppose I'll have to go out front now," Bahar said peevishly. "You know she won't be back for at least another hour."

"Go easy on her, Bahar. This play's really important to her. She auditioned for the lead role, you know. Fiona said she was really good."

"Why am I not surprised?" Bahar said, more grouchily than she felt. The truth was that part of her was proud of Layla. Her younger sister seemed to have quite a talent for finding friends in this new town of theirs, something Bahar had never had much luck with anywhere. Making friends required disclosure, the sharing of secrets and emotions, none of which Bahar could ever see herself doing with perfect strangers. Back in her Green Acres days, her reticence had kept most of her nursing colleagues at bay; she was never invited to aftershift drinks in Doc Watson's Pub, and her lunchtimes were spent not in the cafeteria exchanging notes on petulant patients but rummaging for bargains in the thrift stores that lined nearby Aldersgate Street. Losing herself in the dust of pre-loved knickknacks had comforted Bahar somehow; each bargain buy, be it a tapestry throw from Tuscany or a battered but still lovable copper teapot, kept her mind off how lonely she felt.

With an order pad in hand, Bahar shuffled out to the cacophonous front room, resigned to another afternoon of waiting tables by herself. She rushed back into the kitchen moments later, her face filled with concern. "You better get out there, Marjan. Mrs. Delmonico doesn't look too good. Her skin's bright red and she's drenched in sweat."

Marjan dropped the fried chicken salad she was preparing for the Donnelly twins and hurried through the kitchen doors. Even from across the room it was obvious that something was wrong with the old lady.

Ever since the day she brought her new tenants her famed osso buco, Estelle Delmonico had been one of the Babylon Café's most devoted fans. Although plenty of women her age sat nearby with their daily doses of rosewater-infused treats, Estelle always took her tea alone. She would close her eyes and lick the sugared sweat from her upper lip before sipping her favorite brew, bergamot tea, and biting into an elephant ear or two. Sometimes, the Italian widow would even hum a low aria to herself, one of the many songs her Luigi used to belt out of his robust lungs as he scraped curlicues from a chunk of dark chocolate at the kitchen island.

Marjan usually waited until Estelle had finished her first cup of tea before sitting down at her table for a chat. Lunchtime boom or not, she always spared a few minutes out of the kitchen chaos to say hello to the little old lady with the rickety frame and hearty appetite. She had never watched Estelle for prolonged periods of time, though. As Marjan stood observing Estelle at her lone table now, it dawned upon her that the widow's self-imposed seclusion was not entirely voluntary.

Estelle Delmonico's eyes gave her away. Every thirty seconds or so they would dart over to the long communal table where the ladies of the Patrician Day Dance committee sat, before flicking back to the spoon on her table. She would then dab at her swollen nostrils with an embroidered silk handkerchief taken from her small patent leather handbag. The committee ladies were too busy deciding on the Dance's decoration theme (should they stick to the usual tricolored salute or take on a Caribbean flavor with the colors of terra cotta, pacific aqua, and hydrangea pink?) to notice they were being watched. They did not detect Estelle's quiet pleas as Marjan did, recognizing the signs of desperate loneliness.

Perhaps she could ask Marie Brennan to include the Italian woman in the next week's committee meeting, thought Marjan. Surely, the ladies of the Patrician Day Dance committee could use an extra hand with all the activities they had planned. And, Marjan reasoned, once Estelle felt she was needed, she wouldn't feel so shy about taking the initiative to make new friends herself. Pleased with her idea, Marjan eagerly approached Estelle's table and was about to greet her kind landlady when something in the old woman's face made her pause. Estelle Delmonico's complexion was growing a more dangerous shade of red by the second, and sweat was streaming liberally down her cheeks now, too quickly to be wiped away. Startled, Marjan peered closer at Estelle's flushed face and realized that the sweat was, in actual fact, tears. Large, fat tears. She dashed forward just as the Italian widow fell toward the floor, letting go of the crushed rose she was holding to her heaving chest.

AN OPPRESSIVE MELANCHOLY set in that lasted the rest of the afternoon.

The Donnelly twins helped Marjan lift Estelle from her fainted slouch and carried her to the back of the green hippie van. Father Mahoney, who had stopped by for a lamb and cucumber sandwich to go, climbed in next to Estelle's limp body and held her soft hands, praying hard as the van careened toward Mayo General Hospital in Castlebar. Soon, the rest of the diners also abandoned the café, scattering as if driven away by bad weather, leaving their half-eaten baklavas and sweet syrup drinks behind in a congealed mess.

Bahar locked the café door and set about gathering the rose petals from underneath Estelle's table. She would be the first to admit that the old widow's collapse had shaken her to the core. It had reminded Bahar that not everything was as secure as Marjan would have them believe. Any accident could uproot them again, send whatever success this café had been experiencing into distant memory. What would all their regulars think now? Probably that their food was indigestible, unhealthy, cooked in a kitchen rampant with rats and other diseases. That perhaps it was something Estelle ate that made her fall into a deathlike trance.

Marjan and Layla may have been too busy with their own fantasies to notice, Bahar told herself, but she wasn't blind to the stares thrown her way whenever she stepped out of the café doors. How could she ignore the obvious cuts of silence, the breaks in street conversations whenever she walked by a cluster of townspeople? Why, it had happened in the butcher's just the other day, as she was paying for the café's weekly order of lamb and ground meat for shish kabobs. Three crotchety gossips, standing near the Galtee back bacon rashers display, had scanned her up and down with their myopic eyes when they thought she had her back turned. She should have returned their disapproving looks with a piercing stare of her own, thought Bahar. Put those old bags in their place. But all she had done was keep her head bowed as she hurried out of the shop, glad to have escaped the old women's merciless scrutiny.

Well, what else could she have expected from such a small-time town? And now who knew when all their regulars would feel comfortable enough to come back, or if they would at all. Bahar sighed as she swept a pile of food crumbs into a dustpan.

Really, as long as they were able to survive, to plod along in this sleepy town, she didn't care much about its size, its prejudices. So long as no one in the outside world, beyond the craggy boundaries of the western village, knew that they were there. That was all that mattered.

ESTELLE DELMONICO AWOKE in her hospital bed, rehydrated and cool after the heatstroke and heartache that had caused her to faint. At least that was the doctor's explanation for the old lady's extraordinary coloring and bubbled breathing when Marjan and Father Mahoney admitted her to Mayo General. An hour later, after she had been thoroughly replenished with nutrients from a much-needed IV tube, the Italian woman shared the real reason behind her fainting spell.

"Please! Heatstroke! There is no heat outside for a stroke!" She paused for a moment, her eyes traveling to the hospital room window and its view of green and brown hills that rolled under gray, fast-moving clouds. "I tell you the truth. Today my Luigi and I, we are married fifty years. I was just not feeling happy, you understand?"

She stopped there, all of a sudden aware of Father Mahoney's presence, of Marjan's concerned nods, and reddened again. In all her forty-five years in Ballinacroagh, and especially since her husband's death five years ago, Estelle had never shown her vulnerability, her raw need for company, to any of its townspeople. Not even in her weekly confessionals to Father Mahoney, where she would expound on the loving yet distant relationship she had with her niece, Gloria, would Estelle mention her isolation, her longing to connect to life-forms besides the achingly beautiful rosebush outside her little cottage. And now, on the day when as a young bride she had expected to receive the golden platitudes of loving grandchildren gathered at her knees, she had taken one look at the table of involved, comforted committee women, all in the bosoms of elderly friendships, then looked at the vacancy of her own table, and released the last hold on her privacy—only to find herself fainting, of all things.

Luckily, Father Mahoney rescued the pained silence with his own mark of humility and comedic grace. "Sure, Estelle, we'll be needing your fine expertise for play rehearsals. A modern *Bacchae* of sorts—all that lovemaking and wine drinking—it's all Greek to me. It'll be up your alley, now, I'd say."

It had made Marjan blush to hear the word *lovemaking* from the old priest's smiling lips, but Estelle Delmonico just giggled out loud. Father Mahoney's generosity had broken the ice, giving the once lonely widow an invitation to the camaraderie and community she had longed for for four decades.

"WHERE IS SHE, MARJAN? It's nearly six o'clock! What if something happened to her on the way home?" Bahar looked like an asylum escapee, pacing up and down the empty café aisles as she wrung her hands. Five hours had passed since Layla left to check the audition results, an excursion that, in Bahar's opinion, should have taken her an hour at the most to complete.

"I already told you, Bahar. I called Fiona. She saw her last outside the school offices, with Malachy. They both got the lead roles in the play. She's probably out celebrating with her friends," Marjan replied quietly, trying to sound calm.

"Malachy! Who is this Malachy, really? Yes, I know he's polite and smart, but do we know anything about his family, about what kind of people his parents are? What if they're crazy murderers?"

"Bahar. Please." Marjan shook her head. Her sister could be so dramatic sometimes. Any moment now she might crumple up in a ball of hysterical tears, right there in the middle of the café floor. At least she had stopped cleaning. Marjan had known something had gone awry as soon as she arrived home from the hospital. She found Bahar inside the kitchen with a copper scrubber and a bottle of bleach in hand, deep in a frenzied cleaning match with the oven door. Bahar resorted to such crazed cleaning only when she was too upset to complain; she would scour the floors and countertops until she had spent most of her nervous energy.

"Okay, fine, maybe not murderers, but we still don't know much about Malachy, and she's out with him every day. She should be helping me wait tables instead of doing God knows what with that Irish boy. And you, Marjan—you're not helping!" Bahar pointed her finger at her sister accusingly.

"Me! What did I do?"

"Letting her go off without a curfew. It's almost ten past six now!"

"All right," Marjan acquiesced, not wanting to argue. "I'll check the school. She's probably still there. Just stay calm, okay?"

Marjan hopped into the van and gunned anxiously out of the alleyway for the second time that day, working hard to silence the murky, fearful thoughts that rumbled through her mind. She might have acted composed with Bahar, but she too was extremely concerned. Layla had been gone for nearly five hours now, without so much as a phone call to let them know where she was. Of course, Marjan reasoned, Ballinacroagh was by no means the most dangerous town they'd ever lived in; Layla could be testing out her adolescent boundaries in far worse places. But still, one could never be completely sure.

Saint Joseph's Secondary sat on a low hill about a quarter mile from the high end of Main Mall, so Marjan pulled into its gravelly driveway within minutes of leaving the café. She felt her level of panic rise abruptly as her eyes scanned the school's empty, rain-drenched front lawn. The main building's front doors were stopped open, but its towering, Gothic windows were dark. The only sound she could hear was the clangor of Saint Barnabas's rusty church bell tolling in the distance. It was Saturday after all, Marjan reminded herself, trying to regain her composure. She parked the van outside the front doors and hurried into the building's shadowy corridors.

Heavy wooden classroom doors lined either side of the hall, contrasting with walls painted in pistachio green. Every ten yards or so, muted light fixtures attached to dividing archways cast eerie pools on the speckled moss tiles beneath her feet. The offices must be along this way, she told herself as she rushed down a long passageway. Layla might still be in there with Malachy and her friends, clustered around the audition notice, too excited to see the night falling quickly outside. Marjan was rounding a hallway corner when she bumped into the dark veils.

They came upon her so swiftly that she shrieked in horror. She grabbed a nearby trophy case for support, her knees suddenly buckling under her.

The veils, habits to be precise, belonged to two elderly nuns. Sisters Agatha and Bea were on their way back to the convent, having just finished a meeting of the Popular Canticle Club held in the school's new gymnasium.

Marjan recovered from her shock and found her voice.

"Ah, excuse me. Is the school closed?"

Sister Agatha, a woman who had renounced a life of Jazz-era partying for Christ, smiled at her kindly.

"You're the girl who's taken over Estelle Delmonico's place, aren't you?" She poked Sister Bea with her elbow. "This is the one Father Mahoney was telling us about! *Father Mahoney!*" She yelled into the shorter nun's ear. "She's hard of hearing, Sister Bea is," Sister Agatha explained.

Sister Bea looked confused and stared at Marjan with vague, opaque eyes.

"Oh. Yes. I'm actually looking for my younger sister. Layla Aminpour? She's in third year?" Marjan's heart slowed down its frantic beating.

"Well, I can't say I know any of the students nowadays. Sister Bea and I haven't taught for quite a few years, you see." Sister Agatha leaned into Sister Bea's right ear. "Not taught here for a *long time!* *Have we, Sister?*"

Sister Agatha's croaky voice finally registered with the deaf nun. Sister Bea smiled broadly and nodded, showing her pearly dentures.

"You won't have much luck today, I'm afraid, it being Saturday and all. Though it's a great thing Sister Bea and I finally have the chance to meet you. I was wondering now, can you tell me where to find some of that lovely saffron stuff Father Mahoney has been telling us about?"

Because of the priest's many praises, both nuns were well aware of Marjan's potent *abgusht*. Even the half-deaf Sister Bea had heard about the stew's divine ingredients, the recipe reverberating against the convent walls long after their last prayers were whispered. After answering the two nuns' string of cooking questions as best she could, Marjan quickly retreated to the van. With her heart still hammering, she climbed into the driver's seat and jammed the key into the ignition but stopped before she turned it. A strange clamminess had chilled her skin, causing her teeth to chatter uncontrollably. As comic as the nuns were, those navy habits were just too close to the choking chador for her liking. Had she not been in peaceful Ballinacroagh, Marjan would surely have taken them as a sign of impending doom.

A STROKE OF AMBER, the last sigh of a darkening horizon, guided Bahar on her own search for her errant sister as she hastened up Main Mall. She had never been this far up the street on foot before. Her shopping errands kept her in close proximity to the café; the butcher's and the mini-mart were only a couple of minutes away from the Babylon's front door. Nevertheless, Bahar had decided to brave the unknown, sure that she would go mad if she waited in the café any longer. If Layla was out with friends (and Bahar hoped to God she was), she might be slurping milk shakes in the burger and chip place on Main Mall, or perhaps trying her luck with a more illicit brew in one of the town's three pubs. Bahar was determined to find her, wherever she was. And when she did, she was going to give that sister of hers a mighty earful.

Layla wasn't in the Blue Thunder burger joint, nor was she in Paddy McGuire's Pub next door. Thankfully, Bahar surmised this without having to step foot in either place; both establishments had large, street-front windows from which patrons could be seen downing pints and scoffing greasy curry chips. Perhaps she should try asking some of the shopkeepers along the Mall if they had seen a dark-haired girl with too much time on her hands, thought Bahar. She stopped abruptly in front of the first store that looked open, Corcoran's Bake Shop. As good a place as any to start inquiring, Bahar decided, nodding silently to herself. Pushing through its yellow door, she stepped innocently inside, entirely unprepared for the chilly reception she was about to receive from Assumpta Corcoran.

A lot had changed in the Corcoran household since Layla had crossed paths with Benny Corcoran and his bread-filled wheelbarrow, nearly seven weeks ago to the day. Layla's youthful promise had thrown the reluctant baker into a kaleidoscope of regrets, prompting him to examine his choices in life.

Benny's loveless marriage and his particularly close friendship with Mr. Jack Daniel had turned his once athletic body into a pitiful lump of fat and freckles, the glorious head of red hair he had as a young man reduced now to a handful of unruly strands. Once inspired, though, Benny threw himself into a full exercise regime worthy of the harshest boot camps. He installed a pull-up bar over the bake shop's back door, from which he pumped up and down at three in the morning, and began to experiment with comb-overs and hair volumizers, purchased from Athey's Shear Delight (but only after swearing Fiona Athey to secrecy). Benny even dug out his wide-lapeled leather jacket from the bake shop's cobwebbed attic, along with the Gaelic football trophies he had won as a teenager, awards he had forgotten in all these years of kneading the unsavory rolls of both his profession and the body of his cold wife, Assumpta.

Though named in honor of the ascension of the Virgin Mary, Assumpta Corcoran considered her own soul eternally damned. Her weekly church confessions were filled with the guilt of bodily functions, of her husband's carnal demands, and of the wifely responsibilities that she could never live up (or down) to. After each confession, Assumpta would rush home to cleanse herself with a scalding bath and a harsh loofah, hoping to scrub away her own confused soul in the process. When Assumpta noticed that Benny's gut was no longer straining against the last hole of his belt buckle, and that his florid complexion had toned down to a pleasantly muted pink, she knew that all her praying had come to nothing—her husband had finally given in to his dirty ways and taken a mistress, just as so many in town believed he had for years. Frigid as she was, Assumpta had always assumed that the sanctity of her marriage was safe despite the gossip. But a new

Benny who refused his drink and pored over diet cookbooks was by no means playing by the rules. Benny Corcoran was changing, and it wasn't for her benefit, that was for sure. But who was the floozy who had caught her husband's degenerate eye? The pieces of the puzzle did not fall into place for Assumpta until that very moment, when a flushed and worried-looking Bahar stepped timidly into the bake shop.

"Hi, I'm Bahar Aminpour. My sisters and I own the café down the street."

Assumpta's eyes narrowed. She had passed by the new lunch place several times since it had opened its doors, hoping to catch a sight of the foreigners who were running it. But other than the young girl with the black hair who walked past the bakery on her way to school, Assumpta had never spotted any of the darkie women Dervla Quigley yammered on about. Now she could see that the old gossip's suspicions were well-founded. The brown-skinned woman in front of her was the embodiment of John's warning in Revelation: the Harlot of Babylon had just made herself known. God be with them all.

"What can I do for you?" Assumpta's voice was icy.

"I'm looking for my younger sister, Layla. She's fifteen, long dark hair, about this tall?" Bahar's hand measured a half foot above her own head before dropping listlessly to her side.

"No. Haven't seen anybody like *that* around here," Assumpta replied, making the word *that* sound almost filthy.

"Oh—thanks anyway." Bahar turned sheepishly to leave, feeling another terrible headache coming along.

Just then, Benny huffed and puffed into the shop from the back kitchen. He had finished an agonizing lap around the town center and was sporting velour head- and wristbands that were soaked in his middle-aged sweat. The baker immediately recognized Bahar as one of the three angels from the café, whom he had spotted on his daily bread runs up and down Main Mall.

"Why, hello there. How can I be of service to you today?"

Benny's eyes glazed over, clear confirmation for Assumpta that she was staring at her husband's mistress.

"It's all right. Sorry to bother you." Bahar nodded a shy good-bye and quickly slipped out of the bakery. Overcome by a sudden exhaustion, she pressed her right hand to her thumping temple and continued rather wobbly up the street.

Benny watched her walk off, then turned to his wife. He was taken aback by the look of smug satisfaction spread across Assumpta's normally disappointed face.

"What did ye say to her now, to have her running out the door like a wild banshee?"

"Don't you go telling me what's right or wrong, Benny Corcoran. I know what your jogging and vegetarian diets are all about. Put me to shame, you have! The whole town's talkin'! And don't think I'm going to stick around to see you gallivanting with some foreign hussy!"

Assumpta was close to tears as she grabbed her coat and ran to the door.

"Assumpta!" Benny yelped. "Where are ye going?"

"To Mass! To pray for our souls, dirty thing! And you better be at the pub when I get back!"

MARJAN'S LIME GREEN van idled in the school parking lot, her thoughts floating across the gloomy windshield before her. The nuns' dark habits had resurrected unexpected ghosts, memories she had hoped would lie dead and buried. Maybe some spirits are just not meant for the afterlife, she told herself, their season of haunting lasting forever.

The phantoms had come flapping out of their ghoulish graves when she wasn't looking, the spring day in 1978 when she was released from Gohid Detention Center. The first person Marjan saw when she stumbled into their apartment after her secret incarceration was little Layla. Fattened with buttery dishes, her apple head wrapped in a matronly head scarf, Layla was sitting on the living room carpet holding a photo of a turbaned idol of the revolution in her plump fingers. Snatching the photograph into her own shaking hands, Marjan was about to tear it into a thousand pieces—as many as it would take to erase the furrowed face that was being painted on all neighborhood walls—when she saw the ghosts.

The kitchen was swarming with them. Black chadors and gremlin faces, their gapped teeth slurping at oily broths and overcooked *chelow*. Marjan almost fell over when she realized that one of them was her sister.

At sixteen, and in less than four days, Bahar had become a militant member of the Women's Party.

The darling sister of the male-only Committee, the Women's Party was a local organization led by their neighbor, a large, pointy-faced woman named Khanoum Jaferi. Born to a snake-charmer father and a gypsy mother, whose hobbies ranged from tea-leaf readings to midafternoon trysts with pubescent shepherd boys, Khanoum Jaferi had grown up to abhor all such excesses. She had taken to the veil and chador at the age of twenty and slowly moved up the ranks of pious women's groups by attending monthly summits on the proper length of chadors and techniques for avoiding pleasure during dutiful matrimonial copulation.

In no time at all, the cunning Khanoum Jaferi had pushed her way to the forefront of the revolutionary movement by establishing her own corps of female fundamentalists—the Women's Party. Weekly meetings of the Women's Party were held in her lavishly carpeted apartment. There, devoted members spent hours extolling the virtues of the Turbaned One, the mullah who promised to rid the country of all evil decadence and establish an Islamic society. Over scalding cups of unsweetened black tea and goat's tongue stew, Khanoum Jaferi preached passionately on the need to purge their beloved Persia of Western influence—the Shah, that sweetheart of America, included. She had been waiting thirty years for the Islamic Revolution to cleanse their society, she told the chador-clad women, and she wasn't going to stop until she saw her dream realized.

Khanoum Jaferi, Marjan later learned, had come to the apartment with pots of rice and split pea soup when news spread that she hadn't returned home from the Peacock Restaurant. Never one to miss a recruitment opportunity, the militant matron also came equipped with paint and white banners, setting Bahar to work on writing anti-American slogans while she reheated her tasteless pots of food.

If it wasn't for Khanoum Jaferi and the Women's Party, Layla and I would have starved, Bahar had said, disregarding Marjan's warnings about the group of reactionary chadors proliferating in their kitchen. *Independence, Freedom, Islamic Republic!* Marg bar Amrika, *Death to America,* she exclaimed, before launching into Koranic passages so long and complicated that Marjan was stunned into silence by Bahar's aptitude for rote memorization. The most frightening thing of all, though, was not Bahar's newfound zeal for the revolution, or the weekly Women's Party meetings she insisted that the three of them attend, but the unquestioning loyalty she now had to Khanoum Jaferi's only son, the man who was going to be her husband.

Hossein Jaferi. A salamander of a man, not yet informed on the responsibilities of belonging to the human race. Severely punctured by mishandled forceps at birth, Hossein wore his slashed skin like a badge of honor, proud to have survived the first of life's many obstacles. The metal contraption had marred Hossein's baby face with such deep indentations that his mother had fallen off the high labor bed and broken her hip in two places from the shock of it all. As a young man, Hossein had been arrested by the secret police for burning an effigy of the diminutive Shah, but six years in jail had done little to stem his restlessness, and upon his release, the first place he visited was his local mosque. Inside its cool, mosaic-covered walls, Hossein received divinations encouraging him to establish himself as a leader of believing men. And so, prompted by God and his zealous mother, he joined a local grassroots initiative—the Committee. A perfect platform from which the sadistic, thirty-one-year-old Hossein Jaferi could launch his career in the open territory that was the revolution.

Marjan nearly fainted when she heard the name. The Committee. But her objections carried little weight; Bahar had made up her mind, and a whole community of underground chadors would back her decision.

On the sleepless night before Bahar and Hossein were to be married, Marjan passed the dark hours with her hands deep in sticky dough, trying to think of a way to stop her sister from ruining her life. It was Marjan's job to bake the delicacies for the wedding feast, the baklava, the mulberry-almond paste, and the walnut, chickpea, and rice cookies. As she rolled out the pastry for the baklava (enough to feed the entire militant party of two hundred), Marjan tried to reason with her gnawing stomach, with that voice that was telling her to take her two sisters and run. This Hossein and all that came with him—the Molotov cocktail parties he organized, the martyred uncle he worshiped, his domineering mother, who seemed to have Bahar under an unbreakable spell—were wrong. All wrong. And there was nothing Marjan could do to alter her sister's destiny.

The day after her ill-fated wedding, Bahar moved in with her new husband's family. Her move relieved her sisters from having to attend meetings of the Women's Party every week, but it also left behind such a void, such an empty space in Marjan's heart. And although she lived only a few blocks away, Marjan did not see Bahar until nearly four months after her wedding day.

ASSUMPTA CORCORAN's cold gaze seemed to have imprinted itself on Bahar's temples. The tingling overtures of a headache accompanied her as she stepped inside McGuire's Ale House, hoping to find Layla sitting in one of its ratty booths.

Now Thomas McGuire wasn't the kind of man to let an attractive woman go unnoticed in his establishment. Although he reserved his true affections for the likes of Donna Summer, Gloria Gaynor, and Thelma Houston, and exposed his chunky private quarters only to the embraces of his lusty wife, Thomas was certainly not blind to the swagger of feminine hips. When Bahar walked into the pub, the owner was busy going over the weekly shift roster with his bartender, but he paused in midspeech to gawk at the young woman who had disturbed the stale fog of cigarette smoke and soft flatulence.

That's no ordinary woman, Thomas realized with a sudden shudder. *She's one of those tarts from the café!* He jerked his eyes off Bahar and, curling his thick lips in a soft snarl, gave his bartender a knowing nod. *Bleedin' Arabs.*

Bahar approached the bar counter like a lamb to the slaughter.

"Sorry, hello?" she said, raising her hand like a schoolgirl. The bartender, a pudgy man with heavy ginger sideburns, mirrored his boss's sneer. He turned his back on Bahar and pretended to make conversation with an inebriated old-timer slumped over in his own drool.

"I was just wondering if anyone had seen my—"

All the punters at the bar, from Thomas McGuire to Old Lady Lennon cradling her gin and tonic at the corner table, had turned their backs against her. Silence. Several seconds passed, during which

Chaka Khan's velvety voice could be heard purring from a large juke-box in the corner. Someone coughed as a lazy cloud of tobacco smoke drifted in front of Bahar's eyes. She looked down at the diamond-patterned carpet at her feet, which was gritty with the previous night's revelry of powdered potato crisps, cigarette butts, and peanut casings. Chaka Khan hit an unnaturally high note, and the jukebox lifted the record off, returning it to a fanned stack of shiny black LPs, and went silent. And still, no one turned to look at her.

Angry embarrassment washed over Bahar's cheeks and sent her stomach into a spin. Something was very wrong here, not only in this dirty pub but in the bake shop next door as well. Something that went beyond the sad little curiosities of the old women in the butcher's. Whatever she thought of that kind of small-mindedness, it was noth-ing compared to the bald hatred before her. It was an exclusion as foul as she had experienced in those scary early years in London, when the whole city was under alert of terrorist threats, and anyone who looked slightly foreign was watched with suspicion.

Turning on her heels, which crunched on the littered floor, Bahar pushed through the pub door, anxious to escape the dread that was rising in her chest. Just as the door slammed behind her, a sinister voice called out: "Go back to yer stinking camels!" Raspy smokers' laughs enveloped the rest of the smarting insult.

"OVER THERE. Right next to that cumulus that looks like a rabbit—that's Jupiter. It's always there, even during day-light hours. You should see it at night, though, with a telescope." Malachy's long arm pointed toward the sky over Clew Bay.

"You can see it from your bedroom?" Layla snuggled closer to him on a surprisingly warm patch of sea grass.

pomegranate soup · 141

"Yeah, but I like to bring my gear out here when I can. Even if it gets up my dad's wrong side."

"Your dad?" Layla had forgotten about Emer's warning. She wondered if the rumors were true about Malachy's father wanting the café space but, sensing it would be a sore subject, let it go. Instead, she rested her head on his reclining chest and gazed dreamily up at the sky. "So are all the constellations named after Greek gods and goddesses?"

Malachy, relieved to have sidestepped the subject of his domineering father, smiled and nodded.

"Yup. Though the Babylonians discovered them before the Greeks. They had a whole system worked out." He wiped his hand across the heavens, stopping on a slice of sky that blinked brighter than the surrounding pale clouds. "Next to that patch of sky there is Venus. You can't see it, but trust me, it's there."

Layla gulped and nodded. Venus. Goddess of Love. Yes, it was definitely there.

Somehow, somewhere between the planetary blessings, the gentle lulling of the Atlantic tide, and the canopy of their linking fingers against the sky, they had fallen asleep. The next thing Layla knew, she was staring into the giggling black hole of a toothless six-year-old mouth.

"D'yis tink they're dead?"

"Naw, they're pr'bly jest shagging."

Laughter and spittle landed on Layla's and Malachy's opening eyelids. An urchin gang of three boys and a girl, ranging in age from six to twelve, had surrounded them. The children were dressed in gray and navy tracksuits, their matted red hair and freckled faces streaked with dirt. Globs of mucus lined the corners of their eyes, and their mouths were edged with melted chocolate.

"Go on! Get!"

Malachy shooed them toward a distant cluster of trailer homes parked at the base of a sandy hill. A makeshift clothesline hung between two of the mobile homes, and several plastic foldout chairs encircled a campfire. Three women, wearing tight stonewashed jeans stretched across emaciated thighs, were shivering over the fire as they passed a long cigarette between them. They watched with boredom as a skinny rooster pranced around two mangy, snoring terriers. Layla was surprised she hadn't seen the camp earlier. But then again, her attention had been wholly consumed by Malachy. She trembled just thinking about the boy at her side.

The tinker children laughed loudly and scampered off. The oldest boy jabbed two fingers up in the air, a time-honored insult, before disappearing behind the shoulder of a giant, shadowy dune. As if snapped out of a trance, Layla noticed that everything was suddenly dark around them. Even the stars were beginning to show their twinkling smiles in the night sky above.

BAHAR SAT AT the kitchen table with her head in her hands, crying and, for the first time in a long while, praying. It was all her fault they were stuck in some mean little village at the end of the world, with nothing but cooking burns and the stink of fried onions to look forward to. It was all her fault, and she had no way of remedying it.

"Bahar?" Layla whispered. She was standing just inside the kitchen doorway, afraid to move an inch.

Lifting her wet face from her palms, Bahar stared at Layla in silence. Opalescent shafts from the outside light converged around Layla's head like a halo. Blinded by the bright glow, Bahar was forced to blink hard several times before she could make out Layla's face, but once she was assured that her sister was alive and well, her anger was swift.

"Where have you been? I've been going crazy waiting here!" she yelled, staggering up from her chair.

"I was with Malachy. At the beach," Layla replied casually.

"It's seven o'clock, Layla!"

"I know. Sorry."

Shocked by Layla's carelessness, Bahar stared at her with wide eyes, her mouth falling open. Her sister obviously had no concern for what she had just been through, Bahar thought with increasing anger, searching frantically up and down the street, having to belittle herself in front of such ignorant people. She was with Malachy, simple as that. How dare she? As if she deserved such freedom, as if she had earned the right to go on dates at her age. Had Layla forgotten everything she had been through? Bahar searched for words that would put the fear of men into Layla, but what finally came out of her mouth was: "You'll end up like I did—is that what you want? I forbid you to see this boy again!"

"Bahar!"

"No! I mean it, Layla! We didn't come all the way here so that you could end up in bed with some stupid Irish boy!" Bahar's voice was shrill.

"You just want me to be as bitter as you are!" Layla fired back. "I deserve some happiness, you know! Don't forget it's because of you we had to come here in the first place!"

Layla ran up the stairs and slammed the flat door, leaving Bahar choking on her angry, misplaced fear.

chelow

3 cups uncooked, long-grain basmati rice

6 cups water

2 tablespoons salt

½ cup olive oil

Place rice in a large bowl and wash under lukewarm water. Drain, then repeat two more times. Bring water and salt to a boil in a stockpot. Add clean rice, cover, and cook for 30 minutes, or until al dente. In another large pot, heat oil. Spread an inch-thick layer of cooked rice at the bottom of the second pot. Slowly scoop cooked rice into the pot, forming a pyramid shape so that the top layer is the point. Cover and cook on low heat for 30 minutes. Tadig will form at the bottom.

MARJAN PICKED ESTELLE DELMONICO up from the hospital the following morning. Although the doctors at Mayo General had wanted her to stay on for one more day, in case another fainting spell came along, the feisty Italian woman had insisted on being released as soon as possible.

"I am okay, not to worry so much. And you know, I can't eat one more day of this horrible hospital chicken. No flavor, my goodness!" Estelle protested. Not even in the dark days of the World War, when her family had been forced to ration their weekly supply of linguine and clam sauce, had she ever tasted food as bland and uninspiring.

Remembering Estelle's complaint, Marjan had packed some freshly made elephant ears and a large serving of herb *kuku* in a brown paper bag before leaving for the hospital. One whiff of the fried treats and the taste of boiled hospital meals would be long forgotten, she thought to herself.

Marjan couldn't help but notice how frail the little widow looked in her thin hospital robe. Even so, Estelle had rejected the nurse's offer of a wheelchair and would have walked out of Mayo General all by herself had it not been for her arthritis. Estelle's joints were in-flamed as a result of her spell, the stretched tendons in her fragile hips and knees aching with every step, so Marjan had to hold the old lady steady by her elbow and shoulder for their walk out to the parking lot. Luckily, the sturdy green van was narrow enough to handle the sharp mountain road to Estelle's white cottage. Marjan helped her slowly down from the passenger's seat, and together they tackled the steep gravel path leading up to the bright red door.

"That's a beautiful rosebush," Marjan admired.

"Thank you, darling. Yes, that's my Luigi," Estelle said, pleased.

"How lucky for you to have him so near," Marjan replied, under-standing the significance of the roses immediately.

"He is always close to me."

Estelle handed Marjan a knobby, rusted key on a large metal ring. The door opened to reveal the dim, warm front parlor, a neat little room boasting cushiony cream furniture, lace curtains, and vases filled with gardenias. Both women paused at the threshold as the sea breeze fluttered the leaves of the rosebush behind them, Luigi's own personal welcome. Marjan led Estelle across the cozy parlor's polished flag-stone floors.

"Which way to your bedroom, Estelle?"

"Just down this hall, darling. Make a left."

They turned into a brightly wallpapered hallway lined with framed portraits. There was a young Estelle on her wedding day, her hair in a pert chignon covered by an elaborate lace veil; another sepia-toned photograph with Estelle in her bride's dress, this time standing next to a squat, jolly-faced young man with a thick mustache that curled at its ends. Luigi.

"Ah, so many memories!" Estelle exclaimed. She traced her feeble fingers over the prints, moving along the happy years; the Delmonicos on their honeymoon in Morocco; posing outside Papa's Pastries on its first day of business; even one of her niece, Gloria, in her checkered chef's uniform and tall paper hat.

They passed a sunny, daffodil kitchen on the right, crammed with a wooden table painted purple and chairs and cabinets stenciled with periwinkle blue daisies. Once they were in the bedroom, Marjan helped Estelle into a cotton nightgown and tucked her into her big mahogany and duck down bed.

"Wait here. I've got something for you in the van," Marjan said. She returned promptly with the brown paper bag of treats.

"Elephant ears!" Estelle clapped her hands like a happy child.

Marjan opened the sugary packages on Estelle's handmade quilt and immediately eased the old woman's icicle joints with the lush smells of sweet pastries and a still warm egg and herb pancake. She looked so healthy and calm after eating that Marjan took the opportunity to ask the widow for some precious advice.

"Let the two of them work it out by themselves," Estelle began wisely, after Marjan finished telling her about her sisters' fight. "They are big girls now, Marjan."

"I know, but sometimes I can't help feeling responsible for everything they do. I am the eldest, after all," Marjan replied, twisting the paper bag absently in her hands.

"Big sister, yes. Mother, no. I was never lucky to have children, but I have Gloria, and let me tell you, girls are not easy. This Malachy. You say this boy is good?" Estelle looked skeptical; she knew Thomas McGuire too well to expect much from his offspring.

"He's wonderful. A very good boy."

"Well then, that is okay, yes? I met my Luigi when I was fifteen. I don't say Layla is going to be married now, but if he is a good boy, then that is okay. His father, he is Thomas McGuire?"

"I was meaning to ask you about him," Marjan said. She had heard all about the self-important man who had given Bahar such a hard time in the Ale House the day before. Marjan relayed the information from Emer Athey that Layla had finally remembered to pass down.

"Apparently Malachy's father wants us out of business," she said.

"I tell you something about Thomas McGuire and the rest of those silly people," Estelle said. "They are all scared. You should see them when my Luigi and I moved here. Two, three customers a day for so long! You know what my Luigi did then? He take a table and put it out the window and everything on it was free! Free biscotti, free amaretto delights, free cannoli! Even free espresso! These people love free!"

Estelle sat forward on her bed and gestured excitedly with her warmed hands. "I say don't worry. You smile at them all, at that McGuire, at all the women in church who look like they eat a bad egg. You teach them about being good."

Buoyed by Estelle's wisdom, Marjan decided not to worry but instead to smile and keep her doors open. The café was thriving with its daily patronage of regulars, and she could always rely on Father Mahoney and Fiona Athey to show up, if no one else did. As for the rest of the town, Marjan thought to herself, well, they would eventually succumb to the smell of her fried elephant ears and herb-filled *kuku*. Maybe she couldn't get everyone in Ballinacroagh to come into the Babylon, but Marjan knew there would still be enough customers to keep Bahar, Layla, and her busy from morning until closing time. It was all she had ever wanted for the three of them and now it was coming true.

One thing was certain, though. They had not come all this way to sink to the likes of Thomas McGuire. Or anyone else, for that matter.

CHELOW, OR STEAMED RICE, is vital to Persian cuisine as it lays the foundation upon which other main dishes are built. Not only does *chelow* offer excellent companionship to stews, barbecued lamb, Cornish hens, beef, or fish but the rice can be combined with an assortment of goodies such as pistachios, lentils, dried cherries, and lima beans to make a complete meal in itself. The simplest and most popular recipe, though, is white *chelow*. The rice—each grain a separate pearl of wisdom—needs to be cooked slowly for half an hour before the famed *tadig* can be made.

Marjan busied herself with making the *tadig*, the crunchy bottom layer of the *chelow* that fries into a large rice cake dripping with goodness. She used a deep soup pot to heat the olive oil until it was popping with anticipation, before spreading an inch-thick layer of rice. The *tadig* would need to be covered and gently cooked on low for thirty minutes before it would form into the savory cracker whose crunch attracts diners to the table like nothing else.

The simple touch, the gentle touch, Marjan nodded solemnly to herself as she lowered the heat under the pot of rice. That was the way to approach any situation, whether in cooking or in life. She was glad she had listened to Estelle Delmonico's advice.

The Babylon Café was doing so well three months after opening that Marjan had hired Jerry Mulligan—one of the boys who worked in Healy's Hardware store—to moonlight as a delivery boy. The wiry, nineteen-year-old Jerry valiantly pushed his bicycle up the hilly roads with brown bags of *lavash* and *dolmeh* stacked in the basket behind his seat. The delivery service was available only at lunchtime, which was all that any of them could handle for the moment, especially now that the Babylon was closing later and later. As the summer months opened up, the afternoon tea farers prolonged their ecstasy by turning their pots of oolong and jasmine mint into early dinners, driving Marjan to bursting point as she rushed around preparing double, triple batches of everything. By June, school was out for the summer and Layla was able to help full-time in between play rehearsals, waiting on the busy tables and cleaning up in the kitchen. Her sharing the workload helped a great deal in easing the tension between Layla and an exhausted Bahar, and soon the two sisters were back on good terms, their relationship as calm as the lush valley that surrounded them.

June's warm weather had surprised everyone in town. For, although the sixth month marks the solstice, summers in the west of Ireland are usually plagued by heavy, ominous clouds that send freezing rains to beat down upon the farmlands. Other counties may be basking in the start of sunny days, but for County Mayo, and Ballinacroagh in particular, June usually just meant more rain. But not that summer. June 1986 brought a sultry, steady sun that reminded a bitter Thomas McGuire of the balmy afternoons in Majorca and left the ladies of the Patrician Day Dance committee in a state of panic as to what to do with the upgraded outdoor heaters they had bought only last summer for the usually cold July night festival.

Most Ballinacroagh natives, though, welcomed the dramatic change in climate, and the exuberant pronouncement of sunshine and flora that came with it. Unnamed buds appeared overnight along ivy-covered walls; plain cottages awoke to bursts of magenta, sienna, and lilac flowers that had been slumbering far too long under moss-ridden stones. The soggy grass of surrounding glens rippled with tones of gold, baking in the sun, while the sky over Ballinacroagh took on a shade of untouched blue that previously had been seen only in the cobalt of Pompeii murals. Not surprisingly, this unexpected homage to her Italian homeland gave Estelle Delmonico much reason to rejoice.

Marjan, unfortunately, missed the start of summer's magnificence, as she was too busy filling the daily orders of cherry rice and *dolmeh* that Bahar and Layla delivered at breakneck speed. It was only after the lunch rush had passed that she was able to take a quick breather.

Leaving the kitchen cleanup to her sisters, Marjan would make her way out into the warm, sunny street, crossing Main Mall toward the Butcher's Block. Leaning against a weathered aluminum poster for Clonakilty Blackpudding on the butcher's brick frontage, she examined what she and her sisters had created.

The café windows stood open on their vertical hinges, and the warm afternoon breeze off Clew Bay carried zephyrs of fried cinnamon *zulbia* and cherry preserves, which they had made that very morning. Shoots of lilac and Persian jasmine she had planted were finally taking root, their flowers bursting out of two large hanging pots swinging above the windows. The jasmines fluttered their tiger eyes seductively in the gentle wind. With her own hazel eyes closed, Marjan could almost imagine that she was back in the afternoon gardens of her childhood home, in northern Tehran.

The Babylon Café. The Hanging Gardens of Babylon. This row of shop fronts, Marjan thought to herself, this Main Mall, was their hanging gardens now, their own small slab of paradise.

GRATITUDE FOR LIFE's simple bounties, for the good fortune bestowed upon him, was something that Thomas McGuire, self-anointed nucleus of all that was Ballinacroagh, would learn only too late. Had he not felt the poker of ambition stoke his entrails with such insistence, he would have realized that everything he needed in life was already his—healthy children, more money than he could ever spend, and a randy rhinoceros of a wife who knew how to keep things interesting in the bedroom (with the help of a mail-order catalog sent to her by Hans, a one-eyed Dutch sex toy entrepreneur). All in all Thomas McGuire was a lucky man, but he was the only one in town not to know it.

It had become obvious to the big bully that his boycott and intimidation hadn't stopped the café from thriving. Most of Thomas's cronies and those indebted to him had steered clear of the Babylon's jasmine-tinged threshold, but there were plenty in town who had not. For some, Marjan's *abgusht* was just as powerful a draw as the knowledge that simply stepping foot inside the café was an act of defiance against Thomas. This subtle rebellion was a sleepier, less conscious reason for the Babylon's success than the obvious beauty of the food, but it was a powerful cause nonetheless. The combination of bodily satisfaction and independence of the soul is hard to beat. Still, Thomas was determined to do just that.

Abandoning his boycott, the town bully decided to return to the thing he knew best (next to disco music): competitive pricing and the ousting of rival businesses through the simple laws of supply and demand. Try as he might, Thomas had not been able to unearth the secret behind the Babylon Café's success. Dervla Quigley's scratchily written daily reports had revealed nothing new, and he certainly would never step inside the blasted place to find out for himself. Nor could he send Tom Junior to pick up some *dolmeh* or *chelow* for research's sake—word would be out on the streets within seconds. No, he would have to take his investigation on the road. From Westport to Galway, from Tuam to Killala, he scoured the main streets of towns on the move, trying to decipher for himself why people kept going into the Babylon Café and not the Wilton Inn for their lunches.

Thomas finally found his answer in Galway City's seaside Quay area, where a handful of ethnic restaurants had popped up over the last few years. As Thomas strolled up and down the bustling Quay, past the packed dining rooms of the Real Greek and Dim Sum More restaurants, it dawned on him why the Babylon Café was such a success. The solution had been under his nose all along, really. What Ballinacroagh had been crying out for, what had been lacking from the village all these years, was a bit of the exotic, a taste of the unknown. There was nothing particularly special about this Babylon Café; it had simply arrived at the right time, that was all. Had he not been so busy keeping the whole town plugged with mind-numbing drink, he would have seen it coming sooner himself.

Well, Thomas decided, if it was exotic the village wanted, then it was exotic it was going to get. But none of this Babylon shite for his hometown. Pushing his distaste of all things foreign aside, Thomas chose to look further east for his newest business venture—to a land of fried pork and surprisingly cheap electronic imports. A place where disco music was still thriving and the people revered tyrannical rulers. Thomas McGuire decided to build himself a palace, the Tom Tom Palace, Ballinacroagh's very first Chinese take-out joint.

PATRICIAN DAY WAS still four days away, but already Ballinacroagh was set spinning on its own exhilarated axis. For the first time since anyone in the village could remember, the streets were packed with an influx of tourists that had in all other years kept to the bigger towns of Castlebar and Westport. Tourism had finally hit the village. Big time.

Stalwart devotees of Saint Patrick and pilgrims with a penchant for hiking streamed into town by the busload on Thursday. The religious-minded tourists came from as near as Balla and as far away as Chicago; they meandered up and down humble Main Mall with cameras and Bibles in hand, their mouths hanging open in awe as if they were beholding the relics of some great Mayan city. The excited pilgrims stocked up on bottled holy water and souvenir leather pouches filled with mountain pebbles in Antonia Nolan's religious relics shop, and had their photos taken in front of the weathered Saint Patrick memorial in the town square.

The Donnelly twins, loitering as usual outside Fadden's Mini-

Mart, watched as the tour buses unloaded their cargo of eager pilgrims, many of whom sported sunburnt faces glowing from the combination of miraculous summer weather and the promise of spiritual fulfillment.

"How many minutes would you say, Michael, it'd take someone to notice one of those there buses missing?" Peter smirked, his sly eyes evaluating the line of parked Hibernian Holiday Tours buses.

"We'd be on our way to Dublin before they'd cop on, Peter," Michael replied, reading his twin brother's crafty mind.

"It's something to think about, all right."

"That it is."

Within five minutes the hooligans had telepathically figured out how to hijack a tour bus. They would wait until lunchtime, when all the pilgrims would be packing into the Babylon Café. Michael would lure the driver out of his air-conditioned seat by asking him for directions, and Peter would grab the steering wheel and go. Later, Michael would meet him in nearby Louisburgh for the joyride of their lives.

"Think of the craic, Michael! The parties we could have in one of those things!"

"It's a plan, all right. Let's get a drink to celebrate."

"Paddy's, is it?"

"Na, the Mart for old times' sake."

Ever since graduating from secondary school the month before, the boys had abandoned their beer swapping game, believing the prank to be too childish for them now. Although they still shoplifted from poor Danny Fadden, they no longer replaced the stolen stout with felt IOU notes from Mr. Finnegan the Leprechaun. This omission had far greater repercussions than either twin could have guessed.

"Hello there, Danny. How's that Finnegan of yours coming along?" Michael stood in front of the counter, artfully blocking Danny's view

of the beer shelves, where Peter was busy swiping two brown bottles
of Beamish.

"Not well, laddie. Not well at all," Danny replied sadly. His large
glasses were smudged with countless fingerprints he hadn't bothered
wiping. In fact, the shopkeeper looked like he hadn't washed himself
in days. His meager supply of hair stood on end, and he was wearing
his linty Aran sweater-vest inside out.

The truth was that Danny had grown quite depressed in the last
month, ashamed of having been deserted by both human and fairy
folk alike. It wasn't enough that his wife, Deirdre, had left him five
years ago, but to have his Finnegan leave as well just about pushed the
shy man over the edge. Terribly saddened, he whiled away his lonely
hours behind the shop counter, poring over tattered history texts and
books on Celtic lore, hoping to find some solace in lives more tragic
than his own. And as if he didn't have enough misery in his life,
Danny was now being harassed on a regular basis by none other than
Thomas McGuire himself. The drink baron had stopped by the mini-
mart twice in three days, the last time with a thick manila folder in
his hand.

"Twenty thousand. That's a good price I'm givin' ya, Danny," he
had said, plunking the fat envelope on Danny's counter. "Three times
what this place is worth, you know yerself. I'll leave it with you now,
but I'll be back soon for yer answer. I've got big ideas for this place."
If Thomas McGuire had threatened to knock his head in with a crow-
bar, Danny wouldn't have been more frightened. He just stared at the
envelope, his quivering lips forming a rejection that never came.

What was he holding on to, anyway? Danny wondered. What was
he hoping to accomplish, sitting in this sad excuse for a grocery store
day in, day out, staring at dusty shelves for a leprechaun who never
showed his face? Who was he kidding? As if that sort of magic was

meant for the likes of him, Danny Fadden of all people. And now here was Thomas McGuire, wanting to take this heap of rat droppings and wilted vegetable stalls out of his hands, and all he had done was gawk at the envelope in front of him like an eejit.

Well, maybe he would sell the mini-mart. Spend his days compiling entries for the fairy encyclopedia he had started writing. Now that sounded like a grand idea, Danny mumbled to himself.

Michael Donnelly shot his brother a worried look. Peter nodded, understanding his silent message of concern. He placed the two bottles of Beamish he had hidden in his pants back on the shelf and walked over to the refrigerated section. After paying for two Lucozades, the boys said their good-byes to a crestfallen Danny and walked out onto the busy street.

"Do you suppose it's not having the fairy to look forward to that's got him so down, Peter?"

"I feel like a feckin' eejit, Michael. We're two rotten sods for it."

"I'll dip into Mam's felt box this very afternoon. We'll get his Finnegan back for him," Michael decided.

The twins ambled up the rest of street in silence, each boy blaming himself for taking away Danny Fadden's only companion. By the time they had reached the Ale House, though, they had exhausted their guilt and were ready for a pint. Peter was just about to open the pub door when out flew Tom Junior, thrown in the middle of a grand fight.

A CROWD OF curious pedestrians quickly gathered around the sprawled figure on the sidewalk outside the Ale House. One snap-happy pilgrim, a member of the Long Island chapter of the Saint Patrick's Society, used up half a Kodak roll on Tom Junior's unceremonious expulsion from the pub, catching on camera the young brute's dazed look as he shook his dizzy head and picked his lumbering self off the pavement.

"Fookin' knackers!" Tom Junior yelled, shaking his fists toward the pub door. The pious pilgrims gasped. The Donnelly twins, delighted at the prospect of a midmorning brawl, stood poised on their tippytoes with barely contained excitement. But instead of bulldozing back into the Ale House for a redeeming counterattack on the unseen assailant, Tom Junior pushed his tanklike body through the wall of gawking tourists and stumbled up Main Mall.

He arrived at Saint Barnabas's back gate minutes later. Dropping to his knees, Tom Junior crept stealthily behind a hedge of prickly gooseberry bushes, taking care to avoid any branches that might scratch his already tender face. The right side of his jaw still throbbed from where the tinker had punched him, so he peeked with his left eye through the dark green leaves, across the overgrown back lawn, toward the church's side entrance. Most days he would have been well-sequestered in his brambly hideout by now, but the bleedin' fight had made him late today.

He needn't have bothered with those tinkers, Tom Junior told himself; he should have let Jimmy throw them out of the Ale House, or better yet, called those two lazy shites at the Garda station to come and collect them instead of getting his hands dirty on some stinking knackers. But then again, he couldn't just sit idly by and watch as that lot of drunken trailer trash waltzed into one of his father's pubs as if they owned the place. And how was he to know that one of them was going to come out with a clean southpaw from bleedin' nowhere?

A sharp spasm in his right eye made him recoil in pain, and he hissed under his breath. He was going to have a fecker of a bruise come tomorrow. Still, he would have rather taken another stinger to the jaw than miss his afternoon rendezvous behind the church's impressive grove of gooseberry bushes. Leaning forward on his haunches,

Tom Junior resumed his close guard over the church, aware that Layla would be stepping out of the door of the Sunday School room at any moment.

Tom Junior had been following Layla's every move for months, ever since his father had given him the job of spying on his brother's romance with the girl. At first, Tom Junior had kept his distance from the couple. In a commando move that he practiced many times, he would lie flat on the boggy field adjacent to the cobblestone alleyway behind the café, timing with an army stopwatch the exact minute when Malachy and Layla turned down the side street after school. Pockets of undergrowth in the field kept Tom Junior well out of sight, creating terrific bunkers where he was able to store his spy craft: a Huntsman compass he had bought at Healy's Hardware, a bottle of warm Guinness to quench his thirst, and an old pair of camouflage-colored binoculars that his father had given him for his seventeenth birthday, the year he had seen Sylvester Stallone in *First Blood*.

Disgusting how Malachy cavorted with that Arab girl, with no thought to the damage he was doing to the McGuire name. What was so special about her, anyway? he wondered. Tom Junior had heard the Donnelly twins and some of the younger lads jabbering on about Layla in the pub, as though she was God's gift to men or something. Jaysus. Sure, she was all right looking for a darkie, but he didn't know what all the fuss was about. He much preferred those blond-haired birds with nipples as pink as they come. And to think that she had taken a fancy to Malachy of all people. Well, that just proved she wasn't right in the head, didn't it?

Tom Junior kept up his vigilant watch in the bog every afternoon. When rehearsals for Father Mahoney's play started in Saint Barnabas's Sunday School room, he shifted his hiding place to the bushes that bordered the back of the church, waiting until the three-hour practice session ended to resume his covert operation. Using stone walls and bundles of piled up turf and hay to mask himself from view, Tom Junior would then follow the young sweethearts to Clew Bay Beach, where he had singled out his own private dune for spying. From his sandy fort he was able not only to listen in on the couple's intimate conversations but also finally to appreciate Layla's kinetic beauty. This close proximity to Layla's gazelle legs and glossy black locks was what would finally do him in.

The first time Tom Junior smelled Layla's natural cinnamon-rose perfume he staggered back into a razor-sharp patch of nettle near his dune. His entire body felt electrified; his eyeballs and the inside of his mouth sizzled with longing. When the seizure passed, Tom Junior curled up into his own snail embrace, absolutely stunned. The young man found himself crying unexplainable tears that poured from a dark place in his heart. He kept weeping as Malachy and Layla walked back to town, moaning with confused sadness until the sun went down and the moon was pitying him with her full face.

The next day Tom Junior felt hollow inside but also strangely calm. For he finally knew what was wrong with him, why he had cried so hard, so fast. Layla had shown him what he could do, what he could be without the shadow of his father always looming over him. Riding that wave of her glorious perfume over his pain and anger, Tom Junior had seen himself as the conqueror of his father's empire, the rightful heir to the McGuire throne. He, not Thomas, should be the undisputed drink lord of Ballinacroagh. With Layla by his side, Tom Junior could bring his father to his knees and finally become his own man.

Loud voices startled Tom Junior from his daydream. He jerked his head up too quickly and accidentally rustled the gooseberry branches. Drawing in his breath, he held his body very still and squinted toward the opened church door. The hairdresser, Fiona Athey, strolled out of the church carrying a massive pink binder and a transparent pencil bag full of colored markers. She was tossing her braided hair from side to side, yapping happily. For a second Tom Junior thought the batty beautician was talking to herself, but then Father Mahoney appeared in the doorway, nodding excitedly. Tom Junior strained to hear a snippet of their conversation.

". . . used it in the Puck Fair two years ago. Said we could have it for the whole weekend," Father Mahoney said, beaming.

"An amphitheater! I still can't believe it! It's absolutely perfect!" Fiona did a quick jig on the sidewalk.

"I'll be picking it up from the Arts Center today. Made out of plywood, so it'll need some reassembling. Young Malachy has offered his services," the priest informed her.

"Would you be wanting to go to Castlebar now, Father?"

Tom Junior winced. There was Malachy, that bastard, walking out of the church door with his arm around Layla. His Layla! That gobshite, Tom Junior muttered lowly to himself. How he would love to bash his head in one of these days.

Tom Junior's bruised eye sent another bullet of pain through his skull as he watched his brother embrace Layla and climb into Father Mahoney's clunky black 1975 Cadillac Eldorado. His gaze followed her as she waved good-bye to Fiona and walked the length of the square alone before turning off into a side street that led away from Main Mall toward Clew Bay. Unraveling himself from his leafy hideout, Tom Junior plucked the twigs from his hair and, despite his racing heart, ambled casually up the side street after Layla.

The road was narrow and hilly, flanked by crumbling, three-story Georgian mansions whose expansive doors had been painted in confident shades of blue, green, and red by burgeoning, bustling families in better days. Most of the sad houses were now in disrepair, their limestone porticoes strangled by impenetrable ropes of creeping ivy, their once grand rooms subdivided into musty flats. Tom Junior climbed the steep hill slowly, keeping a safe distance from Layla. By the time he reached the top, she had already rounded the bend that ran past a number of scattered milk farms and was headed straight down to Clew Bay Beach.

Storm clouds were fast gathering over Clew Bay as Tom Junior mounted the sandy bank. Layla was sitting comfortably on her favorite dune, about fifty yards away from him, her head tilted up toward the changing sky. A gentle current of air carried her intoxicating cinnamon-rose perfume to his hungry heart.

Layla sighed with happy relief. The week had been exceptionally hot, and the Sunday School room, built to withstand treacherous gales and long hours of tedious Bible study, was improperly ventilated for the brilliant summer the town was experiencing. Rehearsing in the sweltering room had proven nearly unbearable, so Layla welcomed the cool caresses of sea breeze on her moistened skin. She checked her watch again, eager for Malachy to finish his errand with Father Mahoney and join her on the beach. How romantic it would be if they were caught together in a rainstorm, Layla thought, hugging herself tightly. Straight out of a movie. Grinning, she looked up and winked at grumpy Croagh Patrick, sharing her fantasy with the ancient mountain.

Seized by a sudden, uncontrollable longing, Tom Junior chose that very moment to expose himself to Layla. He dashed feverishly across the dunes, a deep groan escaping from his churning bowels, and jumped on her from behind. His callused fingers pulled at her silky blouse and clumsily groped her bared stomach. At first, Layla thought Malachy had turned into a mad animal, but then Tom Junior's glazed eyes and snorting nostrils came into focus. His mutton lips pressed down into her whole face, suffocating her screams. Gnashing hungrily, Tom Junior's teeth tore into the inside of her lip, breaking its persimmon softness. His beefy paw was just reaching under her squirming denim skirt when, out of nowhere, a knuckled fist came crashing down on the left side of his head.

fesenjoon

1 pound shelled walnuts, chopped

Olive oil

2 ½ pounds skinless chicken breast, cubed

3 large onions, sliced

6 tablespoons pomegranate paste, dissolved in 2 cups hot water

½ teaspoon salt

½ teaspoon ground black pepper

1 tablespoon sugar

2 tablespoons lemon juice

Grind walnuts in a food processor for 1 minute. Fry in olive oil for 10 minutes, stirring constantly. Set aside. Sauté chicken and onions in a deep pan until golden. Add walnuts, pomegranate juice, and remaining ingredients. Bring to a boil. Lower heat to a simmer, cover, and cook for 45 minutes, or until the pomegranate sauce thickens. Serve with chelow.

chapter ten

THE YOUNG TINKER GIRL knocked at the back door at quarter to three in the afternoon. Marjan recognized her as one of the many freckled faces that lingered at the café windows long after other curious schoolchildren had left their mucky handprints behind. The mischievous pack of Irish street urchins, members of the itinerant camp, spent the greater part of their days panhandling with paper cups outside shop doorways on Main Mall. Though never afraid to solicit customers inside the McGuire establishments, for some strange reason the travelers kept a quiet respect for the Babylon Café and never ventured inside its vermilion walls.

"Hello. What can I do for you? Do you want to come in?" Marjan smiled at the girl standing timidly in her back garden. She was a pale, small-boned child, about nine years old, Marjan guessed, a wisp of a thing with wide-set cerulean eyes and long orange hair that hung in a tangled ponytail down her back. The young girl shook her head and looked down briefly, before bursting into a half-intelligible message.

"Yes bettur git te da water. Better git der quick now! We've got yer sis der. She'd hurt just da bit, now, so."

It was enough for Marjan to understand that something was terribly wrong.

Speeding up Main Mall in the green van, Marjan tried her best to make sense of the girl's warbled directions to the travelers' campsite while also keeping her own thumping heart from exploding. They finally arrived at Clew Bay Beach, the van lurching into the public parking grounds just as thunder crackled across the bay. The beach, past the solitary dunes where Layla had been sitting, was filled with summering high school kids and the odd Speedo-suited farmer, all burnt to various shades of pink. As soon as the eager sunbathers heard the thunder, they scrambled for their unused suntan lotions and crisp bathroom towels, stuffing them under folded arms as they ran for their cars and bicycles.

The young tinker girl quickly led Marjan across a sandy pathway scattered with grass and dulled bottle shards, toward a gravel lot crammed with trailer homes. Marjan briefly scanned the large vehicles before her. Fifty-year-old chrome-hooded caravans sat side by side with last year's sleeker models, confidently equipped with the latest in mobile home technology. The entire train of trailers was clustered neatly around a communal area consisting of makeshift crate tables and foldout chairs. Perched on the edge of one white plastic chair was Layla, her black hair tousled and sandy. She was leaning her scratched elbows on her knees as she held a torn piece of tissue to an open cut on her lip. Crouched next to her, and whispering in uncharacteristically angry tones, was Malachy, his usually graceful hands balled into tight fists.

"Layla! What happened to you? What's going on?" Marjan's voice was filled with terror as she rushed to her sister's side.

Layla stood up shakily. "It's okay. I'm okay. I just—" She broke off, not knowing where to start.

Malachy tried to control his anger, but his voice cracked and skipped octaves as he jumped in to explain what had happened.

"I arrived just after it all. I'll never forgive myself," he began, his voice heavy with guilt. "Father Mahoney dropped me off at the beach after we got back from the Arts Center. Layla wasn't in our usual spot, so I sat on a dune and waited. I thought she might have gone to the toilets near the parking lot and would be back soon. I can't believe I was so stupid," he said, shaking his head in utter dismay. At the time he had presumed that one of the tinkers had harassed Layla on the beach and scared her off. Malachy was embarrassed by his assumptions, now that he knew both who had given Layla her bloodied lip and who had saved her from further harm.

Declan Maughan, two-time middleweight champion of the Connaught amateur boxing circuit and chief of the caravan before them, was the man who had rescued Layla from Tom Junior's slobbering assault. As luck would have it, Declan had been just itching for an opportunity to practice the Maughan slide and bounce cut, a combination that would surely make his third time on the ropes a charmed one indeed.

After they had been ousted from their last three campsites (twice by tractor teams in Donegal and once by a herd of menopausal cows in Galway), Declan had moved his caravan to Clew Bay Beach for the spring and summer seasons, knowing how useful the sand would be for resistance training. He had missed his daily beach workout that morning, though, as a result of heavy partying with several of the younger men of the camp the night before. The revelry had lasted well into the morning, as the whole gang caroused down Main Mall with Guinness bottles held high, bellowing songs of rebellion. And then, of course, there'd been the fight in the Ale House with those two eejits, those *amadans*, in which, Declan was proud to say, he and his mates had come out the victors before having to make a hasty retreat to the camp. So, when a still-punchy Declan finally trudged onto the beach that afternoon, the last thing he expected to see was the same gobshite who had picked a fight with him just a few hours before.

He spied Tom Junior groveling on top of the distant dune, his chunky legs sashaying over the sand with all the poise of a ground-hog. Declan slowed down his hoppity jog and squinted into the after-noon horizon. If he wasn't mistaken, that bleedin' bastard wasn't alone. There was a poor girl squirming under him! Declan's sinewy legs sprinted across the sand, flying high over powdery sandbanks and spools of barbed seaweed, landing right behind Tom Junior, on the dune, within seconds.

"I'm going to kill him, Layla. If those bloody guards at the station house don't do anything, then I say we go all the way to Castlebar," said Malachy. His fists were clenched, his knuckles white as he bit down on his words.

"Where's this man who helped you, Layla?" Marjan asked, search-ing the campgrounds.

Several travelers had gathered behind the two teenagers: the imp-ish red-haired girl, Aoife, trailed by a handful of other rascally chil-dren, and four gum-clacking, gold-clad women who looked at Marjan with wary eyes. Two older, scruffy men dressed in frayed football jer-seys sat smoking on chairs nearby, but Declan Maughan was nowhere to be seen. He was, in fact, watching the whole scene from his trailer home, the newest and fanciest one on the lot, but a debilitating shy-ness that always overcame him in the presence of strange women kept the caravan chief from stepping outside to claim his heroic deed.

"He's indisposed ri' now. What can I do fer ye?" The biggest woman there stepped forward. Her teased, hair-sprayed blond helmet reminded Marjan of an overripe kumquat. She had a territorial air about her and was indeed Declan Maughan's older sister.

"I just want to thank him. I can't imagine what would have happened if he hadn't saved my sister," said Marjan, attempting a smile but managing only a wavering grimace. She could feel her composure beginning to unravel.

Buck it up, Marjan, she told herself. Just get yourself back into the kitchen and decide what to do from there. Surrounded by the safety of its warm walls, she might have a chance to make sense of it all.

BAHAR LOCKED THE café door behind Marie Brennan and Mrs. Boylan. After pouring herself a cup of strong Darjeeling tea, she sat down at the kitchen table and replayed Marjan's words in her head.

"Just keep your eye on the *abgusht*, Bahar. Give it a stir, okay? I'll be back soon," her sister had whispered urgently, her face a greenish white as she ran out the back door.

Had Bahar's hands not been full with Mrs. Boylan's order of marinated pepper wrap and red lentil soup, she would have hurried after her sister and demanded an explanation for her stricken appearance. But by the time she stepped out into the cobblestone alleyway, Marjan had already reversed the van and was gone.

Something terrible had happened, Bahar was sure of it. What else could have prompted her sister to run out of the kitchen so hastily, or to ask her to mind the bubbling pot of *abgusht*? Marjan knew how she hated to stand before a hot stove. It was Layla, Bahar told herself. Something bad had happened to Layla.

A tinny sound rang out from the wall behind her. The phone. It was probably Marjan, with the horrible news. Bahar picked up the receiver and slowly brought it to her ear.

"H-hello?" She swallowed hard, a lump caught in her throat.

There was no answer on the other end of the line, just silence.

"Hello? Marjan, is that you?"

She almost didn't hear the low breathing at first. The sound came upon her suddenly, a strange, soft *whoooosshh* like a balloon slowly releasing its air. A deflation of the senses, a deceptively simple expiration that sounded like barely controlled danger. A few seconds later the air spluttered and stopped, ending abruptly in a raspy, barely audible grunt. Then silence.

Bahar felt a sharp, painful depression in her lungs as she stood listening to the void. And then, out of nowhere, she opened her mouth and surprised herself.

"Hossein?" She gulped, the name dropping like lead from her trembling lips. Though he kept permanent residence in a dark place inside of her, months had passed since she had uttered her husband's name. Something in that whispering wind, that creeping *whoooosshh*, had brought him back to her. *Hossein.* The sinister hiss of the middle consonants sent tremors through her entire body. With her hand shaking uncontrollably, Bahar placed the receiver back in its cradle and collapsed into a nearby chair.

A DETAILED REPORT ensued at the Garda station. Shocked by the news of Tom Junior's attack, Kevin Slattery scribbled Layla's and Malachy's accounts in his dusty ledger book while a worried Sean Grogan paced up and down the station's corridor, unsure of how to tackle this new crisis. It would require some serious officiating, that was for sure.

"Rest assured, we'll get to the bottom of this soon enough," Grogan promised as he gently ushered the three of them out of the station. "This here isn't the sort of town where people can go jumping on each other like animals. We're not in Dublin!"

After dropping Malachy off at home, Marjan pulled the van over outside the cobblestone alleyway and turned solemnly to Layla in the passenger seat.

"I want to talk to you about something before we go in." Marjan's voice was thin and raspy. She paused and looked intently into Layla's eyes. "I don't think we should tell Bahar what happened to you."

"Why shouldn't we tell her? I could have been raped, you know!" Layla cried incredulously, twisting her face into a deep scowl.

"I know, *joon-e man*," soothed Marjan. "And we'll tell her, eventually. Just not yet. She's only beginning to calm down after the last time you disappeared, and you know how bad her migraines have been. You and I need to protect her sometimes, that's all."

"But how am I going to explain my lip?" Layla pouted. Her cut lip was clean of blood and sand, but the area around it was swollen and bruised. Bahar would notice it for sure.

"It doesn't have to be a big lie—just tell her that you fell while hiking with Malachy or something like that. Do you understand?" Marjan pleaded.

The younger girl stared sullenly out of the van window, her eyes filled with glistening tears.

"Layla?" Marjan pressed.

"This is history repeating itself," Layla said thickly, voicing the words that Marjan was thinking but could not bring herself to say.

LATER THAT EVENING, Marjan stood before the food processor in the kitchen. She could hear the bolt on the back gate clanging ferociously in the wind. All of her backyard herbs—the summer savory, the mint and tarragon, were bowing down to the storm that had kept the heavens in a headlock ever since they returned from the Garda station. Looking at the sky now, thought Marjan, no one would have guessed that the morning had been so cloudless and benign.

She let the food processor run on, its angry steel blades grinding the walnuts to a brown pulp. She added pomegranate paste and cinnamon, and allowed the blades to whine for several more minutes before snapping the small machine off. She had to keep her wits about her if she was going to make *fesenjoon*, the invigorating pomegranate, chicken, and walnut stew that was Layla's all-time favorite comfort food.

It is the pomegranate that gives *fesenjoon* its healing capabilities. The original apple of sin, the fruit of a long gone Eden, the pomegranate shields itself in a leathery crimson shell, which in Roman times was used as a form of protective hide. Once the pomegranate's bitter skin is peeled back, though, a juicy garnet flesh is revealed to the lucky eater, popping and bursting in the mouth like the final succumber of lovemaking.

Long ago, when the earth remained still, content with the fecundity of perpetual spring, and Demeter was the mother of all that was natural and flowering, it was this tempting fruit that finally set the seasons spinning. Having eaten six pomegranate seeds in the underworld, Persephone, the Goddess of Spring's high-spirited daughter, had been forced to spend six months of the year in the eternal halls of death. Without her beautiful daughter by her side, a mournful Demeter retreated to the dark corners of the universe, allowing for the icy gates of winter finally to creak open. A round, crimson herald of frost, the pomegranate comes to harvest in October and November, so *fesenjoon* is best made with its concentrate during other times of the year.

The *fesenjoon* bubbled happily on the stove, blissfully unaware of the brewing crisis. Even the sweet taste of pomegranate could not cover up the bitterness that had risen among the three sisters. Bahar had been just as distressed about Layla's cut lip as Marjan had anticipated. She gave their younger sister a proper scolding, reminding her of the pitfalls of falling in love, before retiring to her bed with a headache. Layla had opted to lie miserably still on the sofa bed Marjan used as her sleeping quarters, flicking through television channels until she fell asleep with the remote in her hand, a piece of tissue stuck to her lip.

Layla's foreboding words echoed in Marjan's head. *I could have been raped. This is history repeating itself.* It still amazed Marjan how much of the past Layla had retained, especially considering how young she had been back then.

History repeating itself. Was history really that cruel? Marjan didn't know what to think anymore. She lifted the lid off the *fesenjoon* and stirred it again. The pomegranate paste had turned the stew a dark maroon, the broth swimming sinfully with a life of its own. History repeating itself. Maybe it was.

NEARLY FOUR MONTHS after her marriage to Hossein and three days after the momentous Black Friday massacre in Jaleh Square, Bahar had crept into her sisters' Tehran apartment at two in the morning. She slipped so quietly into the single bed she had once shared with little Layla that Marjan did not notice her until the coming of dawn. She had woken up grudgingly with the low light, bracing herself for another day of washing endless dirty dishes at the Peacock Restaurant, only to be confronted by Bahar's soiled body lying in bed.

An orchid and yellow assembly of bruises, imprints of contorted fingers, started at Bahar's neck. Burst violet veins moved up to her left eye and down the side of her right ear, ending in a torn lobe from which hung encrusted droplets of blood, priceless for their shedding. But the worst damage was what could not be seen, not until Bahar uncoiled her chador, winced out of her long gray skirt, woolen stockings, and blood-soaked underskirt. Only then did Marjan see the thick baton grooves embossed upon her sister's upper thighs, a serrated ladder that disappeared deep inside her and left unmentionable wounds in its path.

They packed their bags that very morning.

Out came the two plaid suitcases, bought by their parents at Burberry of London, on that one trip to Europe in the gay 1950s, before any of them were born and when the Shah's palaces still gleamed with a thousand brilliant rubies. The bags smelled of uncertainty, of mothballs mingled with the chalky skins of shrunken pistachio nuts. As little Layla lay sleeping in her bed, Marjan and Bahar went quickly to work, rolling up mementos that were too dear to leave behind in chunky sweaters and tube socks. In went their grandmother's samovar, the old photographs, the brass jewelry box. Clothes, bags of dried fruit, jars of *torshi,* and just-made quince and rose-blossom preserves (drenched in sugar, they would provide energy for hard days to come). The last thing Marjan packed was a folder of stacked lined papers, notes and observations of hundreds of recipes, some inherited from her mother, others compiled over the years from her time at the Peacock Restaurant. Recorded in Marjan's precise hand were the jewels of slivered pistachio baklava, the reminders to introduce pitted sour cherries to *albalou polow* before adding the half cup of sour cherry syrup, and a fat botany guide to herb growing she had picked up during her years at the university.

Early the next day, just before morning prayers were bellowed from the neighborhood mosque, Marjan left the apartment with an envelope containing their birth certificates and most treasured documents tucked under a chador she had borrowed from Bahar. She maneuvered her way down archways and dark side streets to Roosevelt Avenue, the downtown address of the American Embassy. A fortress wall lined with Marines, the embassy was a clear target of hatred for many revolutionaries. On the northwestern side of the cement barrier, a looming teal-colored gate creaked open only at the behest of its keepers—surly-faced, mustached Iranian policemen who looked strangely alien against the brick and marble façade of the embassy building. The line of hopeful visa applicants consisted mostly of bearded young men sprawled on cheap woven kilims and ratty blankets. Spread on the ground before them were the latest leftist newspapers, countless articles forecasting the oncoming revolution, the upheaval of all upheavals that would scald the streets with more young blood.

Praying hard that she would get to file the forms for their American visas, Marjan joined the embassy line on that brisk September morning, but by nightfall the only line that had moved was a steady train of industrious ants on the tall wall overhead. With the Shah's nine o'clock curfew closing in, Marjan was forced to relinquish her spot and hurry home empty-handed. I will hit the line at dawn tomorrow, she decided, as she climbed the dilapidated staircase of the apartment building they had called home for the last two years. Anything to get us away from this living hell, from this Hossein Jaferi, Marjan thought. She was thankful that Bahar had finally come to her senses and left her husband, though she wished her sister's decision hadn't come at such a dear price.

On the tenth floor, Marjan paused to catch her breath, feeling suddenly very weak. She hadn't eaten since the day before and wondered if Bahar had reheated the pot of pomegranate soup for dinner. Marjan hoped her sister had remembered to add the last dash of angelica powder, a good-luck omen, into the simmering pot. Conjuring fortuity was an act of great faith, something they all needed at this fearful moment in time.

The heavy smell of burning pomegranate paste hit her on the twelfth floor, a sad, sweet, but also slightly acrid sensation that harks back to the cloistered tang of a mother's womb; by the fourteenth floor it had manifested into a formidable cloud of bitter, mauve smoke. Marjan shielded her stinging eyes with her chador and frantically pushed forward. Gasping, she stopped short of the apartment door. Splintered and with its golden chain lock broken, the door hung purposelessly off one set of hinges, the wooden frame fanned out in jagged, petrified daggers. She stood in shock before the barbed threshold, unable to move until muffled screams from inside shattered her trance.

Marjan saw his muddy green army boots first, then his gaunt profile. Hossein was bent over as if in prayer, his painfully thin shoulder blades grinding together as his head rocked fanatically back and forward. A piercing, mucusy cry came from the far corner of the kitchen. The pot of pomegranate soup was steaming, hissing, its lid lifting off on a crest of creamy fruit foam as Bahar's small socked feet twitched under Hossein's bony hold. A large object swooped in front of Marjan's eyes, and she ducked instinctively to avoid its assault. The descending pendulum, she soon realized, was her own arm, wielding a wooden stake torn from the doorframe. As if guided by a force outside her body, Marjan squeezed her eyes shut and planted the wooden stake deep into Hossein Jaferi's leg.

He turned in a slow and silent dance, the same man at whose wedding she had thrown rice, praying hard that it would coat her sister through any hardship. The starkness of his long beard and scaly, balding head terrified her; his pitted facial scars pulsed red with anger.

"You motherless whore!"

Hossein lunged for Marjan with the baton he carried to riots—the jagged wooden wedge still implanted in his leg—just as Bahar scrambled up from the floor and grabbed the scalding pot of soup. Left on the stove for too long, the pomegranate soup had become a pulpy mass, the fructose residue sticking to the pot. Half of the soup was already burnt to a black sludge, but the rest flowed freely down upon Hossein's head. He fell, his forehead struck by the hot lip of the heavy pot, as a scalding deluge of pomegranate juice engulfed his unconscious body.

A shrill cry from the hallway pulled Marjan out of a black abyss. She burst into the small side pantry and salvaged her youngest sister from amongst the sea of dried fenugreek leaves and clotted sumac. She kissed little Layla's face and checked for bruises, thankful to find only tracks of tears and brick-colored sumac stains.

"Get the papers! And the chadors! The curfew cars will be coming around soon," Marjan whispered fiercely.

She turned around to find Bahar shaking like *sholeh zard*, saffron pudding that requires a heavy bowl to contain its almondy, spineless matter. All the color had drained from her face and collected at the base of her mottled throat. Bahar's nose was bloody, and a piece of scalp tissue hung at a feeble angle from where her husband had pulled her hair out. Hossein hadn't moved from where he had fallen, but Marjan knew their time was short. With Layla spluttering in her arms, Marjan pulled Bahar out of the kitchen and into the small living room.

"Look at me, Bahar!" Marjan held her sister's chin in her hand and stared into her dazed eyes. "We have to go now, do you understand? We have to go!" Bahar's eyes did not blink but kept staring down at Marjan's chest, where a long tear in her chador exposed her white-collared shirt.

Marjan saw the blood then. Starting at her armpit, it was spreading rapidly across her breast like a blossoming poppy. There, at the juncture where her arm met her shoulder, stood four inches of splintered wood, embedded when she flew past the broken doorframe to save them all.

migraine headache remedy

1 teaspoon ground nutmeg

1 teaspoon ground cardamom

1 teaspoon ground cloves

1 cup warm water

In a clean jar or glass, mix spices thoroughly. A soft brown powder should form. Take 1 tablespoon of medicine, making sure to swallow quickly. Wash down with warm water. Repeat, if necessary, every 4 hours.

chapter eleven

THE CRISP BILL of ownership lay perfectly flat in front of Danny Fadden. Next to the contract sat the bulging manila envelope stuffed with twenty thousand five hundred pounds, five hundred more than Thomas McGuire had previously offered. Ballinacroagh's major publican was hoping the unexpected bonus would induce the lonely shopkeeper to hand over his life's work as quickly as possible.

"You sign that bill, Danny, and we'll be having a pint at Paddy's in no time." Thomas grinned and shoved a fat fountain pen into Danny's pale hand.

Danny stared at the expensive Waterman pen, the kind that important men carried in the breast pockets of their fancy Italian suits. Maybe signing this contract was his ticket to becoming someone important, too. He could invest some of the money in the stock market and live off the rest until he finished his Fairy Encyclopedia. At the moment, Danny was in the middle of the L's, having just edited an entry on "Leprechaun," the trickster shoemaker who plays pranks on human folk.

Yes, selling the mini-mart to Thomas McGuire might have been the smart thing, thought Danny, had his own leprechaun, Finnegan, not come back to him that very afternoon. Danny had unlocked the mini-mart door after his half-hour tea break and walked in to find two bottles of Beamish missing from the beer shelf. That little scally-wag Finnegan had left a piece of emerald green felt and a note in their place: "Hope you didn't miss me, on my holiday, IOU on two stout, till I get me pay. IOU. Finnegan."

"What's the word, Danny? Time to grab the bull by the horns," Thomas said, gritting his teeth through a forced smile.

Danny reached under the counter, into a shelf where he kept all of Finnegan's notes. He rubbed a piece of felt for courage.

"The thing is, Thomas, I can't—"

Just then, Padraig Carey burst into the mini-mart, soaked to the bone.

"Tom! Tom!" he blurted. "You best get yourself down to the station! It's Tom Junior!" The councilman's face was red and bloated, his tie blown over his shoulder by the wet winds.

Thomas shot Padraig a dirty look.

"The eejit hasn't rammed his car into a telephone pole again, has he? That boy— I'll tell ya, Danny, best stick with girls."

"The shop's n-not—" Danny stammered on.

"Stay where you are, Danny. We'll have this all signed and sealed soon enough," Thomas commanded before stomping angrily out of the store. "This better be good, Padraig. Had the deal shut before you opened yer fat gob." He glared at the councilman.

"That's what I've been trying to tell ya. It's bad news, Tom," Padraig replied.

The two men scrambled into Padraig's tiny Fiat and gunned up rainy Main Mall. On the way to the Garda station, Padraig filled Thomas in on what he had overheard outside the police offices.

"The two of them parked that green van and went inside, with

Malachy right behind them! By the time I crossed the square, that Sean Grogan had barred the door. Said there were some 'confidential matters' at hand and would I come by later? The bollocks on him, Tom!" Padraig cried petulantly. "I had to sneak under the window to make any sense of it!"

Thomas's face hardened to stone as he listened to Padraig. Too furious to wait for the councilman to park, he jumped out of the Fiat as it slowed down in the square. The big bully exploded into the police station, startling Kevin Slattery just as the young guard was making himself a cup of weak tea.

"Kevin, what's this business about my Tom? Where's Grogan? Who's in feckin' charge here, eh?"

Sean Grogan, who was in an adjoining room, quickly tucked away the report of Layla's complaint. He stepped out into the hallway and leaned his arm protectively across the door's threshold, clearing his throat.

"There's probably a fine explanation for everything, Tom. I'll be needing to ask your boy a few questions, that's all. If you could just tell me where Tom Junior is . . ."

"Am I hearin' this right? You're letting some feckin' darkie say what she likes about me and mine? Is that it, eh?"

"Thomas—" Grogan could have said more, could have attempted to calm the steaming man in front of him as his position required, but he was enjoying himself too much to stop Thomas's rant. There was no doubt in his mind that Tom McGuire Junior, that dirty sod, had attacked Layla. He had no reservations about locking the boy away in the station's small jail cell for a whole year, if need be, he told himself. No matter who his father was.

"And you, Sean Grogan, yer calling my Tom on it?" Thomas's eyes bulged out of their sockets. He couldn't believe his ears. It was taking all his strength to keep from hitting the guard in his fat face. And that

Slattery, too, thought Thomas, standing there with his tea mug like the nancy the whole town knew he was.

"The thing is, ah, Tom. There's a witness, so. Nothing I can do about it."

"Witness? What witness—who's this witness?"

"Ah, well now, I can't say. That's strictly confidential, you see."

"Feck you and yer confidential!" Thomas growled. He turned on his heels and stomped down the station hallway, knocking Padraig straight into the corridor wall. Pausing at the station door, he pointed toward the two officers. "You're going to be sorry you did this, Sean Grogan," he threatened and thundered out.

A silent Padraig shrugged his shoulders nervously at the guards and followed Thomas to the car. The short councilman knew precisely what side of the plate his meat was on.

BEYOND THE RAIN CLOUDS, above the constant peak that he was now beginning to detest, was the constellation Hercules. The star was a consolation to Malachy as he sifted through his own personal storm.

The young man stooped in his alcove bedroom stuffing his burlap schoolbag with clothes while his mother and three sisters lingered in the upstairs hallway, watching him with confusion. They were accustomed to seeing Malachy and Tom Junior at ends with each other, but no fight had been bad enough to make one of them want to leave home. Joanne, the youngest of the sisters, burst into tears when she saw Malachy begin to disassemble his telescope.

"Don't cry, Joanne. I'll be back to visit," he said before turning to his mother. "Are you sure you haven't seen Tom today, Mam? Are you telling me the truth?"

"Haven't seen him since the mornin', Malachy. Maybe that foreign girl there was the one to take him. I heard a few things about those three in that café. I hope you're looking after yourself when you're down that end. Never know what one of them would do if she saw your lovely looks, eh?"

She went to pat him on his head, but Malachy swatted her away. It was the first sign of defiance he had ever shown his mother, and it made his head burn with unexpected fury. He was glad he hadn't spilled about his relationship with Layla, as he had been tempted to do so many times in the last four months.

"Whatever it is, it can't be that bad. You'll work things out, now," his mother mumbled vacuously, leaning against his bedroom door. She was decked out in her usual Thursday night getup: a black sequined sweater paired with tight stretch pants that highlighted the grapefruit texture of her cellulite-ridden thighs. Her head was wound in thick, spongy rollers, which she would prop up against four pillows at night to ensure the next morning's do. Cecilia McGuire never went anywhere without her poodlelike curls.

Watching Malachy now, Cecilia couldn't help musing about her long-ago love affair with Juan Carlos Escobar the Second. Being the daughter of a late county mayor had assured Cecilia Devereux the choice of Mayo's most eligible bachelors, but she had chosen Thomas McGuire for his ambition and attractive, muscled thighs. Thomas's ambition had its drawbacks, though, as his lonely wife soon discovered, so Cecilia was grateful when Juan Carlos Escobar the Second's ship came in, that exhilarating summer of 1967. The Spanish sailor taught her words like *amor mío, cariño,* and *pasión* while he strummed her inner strings, and although he disappeared before summer's end, he left her with a living, breathing souvenir in the form of Malachy.

The boy stuffed the last piece of clothing, his favorite football jersey, into his backpack and, swinging his telescope case onto one shoulder, lumbered out of his tiny bedroom. Patting a tearful Joanne on the head, Malachy gave his other sisters, Delia and Helen, a silent nod good-bye, determined never to return to his damp, claustrophobic room. At the bottom of the stairs, he stopped and turned back to the four bewildered faces gaping down at him from the top landing, his anger softening slightly as Joanne's whimpers grew louder. Just as he opened his mouth to say something reassuring, Thomas McGuire nosed the Land Rover into the driveway, honking its horn madly.

By the time Thomas burst in roaring for answers, Malachy had already slipped out of the kitchen door. He looked back one last time at the house of his lonely childhood before disappearing into the shadows of the neighboring forest.

A MILE AWAY, in the upstairs shoe box of a bedroom she shared with Layla, Bahar lay perfectly still in bed. She had been asleep, caught up in a fitful nightmare, the only dream she ever had, when the smell of cooking pomegranate and flashes of lightning woke her. Downstairs, she could hear the back door clicking shut. It was probably Marjan, she thought, running out to the store for a missing ingredient for the *fesenjoon*.

Ripples of pain shot up from behind her ears and washed down the right side of her head to pool in her temples. Bahar turned over in bed and reached dizzily for the small glass jar of brown powder sitting next to her on a wobbly pedestal table. The powder, a mixture of ground nutmeg, cardamom, and cloves, was a potent Baluchi remedy that cured mild migraines within minutes of swallowing. Nowadays, though, it took at least six large spoonfuls to ease Bahar's migraines, and even then it was never as effective as the first time she had tried it, back in the Dasht-e Lut desert.

Bahar brought the spoonful of grainy medicine up to her lips and grimaced. She took a deep breath and swallowed all of it in one go, feeling the powder slide slowly down the back of her throat like hot gravel. She could never get used to the harsh taste, its unforgiving texture. Strange, though, she didn't remember the medicine tasting so bad when it was administered by the Baluchi women. Even now, deep in the fog of another fierce headache, she could clearly recall their tribal kindness.

The Baluchi women, with their patchwork skirts and sunburnt faces, had presented Bahar with two jars of the headache medicine the morning the sisters had escaped from Iran. After two nights spent with the Baluchi tribe in the desert, they crossed the Pakistan border with the help of an illiterate goat farmer from the nearby town of Zahedan. For a three-pound-sterling charge, he drove them in his dungy truck to the Red Cross refugee camp erected outside the Pakistani town of Quetta. Surrounded by other frightened Iranians on the run, the girls took refuge in the camp for five months before they finally secured visas to the United Kingdom.

They arrived at Heathrow Airport to the scrutiny of thick-necked immigration officers. Interrogations were fired and passports checked, then double-checked, before the three sisters were granted the sweet stamps of entry. The girls stepped out of the gray, colossal airport and straight into the South London concrete block of apartments appointed to them by the Red Cross. The Brixton Bay View housed an array of personalities: Castro defectors and disco mavens shooting up under rusty stairwells, drag queens who moonlighted as Avon ladies, and half-naked latchkey kids practicing their break dancing in the parking lot. Before long Marjan was working as a pita stuffer in A Thousand and One Kabobs, a shish kabob and falafel takeaway near Trafalgar Square, while Bahar and Layla rejoined the daily humdrum of school life. Things were going well, despite their meager existence on oily couscous and fatty rinds of questionable impaled meats. Within four years Bahar had been accepted into Saint Bartholomew's

School of Nursing and Marjan had moved up in the culinary world, working as a sous chef for Plantain, a Jamaican fusion restaurant in the trendier suburb of Notting Hill. Soon they were able to move from the projects to a nice two-bedroom flat in Lewisham, where Layla could play in a cul-de-sac without running across used needles, and where Marjan could encourage a few precious herbs to grow. Someplace where Bahar could really forget the bruises. But, despite this hard-won tranquillity, it was difficult to ignore what was happening in their homeland.

Iran in the early 1980s was suffering the digestive heartburn of a revolutionary feast gone on far too long. Civil war had broken out, pitting militant mullahs against Islamic Socialists, each vying for the seat of power and getting nowhere in the process. Reverberations of the revolution were felt across the Saharas, as honey-fed princes in the shaken sheikhdoms of Qatar, Saudi Arabia, and Kuwait scrambled to stop their dripping reserves of liquid gold with white robes. And caught in between these upheavals were the young: the thirteen-year-old soldiers who had forsaken puberty for the religious cause. In cemeteries throughout Iran, laminated cardboard tombstones declared their short lives, while shrouded mothers mourned the unnatural reversal of time.

Marjan watched the worldwide demonstrations against the growing Islamic regime on the BBC nightly news with a mixture of awe and relief. Thank God they had gotten out in time, she would tell herself. Her sister, by contrast, was not so optimistic. Bahar would never sit through the televised images of bombed-out streets filled with men who looked like they could all be Hossein. She was afraid not that he might be one of the dead but rather that he *wouldn't* be among the bodies strewn across their television screen. She never should have believed in such a cause, in such a man. What had made her do so? Bahar could no longer remember the reasons she had given herself or

Marjan for marrying into it all, for believing, so whenever Jim Muir's pasty face came on with his nightly reports from Tehran's bloody streets, she would hastily retire to her bed with the headache that was fast becoming her best friend.

Time passed again. Marjan got a new job at Aioli, a chichi Italian joint in Lewisham, where she befriended the head chef, Gloria, and was able to unburden some of their pain onto her sympathetic new friend. Bahar graduated with top honors from nursing school and started work at the Green Acres nursing home, an occupation which, if it did not provide close friendships, did at least ease the acute depression she had been suffering under for over half a decade. By the end of 1985, Bahar had returned to stretches of headache-free days and the occasional laughing fit as she and Marjan watched Layla grow up into gawky adolescence. Then, one night in March, just over four months ago, the telephone rang in their flat.

Bahar was first to answer. "Hello?" Was that an electrical shock in her ear as she picked up the receiver, or was it the chime of Hades' bell?

"Did you think that God was on your side, Bahar? That I would let you and your dirty sisters make a fool of me?" The voice grated through the telephone lines like sheets of sandpaper. "I can't even show my face at meetings anymore, did you know that? My mother won't leave the house for the shame you've brought our family, you whore. If I were you, I'd start praying. Pray for mercy, wife, because the next knock you hear will be mine." The phone clicked off, so chirpy and correct that it made Hossein's threat sound even more sinister. Bahar stared at the receiver in her hand with disbelief, feeling sick to her stomach. The BBC news show on the television went to a commercial break, and Marjan turned to her sister.

"Bahar, who was that?"

Bahar's eyes rolled back into her head. Shadows took over.

Could it be happening all over again? Bahar wondered, wringing the bedsheets in her fists. Had Hossein found her here in Ballinacroagh? Was the eerie hissing on the telephone line this afternoon another warning?

And what about Layla's weak explanation later for the cut on her lip? A hiking accident with Malachy. Who knew if any of it was true? Maybe her sisters had not wanted her to know what had happened, what was going to happen, but Bahar had seen it all play out in their eyes. They had wanted to protect her, bless their hearts, but she knew the truth, the real reason behind Layla's bloody lip and the tremor at Marjan's chin. The signs were all there; that silent phone call had been for her.

Bahar sat up quickly in bed. The tribal migraine medicine had worked its magic, dulling her painful headache considerably, but she knew its effects wouldn't last long. There was no time to lose, she told herself.

Layla was still asleep on the living room sofa when Bahar took the remote control out of her sister's fist. She turned the TV off and pulled the blanket up to Layla's chin, pausing a moment to admire the young girl's beautiful face. She should have been nicer to Layla, more understanding of her needs, Bahar told herself. Layla was only fifteen, after all. Bahar bent over and gently kissed her sister's forehead, then turned and crept toward the creaking staircase. A chill ran down her back as she reached the bottom landing. The kitchen had gone so cold so quickly. Bahar's eyes rested on the pot sitting on the stove. She was right, it was *fesenjoon*.

The pomegranate was calling her back. It wanted her to return, to face up to the pact she had made so long ago, a promise she hadn't kept. There would be no running away this time. Hossein had finally found her.

AT MIDNIGHT, the lights in the café's kitchen could be particularly harsh. Without the comfort of daylight streaming in through the stained-glass window, everything in the room looked grim and strangely utilitarian.

Marjan and Layla sat at the round table in morose silence. Scattered on the tabletop were trails of brown powder, where Bahar had hastily mixed her special headache remedy before leaving. Marjan absently traced a finger through the grainy remains.

"She must have taken the medicine with her. I can't find the jar anywhere," she observed somberly.

"We can't just sit here, Marjan!" Layla jumped up, determined to do something, anything. After a frantic search of the nearby flooded streets, they had returned to the café and sat waiting for over two hours, hoping that the note in front of them was a big mistake, praying that Bahar would realize her folly and come back. She had taken her clothes and personal belongings in one of the plaid suitcases, leaving behind a quick note propped against a yellow enamel jug filled with bluebells:

> *This is wrong. We've been running because of me.*
> *I can't anymore.*
> *Bahar*
> *—I'll call soon. I promise.*

"Why is she doing this? I've told her over and over again that we're safe here. There's no way Hossein's going to find us." Marjan shook her head.

"Call the police again!"

"I have—twice. They just said to wait. She's not considered missing for another nineteen hours, apparently." Marjan laid her face in her hands. She could taste the gritty spice mixture everywhere. "I was only in the butcher's for ten minutes, fifteen at most."

"Yeah, but you didn't find the note until ten o'clock," Layla said pointedly.

Marjan slowly raised her eyes and met her sister's gaze. Layla's face was filled with disappointment. Layla was right, of course, thought Marjan. She hadn't noticed the folded sheet of paper leaning against the jug until the *fesenjoon* had finished cooking and she was getting ready to go to bed. And even then she hadn't known where to search for Bahar. What was wrong with her?

"You're sure Bahar didn't say anything before you fell asleep?" Marjan said.

"No, nothing. She was in the bedroom the whole time. Where could she go, anyway? No one can stay out in this rain for long." The storm was still lashing out in anger, with spidery electric bolts illuminating the sky above the alleyway. "Look, just give me the van keys. I'll go find her myself!" Layla cried, stamping her foot impatiently.

"No, you're staying right here," Marjan said, getting up from the table. "Don't let anybody in, okay?"

Layla nodded, reassured to see her sister in action once again. Her relief was short-lived, however, as a heavy knock sounded at the back door.

"Marjan?" Layla whispered, frightened.

"Shhh . . ." Marjan crept slowly across the kitchen. It was too dark outside to see through the door's glass partition. The shadow of a tall figure moved back and forth across the glass, then there came another booming knock. Marjan's fingers touched the cold doorknob, pausing a beat before she jerked the door open. Before her stood Malachy, drenched and dragging his telescope and backpack behind him.

pomegranate soup

2 large onions, chopped

2 tablespoons olive oil

1/2 cup yellow split peas, rinsed twice

6 cups water

1 teaspoon salt

1/2 teaspoon ground black pepper

1 teaspoon turmeric

2 cups fresh parsley, chopped

2 cups fresh cilantro, chopped

1/4 cup fresh mint, chopped

1 cup fresh scallions, chopped

1 pound ground lamb

3/4 cup rice, rinsed twice

2 cups pomegranate juice

1 tablespoon sugar

2 tablespoons lemon juice

2 tablespoons angelica powder*

*Optional

In a large stockpot, sauté the onions in olive oil until golden. Add split peas, rice, water, salt, pepper, and turmeric, bringing to a boil. Lower heat and simmer, covered, for 30 minutes. Add parsley, cilantro, mint, and scallions. Simmer for 15 minutes. Meanwhile, roll ground lamb into medium-size meatballs. Add meatballs and remaining ingredients to the pot. Simmer, covered, for 45 minutes.

chapter twelve

"I HEAR THE MIDDLE one took off at the same time as Thomas's boy. Wouldn't be surprised if she's got her hands on Tom Junior by now." Dervla pursed her lips over her teacup the next day and scanned the room of women before her. "They're all sluts— mind now, I have to say the word—*sluts*, and they get what's coming to them. I'd lock up your sons if I were you, Joan," she warned.

The congregation of sour-faced women, most of whom were regulars at Antonia Nolan's religious relics shop, nodded their heads in agreement. Dervla, happy for such quick compliance, continued to slurp her watery brew. Ballinacroagh's Bible study members, who gathered every Friday afternoon at Reek Relics, were a complete contrast to the pleasant ladies of the Patrician Day Dance committee. The sanctimonious assembly consisted of the usual spinsters and elderly matrons but had recently gained younger members in Joan Donnelly and Assumpta Corcoran.

"She had her eye on my Benny, you know," Assumpta informed them.

"Sure, my boys won't even come home anymore. Ever since that hussy started strutting her stuff around the place. They could have been priests, those two. Priests!" Joan protested.

The old biddies nodded simultaneously in a geriatric chorus line. Dervla tisk-tisked and shook her head. "I'd tell that sister of yours to keep out of that café, Joan. I saw her going in there just this morning. Knocked on the door with Evie Watson at her side. I thought that café was closed for the day," she said.

"Fiona's never been one for sound judgment. Sure, she's still letting those tinkers in for cuts. Driving out decent business without a thought to myself. And she won't listen. She won't listen," repeated Joan, feeling the pressure of judging eyes upon her.

All heads turned as the café door opened across the street. Mrs. Boylan and two goodwilled ladies from the committee emerged, without the large casserole dishes they had carried inside just half an hour earlier. The stinging drizzle had picked up again, and the three elderly women linked arms and ran up the main street like a trio of carefree schoolgirls.

"Did you see that then? Geraldine Boylan taking them her best dishes. Sheer wastage," said Dervla, spitting out her words.

The Bible study ladies nodded, although most tried their best not to think of the delicious food piling up inside the Babylon Café.

The café's kitchen was indeed teeming with a vast array of delicacies. Mrs. Boylan had made two casseroles of her buttery potato champ, and Maura Kinley brought by three loaves of barmbrack, that wonderful medley of marmalade and dried fruits. There was a chunky rabbit stew, moist brown bread, and creamed vegetables, as well as the minestrone Estelle Delmonico was cooking.

There was nothing like a good bowl of steaming minestrone to put things into perspective, thought Estelle. The old widow sat at the kitchen table, chopping carrots into fine slices. She was making the soup for Marjan, who was lying upstairs recovering from the flu—

a result of staying up all night looking for Bahar. Marjan had bravely maneuvered the green hippie van in the pouring rain, taking all the main roads out of town, hoping to spot her sister somewhere along the way. But in the end she had come home alone, chilled to the bone and shivering with fever.

As soon as the chunky vegetable soup had finished cooking, the little widow climbed up the stairs, balancing a bowl in her arthritic fingers. She walked into the flat's tiny living space, still surprised at how much it had changed since Luigi had used it as an office. Back then it was filled with yellowing receipt books and boxes of quick-rising yeast. Now there was a small woven rug on the scratched wooden floor, a pretty paisley coverlet spread over a futon, and sitting on a spare café chair, a secondhand television Marjan had picked up in Castlebar.

Marjan was lying on the couch, still sniffling and surrounded by crumpled tissues. Though her face was gray and clammy, she looked much healthier than she had the night before.

"Here you go. Some minestrone, yes? Don't get up." Estelle bent down toward Marjan's open mouth to lovingly administer teaspoonfuls of soup.

"Where's Layla? Is she downstairs?" Marjan asked, before coughing into a wad of tissue scrunched up in her hand.

"Shhhh . . . she is okay. She is with Malachy and Emer. They went to Castlebar today. To look for Bahar. They will find her, you will see," said Estelle, smoothing strands of hair from Marjan's eyes. Had Estelle borne a daughter, she had no doubt that she would have looked a lot like Marjan. Such a Roman nose, such an Italian complexion. "Shhhh . . . you go back to sleep, okay?"

Marjan sank deeper into the couch, tears springing up in her reddened eyes.

"What if they don't find her? What if she's gone and they never—"

Marjan broke off and looked away for a moment. She hadn't told Estelle much about Bahar's disappearance, only the fib she had told everyone else who had already paid her a visit: that Bahar had felt so badly about Tom Junior attacking Layla she had decided to skip town for a while. Marjan knew it was a weak explanation, but the alternative would mean opening up too many wounds.

"I'm sorry. I just don't know if we'll find her. And . . . God—" Marjan surrendered into coughs and tears once again. Estelle shushed her gently and wiped her forehead with her wrinkly fingers.

The old lady's touch reminded Marjan of her mother's caresses. Shirin Aminpour had often lullabied her daughters to sleep with fantastic tales of Scheherazade and her courageous storytelling. On such warm nights, as was the custom in Iran, their whole family would gather on their house's flat roof. Sunken and completely cleared of stones or rubble, the roof was lined with back-to-back rugs and ornate pillows, upon which they would all sleep the humid night away, dreaming of golden arches and flying Arabian horses. Someone always had an instrument on hand, usually a *tomback,* the gourd drum of poets, which would *thump, thump, thump* to the stories that were being passed around.

Marjan doubled over from the pain of the memory. They were so young then. Nothing to regret. Nothing to run away from.

Estelle sat quietly by Marjan's side, tenderly stroking her hand as the younger woman sobbed her heavy tears.

"You lie down and don't move," Estelle said, propping several pillows behind Marjan's back.

Marjan marveled at how their situations had reversed; only a couple of months ago *she* had been the one helping Estelle into bed after her fainting spell.

"You need to rest. No more sadness, okay?"

Marjan nodded tiredly, her cheeks burning with fever.

"Now, open your mouth. This is going to make you feel much better, you will see," Estelle said gently. She scooped a big spoonful of broth-softened zucchini and carrot from the bowl in her hand, offering it with a soothing smile. Finally, she thought, someone to take care of. She was going to look after all three girls from now on, just as a mother should.

EVERYONE FELT THE absence of aroma when they stepped inside the café on Saturday morning. The heady steam that always surrounded the golden samovar had deserted its keeper, giving it the look of a barren woman. But for a few stale *zulbia* and a half plate of almond delights, the pastry counter held only the crumbs of past sweetness, an emptiness that further stressed the importance of their mission.

Father Mahoney led the search party that had gathered in the café's closed front room, outlining his reconnaissance plan like a seasoned general out to conquer.

"I'll take the old Cadillac to the east—Westport, Ballintubber, Claremorris," he said, unfolding an old, dusty map of Western County Mayo on the long communal table. "Who wants the coastal road?"

"Evie and I will take it," Fiona volunteered.

"Fine. Malachy, Layla, and Emer can try Castlebar. You'll need a full day for that, I'd say."

"We only got as far as Bridge Street yesterday," Malachy said apologetically

"Right, everyone. We're as good as we'll ever be, so. Time to pull out. Now remember, meet back here at o—eighteen hundred. That's six in the evening if you didn't know. And good luck!"

Father Mahoney attempted a half salute but stopped midway when he realized that he was not in a Bob Hope war pic and the troops were in no mood for light entertainment. Nevertheless, the search party rolled out of the Babylon in regimented strides. No one noticed Marjan's pale face watching through the kitchen door's round windows.

It had been just a day since she had taken in Estelle's comforting minestrone soup, but after five healthy bowls Marjan was finally able to walk up and down the stairs without feeling her legs tremble. Estelle had stayed awake all night to nurse her and instruct Layla in making the footbath, a recipe of salt, vinegar, and hot water that Marjan had herself made many times when her sisters had fallen sick. Only after she was sure that Marjan was free from the flu's hold did Estelle let Mrs. Boylan drive her home to her little white cottage by the sea. For the first time in the four months they had been in Ballinacroagh, Marjan was all alone in the empty café.

Four months. Marjan backed up against the staircase banister as though propelled by a sudden blast of wind, the magnitude of her swirling emotions momentarily sucking the breath out of her. Resinous grief, the echo of guilt, and yes, simple gratitude. Observing the efforts of the kind people gathered to help them, she could not fail to feel grateful. After those lonely years of running and barely trusting anyone, Marjan and her sisters had finally found a home. A real home. So why hadn't Bahar seen that? Why was she giving up on it all, to go—where?

Marjan sank down into a nearby chair. The kitchen seemed to be suffering from a fast of seasons, looking so desolate with its creaking appliances. She had insisted that Estelle and Mrs. Boylan take home the remaining food, the lovely casseroles and stews cooked by the generous ladies of the committee. The groaning refrigerator was now empty but for some ground lamb, three eggs, and leftover *fesenjoon*. She should really throw it away, thought Marjan. Start a new batch, maybe some other kind of stew, or perhaps some pomegranate soup. It had been a long time since she had made pomegranate soup.

FOR THE FIRST TIME since December 1981, when he bought Boney M.'s *Christmas Album,* Thomas McGuire was back in Kenny's Record Shop, thumbing through the latest dance singles with a look of consternation on his fleshy face.

Hi-NRG, Snap!, Industrial, Renegade Soundwave, Techno, House. It was mind-boggling, but according to his teenage daughter Helen, this was the music that everyone listened to nowadays. The new beats were not fit to be called dance music, if you asked him. With their overpowering bass lines and unintelligible lyrics, the whole lot sounded more like a hemorrhoidal computer on its last legs. Nothing like his beloved disco tunes, with their dignified synthesizer beats. But, Thomas reminded himself, after seeing how Ballinacroagh had taken to the Babylon Café, he would have to be more adventurous in his choices.

The bar owner stole a peek outside the record shop window. Although the café was too far down Main Mall for him to see the Closed sign on its door, he knew all about Bahar's disappearance. Three days now. Same as his boy Tom, although he for one was sure the two had nothing to do with each other.

He had to admit, thought Thomas, he was proud of Junior. Maybe not for his choices but for his impeccable timing. With one sweep of his Neanderthal paws, Tom Junior had achieved what Thomas, even with all his influence over the town, had not been able to accomplish in months. That stinking café was finally closed. Good feckin' riddance, if you asked him.

And as for Malachy—that good-for-nothing bastard was no

longer his son. Thomas had gone so far as to give his lawyer a call to change his will, so certain was he of the excommunication. Nothing and no one, not his wife's mewling pleas, not his youngest Joanne's crying, not even his sister Margaret, with her bullish force, could convince him to go back on his pronouncement. That boy was as good as dead to him.

To satisfy his jivey fingers, which kept crawling over to the Disco section in the record shop, Thomas picked up the first album he saw, the Bee Gees' *Saturday Night Fever*. He paid for a rake of dance cassettes that the puzzled shop boy stuffed into two Kenny's Knows Kool Music plastic bags and worked his way down Main Mall toward Paddy McGuire's Pub.

Thomas's eye flitted over the café's silent façade with satisfaction. No sign of activity, not even the golden glow he had peeked at that first day. There was only darkness beyond the half-drawn drapes. A slimy round of phlegm flew out of the bar owner's mouth and landed on the sidewalk between two pots of African violets outside the café's windows. With the expelled spit came a sort of peace that he hadn't experienced since his pre–Turbo Tanner days. Back then, everything around him ran like a well-oiled machine, and there was no competition to worry about except the one waged in his own head. Why had he doubted the outcome? Thomas wondered. Of course the café wouldn't have worked out; the strange spell Ballinacroagh had fallen under these last few months would eventually have been broken, one way or another. Smug and warm all over, Thomas had his hand on the pub door when he heard his older son's voice.

"Dad?"

Tom Junior was standing outside Fadden's Mini-Mart, desperately trying to keep his emaciated knees from knocking against each other every time a gale tunneled down Main Mall. A long minute passed before Thomas recognized his son, for although he had been away only three days, the boy had experienced a complete and utter meta-morphosis. Tom Junior had lost an incredible amount of weight. Gone was the premature beer belly of too many yeasty pints, replaced now by a concave pit of ribs and wrinkled skin. Instead of his puffy jowls, Tom Junior's jagged cheekbones now fell into hollow recesses, while his sunken, saucer eyes were devoid of their usual insolence and cruelty.

"Tom? Is that ye?" Thomas walked toward his son, squinting as though doing so would help flesh out the carcass staring back at him. "Get in the pub right now. Do ye plan fer the whole town to have a look?" said Thomas as he pushed his son up the street. "Thought you'd know better than to get yerself back here in a hurry."

A lone figure occupied the long, oak-paneled bar, slouched over a bottle of scotch. Thomas immediately recognized him as that drunk of all seasons, the Cat. Had it been any other time, the poor sod would have been thrown out on his sclerotic spine, but at the moment there were more important matters for Thomas McGuire to attend to.

"What happened, son? Thought you'd be in Galway having a laugh for yer old man. What's this, now?" He grabbed a crinkly piece of notepaper from Tom Junior's gaunt fingers and peered at it. Thomas could make out only a few words in the dim pub lighting, but his meaty hands started to shake with anger when he saw his son's sloping signature at the bottom of the page.

"It's my note of apologies. I was going to give it to Sean Grogan to give to the Ara— to the girl there. I shouldn't have done it, Dad," Tom Junior said, looking down at his dirty sneakers.

The apology was genuine, the culmination of three of the longest days of Tom Junior's life. His journey had begun when he swallowed a whole bottle of tequila, purchased from the Dew Drop Inn outside Westport, and had ended with Junior squatting in a one-room dustheap better known as the Cat's moldy cottage. And all the while, without his knowledge, Tom Junior's insides were being gnawed at by a ravenous tapeworm.

Posing as a tequila worm, the parasite had been biding its time at the bottom of the now emptied José Cuervo bottle, just waiting for a healthy farm boy to cross its path. The worm had eventually worked its way into Tom Junior's bland soul, boring deep holes from which his ignorance and pent up frustration had seeped out. Gone with the unnecessary bulk of fat was the anger that had burned indiscriminately toward all who stood to oppose him, especially his overbearing father. Tom Junior now realized that Thomas had been suffering under similar strains of unfulfilled dreams, and that he had wrongly compensated for his failures by steamrolling and manipulating everyone in his path.

All in all, these three days had been a spiritual fasting for Tom Junior, from which he had emerged thinned and complete, bereft of any desire to rule over Ballinacroagh or his father's weighty legacy.

Thomas was not so understanding.

"What are you talking about? Have you gone feckin' daft, Tom? Leave this to me," he said, crumpling the written apology in his shaking hand. "Get yerself home to yer mother. She's been driving me up the wall with her crying. Go on, now," Thomas ordered, then added, "And for God's sake, eat something while you're there."

"Da . . ."

"What? What, Tom?" Thomas glared at the ghost of his once hardy son. Was it just him, or had the whole town gone mad?

"I'm not going home, Dad," Tom said firmly. "I'm leaving today. For America. To sort meself out. Find myself."

There was no denying it: Tom Junior was a changed man, through and through. Two days of squatting with the Cat had done more for his mind and soul than the two decades he had lived under his parents' damp roof.

Tom Junior had met his raggedy alcoholic host in a water ditch, where he had spent his first night on the run from the law. What no one in town knew about the Cat, and what Tom had come to discover, was that the old drunkard was once a well-known philosopher in his native Bulgaria. Growing up in a quiet hamlet near the Balkan Mountains, he had been untouched by the seemingly endless Russian-led coups that rocked the little Slavic country toward the end of the nineteenth century. This quiet existence had allowed the Cat to concentrate on his dissertation (via correspondence with Trinity College in Dublin) on Kierkegaard and the missing fourth stage in his existential approach. It was a thesis he was working on well into the second decade of the twentieth century, when out of the blue, Bulgaria found itself caught in the international game of war, choosing the wrong side to cheer for. The Cat escaped the fighting for his Irish alma mater and, after several unrequited love affairs in the capital city, soon found himself in Ballinacroagh of all places. And in Ballinacroagh he had come to stay.

When Tom Junior, with his body thoroughly ravaged by the tequila tapeworm, first stepped inside the Cat's one-room, thatched-roof cottage, he was struck dumb by the library amassed before him. Crammed into every corner of the modest space, and piled high in teetering columns, were hundreds of books. Books everywhere. What windows there were had been blocked by barricades of well-thumbed Mills & Boon romance novels (which, if asked, the Cat would vehemently deny were his), and the old philosopher's Louis XIV daybed was raised on a stack of esoteric Egyptian texts, bought from a Berber peddler in Bulgaria. Tradition had given way to innovation when it came to the cottage's floor; the customary dirt ground was paved in encyclopedias, thesauri, and dictionaries from every language imaginable, with prominence given to the Afro-Asiatic idiom, which was the Cat's favorite tongue to date.

Never a bright student, Tom Junior felt he had died and landed in his own personal hell. Collapsing on the book-strewn floor, he slept four solid hours that felt like four long years, and awoke to find a stack of feathery paperbacks supporting his neck. Next to him, on a dainty white plate, was a glass of milk and two orange crème biscuits, and in a corner across the room sat the Cat, in one of two rocking chairs, with Samuel Beckett's *Waiting for Godot* clutched in his liver-spotted hands. The old tramp did not look up as Tom Junior made his way to the other rocking chair. He just kept rocking away as he read about his favorite limbo contestants, chuckling to himself over the many highlighted passages.

Thirty-eight hours passed before the Cat ceased his slow rocking and looked up to find himself under siege in his reading corner. Stretching from one side of the wall to the other, and cutting him off from the rest of the small room he used as bedroom, parlor, and kitchen, was a wall. Four feet high and eight feet across, the wall was made up entirely of books, many of which were the Cat's personal favorites: from the entire works of Nietzsche, including a frayed edition of *Also sprach Zarathustra;* from Camus and the Absurdists of the theater (Ionesco, Beckett, and that prisoner of life Genet) to the gossamer stanzas of Kahlil Gibran, the Lebanese poet with a heart of gold.

Tom Junior had built the wall while the Cat was deep in a mental soliloquy on the meaning of meaning. Assuming that the young lost soul had made a hasty escape, the old thinker was overcome by a great sadness, but after using a wiry finger to nudge a book out of the precariously built barrier, the Cat discovered a new Tom Junior, thinned to the bone but present and more alive than ever. Tom Junior's eyes, encircled in blue-black rings of exhaustion, were nevertheless filled with a renewed sense of being. On his lap sat the opened pages of *The*

Prophet, and through his cracked lips came the words he had been reading over and over again:

> *It is when your spirit goes wandering upon the wind,*
> *That you, alone and unguarded,*
> *commit a wrong unto others and therefore unto yourself . . .*

Tom Junior's spirit had come home for a landing. He was beginning to see that his attack on Layla was just the symptom of an even deeper disease. A sickness he would tend to from this day on, starting with his sincerest apology.

"I tried calling the café the night it all happened. A woman answered the phone, but I couldn't find the right thing to say. I don't know, but it was like I suddenly ran out of breath. So . . . so, I hung up. I thought a note would be best."

"What were you thinking calling those darkies?" Thomas McGuire said, bristling with anger. "You listen to me, boy, it's taken a mighty hand to get Sean Grogan off me back. I'll not be the one holding me bollocks in all of this, you hear? Feckin' 'find meself'! I'll find ye all right." Thomas slammed the crumpled apology note at Tom's feet. "You look in on your mam, then get yer arse down to the Ale House, where I'll be waiting. Don't even think about getting out of work tonight."

He stormed out of the pub just as the Cat awoke from his alcoholic stupor with a loud belch that told little of the innovative theories running through his inebriated yet brilliant mind. Jimmy the bartender grimaced at the sour smell emanating from the darkened slump in the corner.

Tom Junior picked up the ball of paper and smoothed it out so that his words were legible once again. He hadn't really expected his father to give the note to the guards, let alone understand the epiphany that would forever mark his path.

Hoisting a heavy, book-filled satchel (a going-away present from the Cat) onto his back, Tom Junior sidled up to the old drunk at the bar.

"Jimmy, take care of my man here," Tom said. He slapped the Cat on his hunched back, causing the crinkly old man to double over in a coughing fit. "Give him all the drink he wants on me. See you, Cat."

Tom Junior gave the Cat a thumbs-up before slipping a hundred-pound note into his soiled coat pocket. He then walked down to the pub's back room, a cavernous carpeted ground of mismatched tables and chairs all facing a rotting dartboard. Pushing the emergency exit door open, Tom Junior stepped out into the wet cobblestone alleyway. He looked both ways to make sure that his father was nowhere in sight before creeping quietly up to the café's squeaky back gate. There, with bated breath, he slipped his refolded apology note between two of the fence's wooden boards, then turned and left the town of Ballinacroagh forever.

MOMENTS LATER, JUST as Tom Junior disappeared down the alleyway, Marjan walked out into the café's backyard. She knelt down among the dewy, bottle green cilantro and, encircling the stems with her thumb and forefinger, tugged firmly at the herb. She was careful to leave her other hand on the plant's base to protect its roots. The tempest that had raged over four days had decimated her garden, tearing the delicate bluebells and velvety purple violas that had blossomed in June from their comfortable beds. The dead flowers lay scattered about the yard now, their once vibrant inner petals turned to clomps of rotting brown. The hardy cilantro, parsley, and mint, Marjan was happy to note, had fared better in the storm. As she pulled the last sprig of tall cilantro, she whispered safe keepings so that Bahar would come back home quickly. For this was home, she was sure of that now more than ever.

Marjan walked back into the kitchen with her handful of herbs just as the phone rang. Fiona's bright voice greeted her on the other end.

"We've taped the Missing flyers on every tree and lamppost," Fiona informed her. "Don't worry, Marjan. We'll find her. There's not many petite, olive-skinned brunettes around these parts. Someone would've noticed her."

"I hope you're right, Fiona," Marjan replied, trying hard not to think of the multitude of hiding places in Ireland. Surely the endless green quilted fields, separated by the tidy pilings of rock borders, were ideal coverlets for escape.

After several more minutes of reassuring conversation with Fiona, Marjan hung up the phone and began chopping the parsley, cilantro, and mint. She mixed the herbs in a bowl with ground lamb, onions, and seasoning, the meat squishing between her fingers, feeling like warm mud inviting itself between bare toes on a hot summer's day. The familiar rhythm of mixing was soothing, and by the time she added the meatballs to the pot of hot broth, her hopes were singing once again.

Unlike *fesenjoon,* in which the pomegranate taste is balanced by a robust walnut companion, pomegranate soup relies entirely on the fruit for its inspiration. A shimmering magenta when fully cooked, the pomegranate juice gives the broth a sour-sweet taste and is usually enjoyed as an appetizer rather than a main meal. There was no other dish with such a perfect balance of *sardi* and *garmi,* in Marjan's opinion, the *sard* pomegranate and cilantro equaling out the *garm* lamb and split peas. She wished Bahar could smell it now. She would realize that there was nothing to fear—real or imaginary.

Marjan stirred the luscious waves of pomegranate beneath her and thought about her sensitive sister. Had she done enough to help Bahar? she wondered. She certainly tried to be understanding and protective, Marjan told herself, but maybe she could have tried harder to ease Bahar's painful memories, those headaches that plagued her daily. She knew how hard it was for her sister to trust her surroundings, but had she been as sympathetic as she could have been? Or had Estelle Delmonico's observations been right; was she still playing the mother to her sisters?

Perhaps the little Italian woman was right in her advice; there were some things that were out of even her control. Some things had to play themselves out, burn themselves cold, without her stirring hand, without her help. Because, maybe, it wasn't all up to her.

Marjan nodded silently, admitting a welcomed defeat. It was necessary. Bahar and Layla would just have to find their way without her always being there. Because she couldn't do it anymore. She would have to learn to put her trust in something greater than them all; she would have to simply believe everything would work out in the end.

Placing the lid back on the hot pot, Marjan turned away from the stove and exhaled.

Bahar was going to be all right.

Layla was going to be all right.

She was going to be all right.

The lightness of her surrender carried her up the stairs and to an afternoon sleep that had been a long time coming. And behind Marjan, left bubbling on the stove for the first time in all her life, was the unattended pot of pomegranate soup.

LIKE HER SISTER, Bahar was about to be lifted, rising to higher grounds. At the moment, though, as she looked around her hostel room, hope was the last thing on her mind.

The patch sewn onto one corner of the checkered duvet read "Property of Castlebar Castle," but the chipped plaster ceiling contradicted such grandiose claims. There is definitely nothing regal about this hovel, Bahar thought to herself. She couldn't get used to the springy mattress or the shocking chartreuse walls of the stuffy room, even after two long days. The shag carpet, a psychedelic pattern of orange circles against a dark brown background, still smelled like deviled eggs; and the faded window blinds with their missing slats let in the gloomy gray light far too early every morning. The room's only redeeming feature—a white, Victorian cast-iron fireplace carved with two cherubic angels on either side—was marred by a faded, larger than life, beaming portrait of JFK that hung in a gilded frame over the mantelpiece. The dead president's glazed eyes had followed her as she stumbled into the room that first night, falling straight into the musty single bed in her wet clothes.

She woke up with the worst migraine the next morning. After swallowing eight spoonfuls of the headache medicine she had packed in her suitcase, she pulled a creased piece of paper out of its side plaid pouch, and stared at the phone number scribbled on it in Persian numerals. The page had been torn out of an old address book that Bahar had flipped through the previous night, just before leaving the warmth of the café. She found the phone number sitting under the letter *J,* nestled innocently between the names and addresses of two of Marjan's old schoolmates.

Her plan was simple enough in theory: remove the dangerous element (herself) from the café, book a room at the Castlebar hostel, the same room she and her sisters had stayed in when they first arrived in County Mayo, and call Khanoum Jaferi's apartment in Tehran. Then she would just wait until Hossein found her. Bahar was sure it wouldn't take him long to come to the hostel, especially if he was already in Ireland. She would let him do whatever he wanted with her, take her back to Iran even, just as long as he left Marjan and Layla alone. Yes, it was a clean enough solution, thought Bahar. And it would have worked, had she actually had the courage to make the call. Instead, she had spent the last two days and nights locked away in her hostel room, pacing the expanse of the shag carpet and counting the water spots on the plaster ceiling above her.

Bloody coward, that was what she was. She couldn't even run away right. Can't even go downstairs to the lobby and make a phone call, Bahar thought disgustedly, as she pushed her aching body up from the bed. Casting her eyes down to avoid John F. Kennedy's disconcerting stare, she slowly crossed the room to the fireplace. Using her shoe, Bahar tentatively poked the small pile of turf ash inside the hearth, ready to jump back in case anything moved in the chalky residue. I could die in here and nobody would notice, she thought morbidly. Sighing, she stretched her arms wearily across the freezing iron mantelpiece and hung her head.

Her stomach growled angrily. She would have to leave the room sooner than later, if only to get reinforcements; the food she had bought the night she arrived at the Castlebar Castle was nearly gone. All that was left was one green apple and a half-eaten package of Knorr crème biscuits sitting forlornly on the bedside table. Weakened suddenly by the thought of her meager food supply, Bahar lifted her head and stepped away from the mantelpiece. She turned around, about to flop dejectedly back on her checkered bed, when her eyes suddenly fell upon several brochures scattered across the mantelpiece. She had forgotten about the glossy leaflets, which the receptionist had handed her along with her room key the night she arrived. The pamphlets showcased the usual destinations favored by American tourists: Knock, Leenane, the Aran Islands. And Croagh Patrick.

Bahar grabbed the first brochure from the pile: Hibernian Holiday Tours of Croagh Patrick. It contained a garish green and yellow foldout of the mountain with a brief history of Saint Patrick on one side and archaeological facts on the other. Gift shop hours. Mass times.

Pilgrimage season. "Let Hibernian Holiday Tours take you up the mountain!"

Hibernian Holiday Tours. It was the same tour bus company that had picked her up on the stormy road out of Ballinacroagh. The Irish bus driver, a portly man with a light case of eczema, had kindly agreed to drop her in front of the shabby hostel in Castlebar before driving off toward the more expensive lodgings, like Mountain Manor on Bridge Street.

"Picking up the Americans at the Manor there. Irish Americans, they call themselves. Out here to have a look at the Reek. Better off going to the Bahamas, if ye ask me," the driver had said, before winking at her in the rearview mirror.

Bahar's heart began to pound furiously. The Reek. Of course. That was it.

She had been spending all this time moving, running, avoiding—but never in the right direction. Not across lands and small seas, not through valleys or shifting deserts, but up. Up! The source of the calling was mysterious; Bahar didn't know where the soft voice in her head had come from, but all of a sudden it was telling her to go up. There was no other way but up.

THE FLIRTATIOUS BUS DRIVER winked at her as she climbed up the bus's steep, rubbery steps.

"Back again I see. I'm not complaining, mind you. Always happy to see a pretty young face," he said, throwing her a lopsy-sided grin.

Hoping to avoid further unwanted attention, Bahar crouched low in her seat. She was thankful that none of the bus's passengers—Irish American retirees who were retracing their fractioned ancestries—had tried to strike up a conversation with her. The jolly senior citizens were swapping addresses and sharing wallet-size pictures of their smiling grandchildren and took no notice of the young, dark-haired woman sitting in the front seat. As the bus pulled out of Castlebar bound for the mountain, Bahar kept her eyes glued to the rolling countryside. The rain-soaked heather and forests of oak with their awnings of dark green alder suddenly struck her as very beautiful. Ireland was an enchanting country, Bahar thought to herself.

The Hibernian Holiday Tours bus joined a pack of fifteen other buses in a large car park situated at the eastern base of the mountain. Pilgrims, mostly well-fed Americans with new Nikes and bulging fanny packs, spilled out of the tour buses, some whistling sprightly renditions of "Danny Boy" as they all headed for a small brass-and-marble plaque at the base of the mountain.

"Saint Patrick," the tour guide started. "Patron Saint of Ireland. Tormented visionary. Benevolent missionary. Savior of the heathen Irish." She paused, flashing the crowd an ironic smile.

"Battled his own demons when he climbed the mountain. The devils came to him in the shape of blackbirds, shrouding the sky with their dark wings. But Patrick kept on praying, not stopping until the sky shone bright again," she said, passing around complimentary shamrocks laminated onto small cards. "There'll be no Mass as today's Saturday, but don't let that stop you from saying your prayers if the need strikes. I'll be saying my own thanks, now that the storm's gone."

The tour guide directed everyone to a narrow walkway that zig-zagged up the steep mountain. Though a wispy veil of mist obscured the path ahead, and the short, pale grass on either side was littered with jagged stones, it did not stop a couple of the more dedicated climbers from walking with feet bared and souls opened. Bahar trailed behind the tour group, taking her time to breathe in the thin mountain air.

Prayers, the tour guide had said. What sort of prayers could help her now? Bahar wondered. What did she have to be so thankful for? There was no way of undoing what she had done, the misery she had brought on her sisters when she married Hossein. And she was still causing Marjan and Layla pain. Right this very minute, even as she was climbing this mountain. She knew they would be worried sick about her, thinking the worst had happened, but she still hadn't phoned to let them know she was all right. All she had done was run away again.

Bahar shook her head and grimaced. She was always running away. Not once, not one single time had she ever taken responsibility for her actions, apologized for not listening to her older sister's warnings about Khanoum Jaferi and her disgusting, pock-marked son. Instead she had hidden behind her headaches, forced Marjan and Layla to tiptoe around her all these silent years, as if she was some sort of helpless invalid. Prayers. She was going to need a lot of prayers, Bahar told herself, as she hoisted her body up onto a granite ledge.

As Bahar reached the last leg of her hike, the steepest, rockiest part of the mountain, a most curious thing began to happen. It seemed that the higher she climbed, the more lucid her thoughts became. She was well ahead of most of the American tourists by now, and had almost caught up with the sprightly tour guide, who had the happy advantage of toned calf muscles and a trusty walking stick. As she scaled the stony mountain path, Bahar found herself suddenly bursting with energy, her morning migraine long gone.

Why, she asked herself, had she assumed that that strange sounding phone call had been from Hossein? The fact that he had found them in London, frightening as it may be, didn't mean that he was going to follow them all the way to Ballinacroagh. And really, if she thought about it rationally for a moment, the phone call in the café could just as likely have been a wrong number or some neighborhood kids playing a prank. So why had she chosen the worst possible explanation and allowed her headaches and hysteria to fog her judgment? If she wanted to survive, if she wanted to move forward, then she'd have to learn not to expect the worst from situations—or people, for that matter.

Yes, Bahar told herself, she had her own set of penances to pay. Layla had her youthful cinnamon-rose promise and Marjan, the ability to create one spectacular dish after another, but those were their journeys, not hers. She didn't know what her strengths were just yet, but she did know they were there to be discovered.

At Croagh Patrick's summit, Bahar stopped hiking and turned around, toward the dazzling blue waters of Clew Bay. The gray clouds were fast departing across the horizon, their liquid wings reflected in the bay below. Climbing this ancient mountain had given her the clarity to claim her ill spirits, she decided. Each rock-strewn step forward had made her feel stronger, as if she was indeed casting off her fear and loneliness, the monsters who had been riding her for such a long time. Just as Saint Patrick had done so many centuries ago, thought Bahar. Whatever miracles that old bishop had performed among these thick clouds, they were still working their magic on her. Even Hossein could not reach her at these heights.

She stretched her arms and, closing her eyes, drew in a deep, loud breath that made even the more extroverted of the American tourists do a double take. The sweet innocence of their stares brought a small smile to Bahar's face.

BELOW ON MAIN MALL, a scowling Thomas Mc-Guire was also experiencing the first of many belated epiphanies. His sense of smell set off the initial alarm.

The burly publican smelled the soup as he was stomping his way down to Fadden's Mini-Mart. He had little clue about his own approaching demise. In fact, when he would later recall the whole incident to himself, curled up on the many sleepless nights that would follow him to his dying day, Thomas would swear that it was not the smell that had brought him to the café's kitchen but the duties of a concerned parent and citizen who had finally had enough. Such, it seems, are the altruistic fantasies of many a skewed, criminal mind.

Thomas never made it into the mini-mart for another round of badgering poor Danny Fadden. Smelling the cooking pomegranate as soon as he stormed past the Babylon Café, he turned and marched back up Main Mall with a renewed sense of purpose. He veered into the alleyway, sidestepping overturned rubbish bins and a pack of rabid cats to reach the café's backyard.

Ballinacroagh's beer baron didn't stop to knock on the gate but chose instead to kick his way in. He raised his foot and was about to karate chop through the gate when he saw the note. It was the same lined sheet of blubbering apologies he had crumpled up not two hours ago, Junior's words living on to taunt him once again. With blood pumping in his ears, Thomas shoved the gate door open and stumbled into the café's backyard, trampling the remainder of Marjan's standing herbs with his heavy work boots. The unlocked back door gave way easily to his fist, and he staggered into the kitchen, a place he had secretly dreamt of since he was a little boy, when the Delmonicos still ran their little pastry shop.

Expecting to be confronted by Marjan chopping up questionable chunks of rotting meat and animal parts, Thomas was somewhat disappointed to find the opposite. There were no intestines flying about or globular fish eyes staring back from bloody chopping blocks. Before him stood a round table spread with a frilly, blanched tablecloth printed with cherries. A little ways beyond, in the middle of the kitchen, was the wooden island, clean but for a bowl of blushing apricots. And on the stove was a bubbling, half-covered silver pot, from which escaped taunting tendrils of pomegranate.

The perfumed fingers reached Thomas's curved chin, tickling his jaws like an animated temptress. He gasped audibly as he stepped back against the wall in horror. Disgusting what some people would put in their mouths, he thought, feeling dizzier than he had in his entire life. His breathing came out in short spats, and his head was swimming. After he had partially regained his composure, he stole another glimpse around the kitchen.

A woven Tabrizi runner that Bahar had bought for twenty English pounds in Portobello Market ran across the room, from the back entrance to the twin swinging doors opening on to the front dining room. Perched above the doors' dark frame was a rectangular slice of turquoise tile, embedded with shards of indigo glass. The mosaic pieces spelled out the words *Nush-e Jan,* a robust Farsi expression whose closest translation is "bon appétit!" The warm gesture was lost on the furious Thomas.

Just look at what those cows have done to his place, the publican thought to himself. That was right; this was his place, always had been, always would be. Where he was standing now, just under his mud-coated boots, was where Polyester Paddy's dance floor would be. Writhing bodies would be commanded to move to fabulous disco beats here, the sexy whirl of a glittering disco ball throwing light prisms around like rainbow confetti. And there, through those doors, there in that feckin' empty place, for God's sake, that was where he'd walk through from adjoining Paddy's, taking his time to give his hellos to the couples that would be strewn across velveteen couches and chairs. Black marble tables would stand crowded with cocktails, drinks he had been dying to try out but for those feckers who just wanted stout and more stout in his pubs. Here he would have been able to do it all. He might even have hired one of the O'Reilly girls, the one with the big knockers, to take to roller skates and bum-filled short shorts, swirling about with her drinks orders. Why the feck not? This was his place. This was Polyester Paddy's, where it was all going to happen!

Caught in his disco dream, Thomas twirled around and around on his boot heels, spinning wildly in the middle of the kitchen, hearing the funky music in his head as he was blinded by the glittering lights. As if possessed, he suddenly lurched forward toward the stove and the pot of cooking pomegranate soup. But for the red tea towel that Marjan had hung on the oven door's handle, Thomas would have fallen straight into the open flame. Even so, he was able to hang on to the linen towel for only a second before letting go of it on his way down to the cold floor.

The plastic bags of dance albums from Kenny's Record Shop shot into the air overhead. They intersected with the airborne tea towel, spinning in such perfect symmetry that for an instant—that brief suspension of time before his skull hit the linoleum floor and his eyes rolled back—Thomas was really in his own discotheque; a fabulous place of rocket-propelled fireworks, falsetto voices, and syncopated synthesizers. But like the era it lived and died in, the disco music came to an end all too quickly, just as Thomas's arteries, strained from decades of pig's blood sausage breakfasts and butter and creamed rashers, clamped shut.

Thomas McGuire's heart stopped the same instant the flying cassettes landed all around him, sounding a lot like the applause of a hundred plastic hands. The copy of *Saturday Night Fever* fell into his open palm, a soundtrack to step over with on his way to a white polyester–suited heaven. The tea towel landed on the stove, erupting into an instant fireball that bounced up the adjoining wall.

Yes, it all came to a stop for Thomas then, everything but the beat that rose above his mammoth body, beyond the insatiable ambition that had led him through all the wrong doorways, all the wrong songs. For it was the eternal beat, the endless tune that stopped for no one, not even him.

after dinner lavender-mint tea

2 tablespoons honey

3 teaspoons fresh lavender flowers

1 cup fresh mint leaves, chopped

½ lemon, cut into thin wedges

Boil 2 quarts of water. Heat teapot with half of the water. Discard.
Fill teapot with honey, lavender leaves, and mint. Add the hot water.
Cover and steep for 10 minutes. Serve with a slice of lemon.

epilogue

EARLY THE NEXT MORNING, just as the more devout pilgrims reached Croagh Patrick's white church to watch the sunrise, the circus came to town. Quite literally.

A train of four wooden, horse-pulled caravans rambled through Main Mall, their canvas and patchwork coverings stretched to reveal banners written in fluorescent orange and pink—THE MCGUIRE FAMILY CIRCUS.

The McGuire Family Circus was really the linked caravans belonging to Thomas's actor brother, Kieran, and his troupe of physical storytellers. The traveling performers parked their train at the far end of the open field, near the pitched tents and foldout tables of the Patrician Day celebrations. From there the circus troupe showcased their theatrics, an extravaganza of torch jugglers, levitation exhibitions, and a hilarious Punch and Judy show. The circus was not only an enchanting surprise for the pilgrims and tourists who had gathered in the field after their arduous mountain climb but a perfect opening act to *Fruits of Labor*, Father Mahoney's play.

Despite the fact that she'd missed some last-minute rehearsals because of the unforeseen dramas of the week, Fiona Athey's directorial debut was a smash hit. Following the fortunes of Gino Pepino, a young apple picker who wakes from an afternoon siesta to find himself the only male left in a village of one hundred very hungry women, the play drew roars of delight from its large audience. Layla and Malachy proved to be excellent romantic leads and carried Father Mahoney's delicious romp to a standing ovation.

Marjan watched the happy priest bite down on a carrot *torshi*, one of the many pickles he had consumed from the jar he bought at the charity table. All of the *torshi*s that Bahar had packed were already sold out, but thanks to a generous Benny Corcoran, who had loaned Marjan the use of his bakery kitchen (Assumpta wasn't talking to him as a result), a panoply of buffet dishes was available for the picking. The pots of *abgusht*, trays of feta and mint wraps, *dolmeh*, and elephant ears were being gobbled up faster than the beer that kept flowing from free taps, the only time the McGuire pubs would be so charitable.

It would have been enough to push Thomas McGuire back through the gates of oblivion had he been there to see it all. As it was, Thomas was in no position to move a toe, even if he wanted to. He was strapped to tubes and machines that kept him barely alive and breathing, though after hearing what had happened to him in the Babylon Café, he sometimes wished he had died.

Thomas had been legally dead for just over a minute when Bahar, dropped off by the tour bus after her momentous climb, burst into the kitchen with exhilaration that quickly turned to alarm. She forced her way through the pink-black pomegranate cloud that had filled the kitchen, the smoke stinging her eyes and throat. Tongues of vicious orange and black flames darted across the wooden kitchen counter and snaked up the walls above. Panicked, Bahar ran for the stairs to find her sisters and tripped over Thomas McGuire's lifeless body

Using her own hot breath to puff out Thomas's chest, Bahar

pumped his torso over and over until his heart began beating once again. Thomas started to cough, his eyes blinking open only to fall back into a faint; the shock of finding Bahar in the midst of resuscitating him was too much for the fallen lord of Ballinacroagh to handle.

Marjan, woken up by Bahar's screams, had tumbled downstairs to find her estranged sister hunched over a large man and the kitchen burning. Thanks to the small fire extinguisher Luigi Delmonico had kept in the pantry, Marjan was able to stop the flames from reaching the refrigerator on the other side of the room, choking the fire just as Thomas McGuire spluttered his first breaths back on earth. By the time Marjan knelt down next to Thomas's body with a glass of water, the devastating fire had been quenched.

Dervla Quigley almost fell out of her open window when she saw the lime green hippie van screeching out of the alleyway in the wake of billowing smoke, heading toward the Westport Road with Marjan at the wheel. The old gossip would have keeled over in an instant had she been able to see the van's cargo that day.

Bahar kept a close eye on Thomas's staccato breathing in the back of the van as Marjan drove to Mayo General. A waxy peach tinge had returned to the bully's flaccid face, but he remained unconscious and his skipping heartbeat was extremely faint. Why *had* he come into their café, Bahar wondered, as she checked Thomas's pulse again.

Marjan thought she had a pretty good idea about Thomas's intentions, until she saw all the dance cassettes piled up into little hills on the kitchen floor. What a strange man, she thought.

Thomas McGuire would never really recover from the heart attack that had briefly sent him to that great big nightclub in the sky. He did his best to forget what had happened in the café but found peace only after he had paid Estelle the hefty sum it would take to restore the café to its former glory. Though neither inept guard filed formal charges against him, Thomas McGuire's long stint of tyranny was as good as over. He would spend the rest of his days listening to his dusty collection of twelve-inches and quietly tending to his wife's libidinous needs (for Cecilia became even more enthusiastic in the bedroom after her sons were out of the house), trying hard not to die in the process. And from that Patrician Day onward, Thomas's sister Margaret took full power of attorney over his business affairs; she acted as both his eyes and ears as she set about fixing the family reputation he had shattered in one fell swoop.

Marjan ambled over to the samovar and poured herself a steaming cup of lavender-mint tea. She and Malachy had carried the big machine out of the café especially for the occasion, using a long extension cord to plug it into the nearby mini-mart's outer wall socket. Estelle had brought down the mint and lavender from her own small herb garden, and together they had arranged the various teacups and sugar spoons for the town's second favorite beverage. The weather was no longer threatening to explode into storms, but it had yet to return to the summer heat of previous weeks, so tea was a particularly pleasant drink that Sunday afternoon.

Taking a sip, Marjan settled into a plastic chair set under a pink and turquoise striped tent. Sitting close by were some of the people she loved most in the world, as well as some she would eventually come to call family. Estelle was reclining in one of the plastic chairs, also sipping on the lavender-mint tea while she chatted away with Mrs. Boylan about the infinite uses of cold-pressed, virgin olive oil. Seated to the little Italian widow's right were Layla and a skinny young girl with tangled, carroty hair. Marjan recognized the child as the little urchin who had summoned her to the travelers' camp on that stormy Thursday, only four days ago. The young girl had come to town with a group of campers, the proud itinerants streaming through the afternoon festivities with their own brand of a good time.

A heroic Declan Maughan claimed a piece of the field near the stage for his caravan but pretty soon had sauntered over to the pink and turquoise tent with redheaded Aoife, his youngest of thirteen sisters. After a slug of Dutch courage in the form of a Guinness (or two), the boxing champion had seated himself on a deck chair and promptly struck up a rather passionate conversation about the state of amateur boxing in Ireland with none other than a blushing Bahar. Marjan could tell that her sister liked the ruggedly handsome gypsy, despite the fact that Declan was doing most of the talking. Bahar's smile, though quite shy, did not look so different from Layla's own beaming face just about then—hopeful and unabashedly proprietary.

The love between Layla and Malachy was the best kind of ownership, Marjan thought to herself, in which the only commodity was the ceaseless flow of affection. The young couple had arrived well after the fire in the café's kitchen died down. They had bypassed the grittiness to find only blackened kitchen walls and a story that, especially for Malachy, was a bizarre one indeed. It was right that they had not been involved in the commotion, thought Marjan. Their destinies required them for greater adventures, unencumbered by needless dramas. She watched Malachy curl his long fingers around a lock of Layla's straight hair, gently caressing it as he mused on the origins of stars. The young astronomer knew that in Aristotelian times the word *comet* meant "the length of luminous hair," but the word eventually changed to signify the orbiting streak that sometimes, just sometimes, flies a little too close to the sun.

But Marjan knew those two would be just fine. In fact, she thought, they would all be fine. Of course, there was still a lot she and her sisters needed to talk about; too much had been left unsaid since that dark night they left Tehran for good, in the wake of a revolution and a man she hoped would never cross their path again. But that could all wait until tomorrow. For now, she told herself, for now it was enough just to have Bahar and Layla with her, here in this small village called Ballinacroagh, both with sweet smiles on their beautiful faces.

The sun began to set over Clew Bay as Marjan leaned back with her tea to watch members of the acrobatic circus troupe, dressed in jumpsuits of green and gold silk, cartwheel across the modest wooden amphitheater. The impromptu show was a dance based on the festival of Lughnasa, that harvest celebration of ancient Celts, which marked their new year. Marjan marveled at the similarities between this ancient ritual and her own version of the pomegranate myth.

Unlike the classical Greeks, for whom the fruit symbolized the inescapable cycle of bitter death, with a remorseful Persephone returning to the underworld for her six months of required winter, Marjan liked to believe the old stories of Persian soothsayers, who held a different vision of the tart fruit's purpose in life. She liked to remember that above all else, above all the unfortunate connotations of death and winter, the pomegranate was, and always would be, the fruit of hope.

The flower of fertility, of new things to come and old seasons to be cradled.

It had shown even her that some of the best recipes are the unwritten ones, the ones that happen when you pour yourself a generous glass of Shiraz *vino*, pop on a soothing Billie Holiday song, and just let the bountiful ingredients lead you. Because, like it or not, life will go on with or without you, forever blooming in someone else's backyard, giving flavor to yet another pot of pomegranate soup.

Yes, that was how she would like to think of that particular sweetness. The myriad seedling that could only, really, be the flower of new beginnings.

acknowledgments

I am deeply grateful to the following people: My agent, Adam Chromy, for his intuition and tenacity. My editor, the indefatigable Robin Rolewicz, whose steady guidance and sweet laugh made all the difference. Everybody at Random House who have rallied behind this book from the very beginning—Gina Centrello, Daniel Menaker, Jon Karp, David Ebershoff, Claire Tisne, Nicole Bond—thank you so much for your hard work and support. The talented visual and production team of Barbara Bachman, Robbin Schiff, Susan M. S. Brown, Vincent La Scala, and my fabulous publicist, Lanie Shapiro. My Irish family, the Collinses of Mayo and Long Island, who provide me with endless sources of merriment; my brother, Sam, and my parents, who shared my first taste of a pomegranate. And most of all, CRC, my anchor and constant companion. Thank you.

pomegranate soup

marsha mehran

a reader's guide

Question: Pomegranate Soup is your first novel. What inspired you to write this book?

Marsha Mehran: I was living in Ireland in 1999 with my husband, who is Irish.

"Multiculturalism" wasn't even in the vernacular then; I was one of only a handful of "foreigners" living in County Mayo. When I walked down the village's main street, people literally came out of shop doors to stare at the "brown girl" passing by! At the local pub, I was often asked if I was Japanese or Chinese (ethnic groups whose members I do not remotely resemble). During this time I met a Middle Eastern family that ran a deli outside of Castlebar. They sold cans of chickpeas, tahini, and Mediterranean condiments, which are common in supermarkets today, but were a rarity then. This Lebanese family reminded me of my own parents, who had escaped the Islamic Revolution in Iran and moved to Argentina, where they opened a Middle Eastern eatery. They carried the same haunted, lonely looks on their faces that my mother and father did when they had struggled to build a life in a country so vastly different from their homeland. The image of this family stayed in my mind, even as I moved back to New York and began writing my first novel, a story about Iranian women.

Q: Although *Pomegranate Soup* is not autobiographical, how much of your protagonists do you see in yourself?

MM: I am a mixture of all three sisters, actually. There is a little of the maternal Marjan, a bit of the neurotic Bahar, and even a dash of the free spirit that guides Layla, in me.

Q: Pomegranate Soup offers not only a fascinating picture of revolutionary Iran, but also a buffet of traditional Persian dishes. What inspired you to make food such a prominent aspect of the story, and is there a specific Persian dish you love the most?

MM: I'm mad about cooking. Chopping and frying is so relaxing to me; cooking is a perfect expression of love. When you give of yourself through a dish, you aren't just feeding somebody's physical hunger, but a deeper longing for home, for a safe place to rest. I have to say that my favorite Persian dish is *gheimeh*. It's a delicious stew made from tomatoes, yellow split peas, lamb, and french-fried potatoes.

Q: Persian cuisine is still fairly unknown here in the United States. Why do you think this is?

MM: Maybe it's a public relations thing—not enough advertising. There are approximately one million Iranian Americans living in North America, most who moved here after the revolution. So, it probably is just a matter of time, really. I'm definitely ready to spread the word!

Q: In your novel, the image of the bubbling samovar is very central to the Aminpour sisters' café. While coffee is the stimulant of choice for many Americans, it seems the complete opposite in Iran, where an entire ritual surrounds drinking tea. Can you tell us a bit more about this?

MM: There was a period in my childhood when samovars seemed to be taking over our household. My mother had an obsession for them and scoured garage sales and Persian grocery stores for antique, brass, miniature, and electric versions of the water boiler used to make tea. No matter what time of day, visitors to our home were ensured a hot cup of tea thanks to these miraculous machines. Persian tea is easily obtained at any Middle Eastern grocery store nowadays. However, if you're looking for an approximation in the general supermarket, an even mixture of Earl Grey and Darjeeling will do. Persian tea exudes a rich, orangey perfume and a dark amber color. The thing to remember is that Persian tea is always meant to be taken with some sort of sweet accompaniment, such as sweetened nuts, fruit, nougat candy, dried mulberries, or raisins. But beware: Persians never sweeten their tea beforehand. Rather, cubes of crystallized sugar are clenched between the teeth, before a sip is taken, allowing for the synthesis to occur right on the tongue.

Q: Persian cuisine, surprisingly enough, has influenced our own views on healthy eating. The surgeon general's daily nutritional recommendation—the food pyramid we've been taught to follow for so long—has its genesis in the Persian Zoroastrian system of balancing. Where does this balancing theory come from and how is it implemented in Iranian homes today?

MM: Zoroastrianism was founded by the Persian prophet Zoroaster around 600 B.C. and is now believed to be one of the first, if not the first, monotheistic religions. It's dualistic in nature, and its basic concept concerns opposing forces: good and evil struggling for supremacy. This theory of opposites extends to every aspect of life, including diet. Foods, like people, are believed to have natures, hot or cold, *garm* or *sard*. Melancholia or lack of energy can be treated with *garm* foods. Hot tempers, fevers, and nervous tension can be alleviated by *sard* foods. Good health is obtained when there is a balance. Most modern-day Iranians, my mother included, still believe in this system of gastronomic balancing.

During my school years, if I had an important exam coming up or needed to have all my wits about me for an assignment, my mother would insist I eat *ajil,* a mixture made from dried fruit such as raisins and figs, and walnuts, almonds, and pistachios. She believed that this *garm* food would raise my energy levels and help with concentration. (I would always ace a test when I followed her advice!) To calm me down on hot days, or when I was particularly temperamental, cucumber and yogurt dip combined with white basmati rice was a good *sard* remedy. Likewise, in the book, Marjan keeps a close watch over her moodier sister Bahar, feeding her dishes according to her state of mind.

Q: The concept of Zoroastrian balance can be found in your novel, on a number of levels. How did it influence you when you were writing *Pomegranate Soup*?

MM: As I toiled on the manuscript, at some point it dawned on me that something was missing from my story—a sense of joy. A happiness and vitality that is particular to Iranians, to Persian culture itself. I wanted to express the beauty of my birthplace, a vision I knew was incongruous with the dark, violent images Westerners see when they think of Iran. Above all, I wanted readers to almost smell and taste one of Iran's greatest contributions to the world: its delicate, perfumed cuisine. Somehow, all these memories and emotions came together as I began to write *Pomegranate Soup*.

It wasn't a conscious decision of mine to incorporate the Zoroastrian system of contrast, the good and evil characters and the dramatic ups and downs of the plot. I think that without my knowing it, this Persian concept manifested itself in the story, so that when I was done with the first draft, the *garm* and *sard* elements were already there. That is the magic of writing—the synchronicity that directs the story without the writer being fully aware it is happening.

Q: In the U.S. we take our meals wherever we can—at the dinner table, on the couch, in the car—squeezing them into our busy schedules, almost like an afterthought. It's completely the opposite in Iranian homes, with their tradition of the *sofreh*. How does the *sofreh* affect the way Iranians eat?

MM: Not until my late teens did I ever use a dining table for something other than collecting books, errant newspapers, and household bills. All my childhood meals were celebrated on a piece of embroidered cloth called the *sofreh*. Sitting cross-legged along its borders, families are able to "touch base" in the most fundamental of ways. It was a picnic three times a day! A typical meal could last up to two hours, and if the weather was particularly hot, the entire contingent would move outdoors. Rooftops or any patch of grass would do. In the book Marjan has a wonderful memory of spending a hot summer night eating and telling stories on her childhood home's sunken rooftop. I, too, have distinct memories of dining around a *sofreh* on our rooftop in Buenos Aires, while my mother told me fantastical tales of Scheherazade and the thousand and one nights.

Q: Your book has already been translated into thirteen languages, and you have traveled around the world to talk about *Pomegranate Soup*. How has the book been received in different countries? Did any of the local reactions surprise you?

MM: I am continually being surprised by the varied reactions of readers, and it has been particularly interesting for me to see how each country extracts different messages from the book. In Holland, for example, the press has focused heavily on the novel's political side, taking on the very serious topics of immigration and integration. Italians, on the other hand, were more interested in the sensual, culinary side of the story. The jacket on the Italian edition highlights Mrs. Estelle Delmonico, the Italian character in the story, as the heroine, which I thought was wonderful. I realized that, for some people, she was more important to the story than I had previously thought. Each new opinion gives the story another layer, one that even I might not have known existed before. And of course, knowing that readers in America and around the world are now intimately acquainted with the fictional characters I brought to life is a great thrill. I feel very lucky that my first book has found such a warm, enthusiastic audience.

suggested further reading

IF YOU WANT TO LEARN MORE ABOUT PERSIAN CULTURE,
HERE ARE SOME WONDERFUL BOOKS I HAVE COME ACROSS:

Foreigner by Nahid Rachlin

Funny in Farsi by Firoozeh Dumas

Iran Awakening by Shirin Ebadi

The Iranians: Persia, Islam and the Soul of a Nation
     by Sandra Mackey

Journey from the Land of No by Roya Hakakian

Lipstick Jihad by Azadeh Moaveni

A Lonely Woman: Forugh Farrokhzad and Her Poetry
     by Michael C. Hillman

Moonlight on the Avenue of Faith by Gina B. Nahai

My Uncle Napoleon by Iraj Pezeshkzad

Persepolis by Marjane Satrapi

Reading Lolita in Tehran by Azar Nafisi

1. Each chapter in *Pomegranate Soup* begins with a traditional Persian recipe, which is then incorporated into the story like a character. Why do you think the author has chosen to highlight the food in this manner? How do you think the recipes guide the narrative? Is there one recipe that resonated with you more than the others? Why?

2. We first meet the three Aminpour sisters, Marjan, Bahar, and Layla, in the kitchen of the new Babylon Café. How does this setting offer a glimpse into their different personalities? If you have siblings, do you recognize the dynamics between the three sisters?

3. Marjan cooks in accordance to the Zoroastrian system of gastronomic balancing, known as *sard* and *garm*. As one of the world's first monotheistic religions, Zoroastrianism introduced the dual ideas of good and evil, which is also practiced in the Judeo-Christian tradition. Have you ever heard of Zoroastrianism or the concepts of *sard* and *garm* (cold and hot) foods? How is this system relevant to the rest of the story?

4. Why do you think Marsha Mehran has chosen to set *Pomegranate Soup* in 1980s Ireland, instead of in the present? How do you think the village of Ballinacroagh perpetuates the fairy-tale

image tourists often have of Ireland? In what ways, if any, does Ballinacroagh differ from this idealized picture?

5. The Aminpour sisters escape Tehran on the eve of the Islamic Revolution. What do you know of Iran's history, particularly the revolution of 1979? Were you surprised to read that the Shah was as unpopular as he was with many Iranians? If you were around during the time of the revolution, what images do you remember receiving about it through media outlets in the West?

6. Both Marjan and Bahar were romantically involved with men who supported the Islamic Revolution. These relationships led the two women to perform revolutionary activities, which they later regretted. Do you feel either sister has come to terms with her violent past? Have you ever felt like you've lost your moral compass in a relationship?

7. The Babylon Café provides a venue for dreams to flourish. How do the food and the sisters' temperaments influence the villagers to pursue dreams that may have lain hidden, even to themselves? Have you ever experienced a quiet epiphany such as the one that Father Mahoney has over a bowl of *abgusht,* or a more pronounced moment of transformation such as Tom Junior has in the Cat's cottage?

8. What parallels do you find between Thomas McGuire and Hossein Jaferi? What are the differences? Can you think of any other parallels between the sisters' experiences in the Irish village and in revolution-era Iran?

9. Marjan, Bahar, and Layla try to protect one another from the memories of the past. How is this over-protectiveness similar to events you might have experienced in your own life? Do you relate to any one sister's methods more?

10. Croagh Patrick looms protectively over the village of Ballinacroagh. The holy mountain is where the patron saint of

Ireland, Saint Patrick, reportedly took his Lenten fast, banishing the evil spirits that had haunted him his entire life. What roles do Croagh Patrick and Saint Patrick play in Bahar's self-revelation? What do you think initially sparked her desire to climb the mountain?

11. Young Layla and Malachy provide a romantic subplot, but what other purpose do they serve? Discuss their role in the story.

12. What would you like to see happen to the three sisters after the story ends? Do you think they have found a home in Ballinacroagh? Do you think they are ready to heal from the painful events of their past?

Born in Tehran on the eve of the

Iranian Revolution, MARSHA MEHRAN

escaped the upheaval with her family for

the southern shores of Argentina, where

her parents set up a Middle Eastern café.

She now lives in New York with her

Irish husband, Christopher, who is

constantly called upon to taste her

experimental cooking.